THE AUTHOR

S.S. Van Dine is the pen name of Willard Huntington Wright, born in 1888, whose eminent career as a crime novelist opened with *The Benson Murder Case* (1926). Before this he was well known as an art critic, journalist and socialite; he was Editor-in-Chief of *The Smart Set* Magazine, Editor of *The International Studio*, and author of several books, including a study of Nietzsche and works on modern painting. Forced through overwork to take a long rest, and forbidden by his doctors to do any 'serious' reading, Wright read over two thousand detective novels and books on criminology. Subsequently, as 'S.S. Van Dine', he wrote a series of best-selling crime novels, and his detective Philo Vance – one of the most famous amateur sleuths – was immortalised on screen by William Powell in *The Canary Murder Case*.

S.S. Van Dine's novels include *The Canary Murder Case* (1927), *The Greene Murder Case* (1928), *The Scarab Murder Case* (1930) and *The Casino Murder Case* (1934). He died in 1939.

THE BENSON
MURDER CASE

S.S. Van Dine

THE HOGARTH PRESS
LONDON

Published in 1988 by
The Hogarth Press
30 Bedford Square, London WC1B 3RP

First published in Great Britain by Ernest Benn Ltd., 1926
Copyright © Estate of S.S. Van Dine

A CIP catalogue record for this book is available from the British Library

ISBN 0 7012 0677 2

Printed in Great Britain by
Cox & Wyman Ltd.,
Reading, Berkshire

EDITOR'S NOTE

Mr. S. S. Van Dine has, so to speak, patented a particular type of title for a number of his novels of which this title is perhaps the most popular.

Owing to the extraordinary power and lucidity of his graphic pen he has been spoken of as the "newest and greatest mystery writer in the world."

This story is concerned with the elucidation of the murder of Alvin Benson on the night of June 13th:—"His body was found reclining in a large wicker lounge chair with a high fan-shaped back in an attitude so natural that one almost expected him to turn and ask why his privacy was being intruded upon. His head was resting against the chair's back. His right leg was crossed over his left in a position of comfortable relaxation. His right arm was resting easily on the centre-table and his left arm lay along the chair's arm."

You will notice how carefully these details are given: the exact position of the body, the head, the arms and the accurate description of the chair, even to its high fan-shaped back.

The whole book, just like its predecessor, "The Canary Murder Case," has that professional air about it which makes one feel the crime has really happened and that one is not reading a piece of pure fiction.

It is in this exciting and brilliantly written story that the clever detective, Philo Vance, gives his views about circumstantial evidence, a subject which has received a good deal of publicity recently on account of several murder cases that have attracted an enormous amount of attention. He says:

"Circumst'ntial evidence, Markham, is the utt'rest tommy-rot imag'nable. Its theory is not unlike that of our present-day democracy. The democratic theory is that if you accumulate enough ignorance at the polls you produce intelligence; and the theory of circumst'ntial evidence is that if you accumulate a sufficient number of weak links you produce a strong chain."

Philo Vance, the brilliant detective, an outstanding character in "The Canary Murder Case," who elucidated the murder of Margaret Odell, conducts this Benson inquiry with, if possible, even greater ingenuity.

To follow the close, clear-cut reasoning of the analytical mind of this latest and most up-to-date "Sherlock Holmes" is a sheer delight.

It is also in this book that Van Dine divulges how he first came in contact with Vance at Harvard. In contrast with the gruesome nature of his calling, he indulges in a passion for art. He is not only a dilettante but also a man of unusual culture and refinement, who detests stupidity more than vulgarity. He often quotes Fouché's famous line: "It is more than a crime; it is a fault."

The name Van Dine, as we have said in the Editor's Note of his preceding book, hides the identity of a well-known novelist who used this nom-de-plume when he turned his attention to writing detective novels.

During a long and serious illness he had been compelled to give up writing works of philosophy. He began to read detective mystery stories and so was led to study serious crime and its detection. The result has been that he has become the finest living writer of this class of fiction.

THE EDITOR.

CONTENTS

The Benson Murder Case

CHAPTER I

PHILO VANCE AT HOME

(Friday, June 14th ; 8.30 a.m.)

IT happened that, on the morning of the momentous June the fourteenth when the discovery of the murdered body of Alvin H. Benson created a sensation which, to this day, has not entirely died away, I had breakfasted with Philo Vance in his apartment. It was not unusual for me to share Vance's luncheons and dinners, but to have breakfasted with him was something of an occasion. He was a late riser, and it was his habit to remain *incommunicado* until his midday meal.

The reason for this early meeting was a matter of business— or, rather, of æsthetics. On the afternoon of the previous day Vance had attended a preview of Vollard's collection of Cézanne water-colours at the Kessler Galleries, and having seen several pictures he particularly wanted, he had invited me to an early breakfast to give me instructions regarding their purchase.

A word concerning my relationship with Vance is necessary to clarify my rôle of narrator in this chronicle. The legal tradition is deeply embedded in my family, and when my preparatory school days were over I was sent, almost as a matter of course, to Harvard to study law. It was there I met Vance, a reserved, cynical and caustic freshman who was the bane of his professors and the fear of his fellow-classmen. Why he should have chosen me, of all the students at the University, for his extra-scholastic association, tion, I have never been able to understand fully. My own liking for Vance was simply explained: he fascinated and interested me, and supplied me with a novel kind of intellectual diversion. In his liking for me, however, no such basis of appeal was present. I was (and am now) a commonplace fellow, possessed of a conservative and rather conventional mind. But, at least, my mentality was not rigid, and the ponderosity of the legal procedure did not impress me greatly, which is why, no doubt, I had little taste for my inherited profession—and it is possible that these traits found certain affinities in Vance's unconscious mind. There is, to be sure, the less consoling explanation that I appealed to Vance as a kind of foil, or anchorage, and that he sensed in my nature a complementary antithesis to his own. But whatever the explanation, we were much together; and, as the years went by, that association ripened into an inseparable friendship.

Upon graduation I entered my father's law firm—Van Dine and Davis—and after five years of dull apprenticeship I was taken into the firm as the junior partner. At present I am the second Van Dine of Van Dine, Davis and Van Dine, with offices at 120 Broadway. At about the time my name first appeared on the letterheads of the firm, Vance returned from Europe, where he had been living during my legal novitiate, and, an aunt of his having died and made him her principal beneficiary, I was called upon to discharge the technical obligations involved in putting him in possession of his inherited property.

This work was the beginning of a new and somewhat unusual relationship between us. Vance had a strong distaste for any kind of business transaction, and in time I became the custodian of all his monetary interests and his agent at large. I found that his affairs were various enough to occupy as much of my time as I cared to give to legal matters, and as Vance was able to indulge the luxury of having a personal legal factotum, so to speak, I permanently closed my desk at the office, and devoted myself exclusively to his needs and whims.

If, up to the time when Vance summoned me to discuss the purchase of the Cézannes, I had harboured any secret or repressed regrets for having deprived the firm of Van Dine, Davis and Van Dine of my modest legal talents, they were permanently banished on that eventful morning; for, beginning with the notorious Benson murder, and extending over a period of nearly four years, it was my privilege to be a spectator of what I believe was the most amazing series of criminal cases that ever passed before the eyes of a young lawyer. Indeed, the grim dramas I witnessed during that period constitute one of the most astonishing secret documents in the police history of this country.

Of these dramas Vance was the central character. By an analytical and interpretative process which, as far as I know, has never before been applied to criminal activities, he succeeded in solving many of the important crimes on which both the police and the District Attorney's office had hopelessly fallen down.

Due to my peculiar relations with Vance it happened that not only did I participate in all the cases with which he was connected, but I was also present at most of the informal discussions concerning them which took place between him and the District Attorney; and being of methodical temperament, I kept a fairly complete record of them. In addition, I noted down (as accurately as memory permitted) Vance's unique psychological methods of determining guilt, as he explained them from time to time. It is fortunate that I performed this gratuitous labour of accumulation and transcription, for now that circumstances have unexpectedly rendered possible my making the cases public, I am able to present them in full detail and with all their various sidelights and succeeding steps—a task that would be impossible were it not for my numerous clippings and *adversaria*.

Fortunately, too, the first case to draw Vance into its ramifications was that of Alvin Benson's murder. Not only did it prove one of the most famous of New York's *causes célèbres*, but it gave Vance an excellent opportunity of displaying his rare talents of deductive reasoning, and, by its nature and magnitude, aroused his interest in a branch of activity which heretofore had been alien to his temperamental promptings and habitual predilections.

The case intruded upon Vance's life suddenly and unexpectedly, although he himself had, by a casual request

made to the District Attorney over a month before, been
the involuntary agent of this destruction of his normal
routine. The thing, in fact, burst upon us before we had
quite finished our breakfast on that mid-June morning,
and put an end temporarily to all business connected with
the purchase of the Cézanne paintings. When, later in
the day, I visited the Kessler Galleries, two of the water-
colours that Vance had particularly desired had been sold;
and I am convinced that, despite his success in the unravel-
ling of the Benson murder mystery and his saving of at
least one innocent person from arrest, he has never to this
day felt entirely compensated for the loss of those two little
sketches on which he had set his heart.

As I was ushered into the living-room that morning by
Currie, a rare old English servant who acted as Vance's
butler, valet, major-domo and, on occasions, speciality
cook, Vance was sitting in a large arm-chair, attired in a
surah silk dressing-gown and grey suède slippers, with
Vollard's book on Cézanne open across his knees.

"Forgive my not rising, Van," he greeted me casually.
"I have the whole weight of the modern evolution in art
resting on my legs. Furthermore, this plebeian early rising
fatigues me, y'know."

He rifled the pages of the volume, pausing here and there
at a reproduction.

"This chap Vollard," he remarked at length, "has been
rather liberal with our art-fearing country. He has sent
a really goodish collection of his Cézannes here. I viewed
'em yesterday with the proper reverence, and, I might add,
unconcern, for Kessler was watching me; and I've marked
the ones I want you to buy for me as soon as the Gallery
opens this morning."

He handed me a small catalogue he had been using as a
book-mark.

"A beastly assignment, I know," he added, with an in-
dolent smile. "These delicate little smudges with all their
blank paper will prob'bly be meaningless to your legal
mind—they're so unlike a neatly-typed brief, don't y'know.
And you'll no doubt think some of 'em are hung upside-
down—one of 'em is, in fact, and even Kessler doesn't
know it. But don't fret, Van, old dear. They're very

beautiful and valuable little knick-knacks, and rather inexpensive when one considers what they'll be bringing in a few years. Really an excellent investment for some money-loving soul, y'know—inf'nitely better than that Lawyer's Equity Stock over which you grew so eloquent at the time of my dear Aunt Agatha's death." [1]

Vance's one passion (if a purely intellectual enthusiasm may be called a passion) was art—not art in its narrow, personal aspects, but in its broader, more universal significance. And art was not only his dominating interest, but his chief diversion. He was something of an authority on Japanese and Chinese prints; he knew tapestries and ceramics; and once I heard him give an impromptu *causerie* to a few guests on Tanagra figurines, which, had it been transcribed, would have made a most delightful and instructive monograph.

Vance had sufficient means to indulge his instinct for collecting, and possessed a fine assortment of pictures and *objets d'art*. His collection was heterogeneous only in its superficial characteristics: every piece he owned embodied some principle of form or line that related it to all the others. One who knew art could feel the unity and consistency in all the items with which he surrounded himself, however widely separated they were in point of time or *métier* or surface appeal. Vance, I have always felt, was one of those rare human beings, a collector with a definite philosophic point of view.

His apartment in East Thirty-eighth Street—actually the two top floors of an old mansion, beautifully remodelled and in part rebuilt to secure spacious rooms and lofty ceilings—was filled, but not crowded, with rare specimens of oriental and occidental, ancient and modern, art. His paintings ranged from the Italian primitives to Cézanne and Matisse; and among his collection of original drawings were works as widely separated as those of Michelangelo and Picasso. Vance's Chinese prints constituted one of the finest private collections in this country. They

---

[1] As a matter of fact, the same water-colours that Vance obtained for $250 and $300, were bringing three times as much four years later.

included beautiful examples of the work of Ririomin, Rianchu, Jinkomin, Kakei and Mokkei.

"The Chinese," Vance once said to me, "are the truly great artists of the East. They were the men whose work expressed most intensely a broad philosophic spirit. By contrast the Japanese were superficial. It's a long step between the little more than decorative *souci* of a Hokusai and the profoundly thoughtful and conscious artistry of a Ririomin. Even when Chinese art degenerated under the Manchus, we find in it a deep philosophic quality—a spiritual *sensibilité*, so to speak. And in the modern copies of copies —what is called the *bunjinga* style—we still have pictures of profound meaning."

Vance's catholicity of taste in art was remarkable. His collection was as varied as that of a museum. It embraced a black-figured amphora by Amasis, a proto-Corinthian vase in the Ægean style, Koubatcha and Rhodian plates, Athenian pottery, a sixteenth-century Italian holy-water stoup of rock crystal, pewter of the Tudor period (several pieces bearing the double-rose hall-mark), a bronze plaque by Cellini, a triptych of Limoges enamel, a Spanish retable of an altar-piece by Vallfogona, several Etruscan bronzes, an Indian Greco Buddhist, a statuette of the Goddess Kuan Yin from the Ming Dynasty, a number of very fine Renaissance wood-cuts, and several specimens of Byzantine, Carolingian and early French ivory carvings.

His Egyptian treasures included a gold jug from Zakazik, a statuette of the Lady Nai (as lovely as the one in the Louvre), two beautifully carved steles of the First Theban Age, various small sculptures comprising rare representations of Hapi and Amset, and several Arrentine bowls carved with Kalathiskos dancers. On top of one of his embayed Jacobean bookcases in the library, where most of his modern paintings and drawings were hung, was a fascinating group of African sculpture—ceremonial masks and statuette-fetishes from French Guinea, the Sudan, Nigeria, the Ivory Coast, and the Congo.

A definite purpose has animated me in speaking at such length about Vance's art instinct, for, in order to understand fully the melodramatic adventures which began for him on that June morning, one must have a general idea of the man's *penchants* and inner promptings. His interest in art was an important—one might almost say the dominant—factor in his personality. I have never met a man quite like him—a man so apparently diversified, and yet so fundamentally consistent.

Vance was what many would call a dilettante. But the designation does him injustice. He was a man of unusual culture and brilliance. An aristocrat by birth and instinct, he held himself severely aloof from the common world of men. In his manner there was an indefinable contempt for inferiority of all kinds. The great majority of those with whom he came in contact regarded him as a snob. Yet there was in his condescension and disdain no trace of spuriousness. His snobbishness was intellectual as well as social. He detested stupidity even more, I believe, than he did vulgarity or bad taste. I have heard him on several occasions quote Fouché's famous line: *C'est plus qu'un crime ; c'est une faute.* And he meant it literally.

Vance was frankly a cynic, but he was rarely bitter: his was a flippant, Juvenalian cynicism. Perhaps he may best be described as a bored and supercilious, but highly conscious and penetrating, spectator of life. He was keenly interested in all human reactions; but it was the interest of the scientist, not the humanitarian. Withal he was a man of rare personal charm. Even people who found it difficult to admire him, found it equally difficult not to like him. His somewhat quixotic mannerisms and his slightly English accent and inflection—an heritage of his post-graduate days at Oxford—impressed those who did not know him well, as affectations. But the truth is, there was very little of the *poseur* about him.

He was unusually good-looking, although his mouth was ascetic and cruel, like the mouths on some of the Medici portraits;[1] moreover, there was a slightly derisive hauteur in the lift of his eyebrows. Despite the aquiline severity of his lineaments his face was highly sensitive. His forehead was full and sloping—it was the artist's, rather than

[1] I am thinking particularly of Bronzino's portraits of Pietro de' Medici and Cosimo de' Medici, in the National Gallery, and of Vasari's medallion portrait of Lorenzo de' Medici in the Vecchio Palazzo, Florence.

the scholar's, brow. His cold grey eyes were widely spaced. His nose was straight and slender, and his chin narrow but prominent, with an unusually deep cleft. When I saw John Barrymore recently in *Hamlet* I was somehow reminded of Vance; and once before, in a scene of *Cæsar and Cleopatra* played by Forbes Robertson, I received a similar impression.[1]

Vance was slightly under six feet, graceful, and giving the impression of sinewy strength and nervous endurance. He was an expert fencer, and had been the Captain of the University's fencing team. He was mildly fond of outdoor sports, and had a knack of doing things well without any extensive practise. His golf handicap was only three; and one season he had played in our championship polo team against England. Nevertheless, he had a positive antipathy to walking, and would not go a hundred yards on foot if there was any possible means of riding.

In his dress he was always fashionable—scrupulously correct to the smallest detail—yet unobtrusive. He spent considerable time at his clubs: his favourite was the Stuyvesant, because, as he explained to me, its membership was drawn largely from the political and commercial ranks, and he was never drawn into a discussion which required any mental effort. He went occasionally to the more modern operas, and was a regular subscriber to the symphony concerts and chamber-music recitals.

Incidentally, he was one of the most uncanny poker players I have ever seen. I mention this fact not merely because it was unusual and significant that a man of Vance's type should have preferred so democratic a game to bridge or chess, for instance, but because his knowledge of the science of human psychology involved in poker had an intimate bearing on the chronicles I am about to set down.

---

[1] Once when Vance was suffering from sinusitis, he had an X-ray photograph of his head made; and the accompanying chart described him as a "marked dolichocephalic" and a "disharmonious Nordic." It also contained the following data:—cephalic index, 75; nose leptorhine with an index of 48; facial angle, 85°; vertical index, 72; upper facial index, 54; interpupilary width, 67; chin, masognathous, with an index of 103; sella turcica, abnormally large.

Vance's knowledge of psychology was indeed uncanny. He was gifted with an instinctively accurate judgment of people, and his study and reading had co-ordinated and rationalised this gift to an amazing extent. He was well grounded in the academic principles of psychology and all his courses at college had either centred about this subject or been subordinated to it. While I was confining myself to a restricted area of torts and contracts, constitutional and common law, equity, evidence and pleading, Vance was reconnoitring the whole field of cultural endeavour. He had courses in the history of religions, the Greek classics, biology, civics, and political economy, philosophy anthropology, literature, theoretical and experimental psychology, and ancient and modern languages.[1] But it was, I think, his courses under Münsterberg and William James that interested him the most.

Vance's mind was basically philosophical—that is, philosophical in the more general sense. Being singularly free from the conventional sentimentalities and current superstitions, he could look beneath the surface of human acts into actuating impulses and motives. Moreover, he was resolute both in his avoidance of any attitude that savoured of credulousness, and in his adherence to cold, logical exactness in his mental processes.

"Until we can approach all human problems," he once remarked, "with the clinical aloofness and cynical contempt of a doctor examining a guinea-pig strapped to a board, we have little chance of getting at the truth."

Vance led an active, but by no means animated social life—a concession to various family ties. But he was not

---

[1] "Culture," Vance said to me shortly after I had met him, "is polyglot; and the knowledge of many tongues is essential to an understanding of the world's intellectual and æsthetic achievements. Especially are the Greek and Latin classics vitiated by translation." I quote the remark here because his omnivorous reading in languages other than English, coupled with his amazingly retentive memory, had a tendency to affect his own speech. And while it may appear to some that his speech was at times pedantic, I have tried, throughout these chronicles, to quote him literally, in the hope of presenting a portrait of the man as he was.

a social animal—I cannot remember ever having met a
man with so undeveloped a gregarious instinct—and when
he went forth into the social world it was generally under
compulsion. In fact, one of his "duty" affairs had occupied him on the night before that memorable June breakfast; otherwise, we would have consulted about the Cézannes
the evening before; and Vance groused a good deal about
it while Currie was serving our strawberries and eggs *Béné-
dictine*. Later on I was to give profound thanks to the
God of Coincidence that the blocks had been arranged
in just that pattern; for had Vance been slumbering peace-
fully at nine o'clock when the District Attorney called,
I would probably have missed four of the most interesting
and exciting years of my life; and many of New York's
shrewdest and most desperate criminals might still be at
large.

Vance and I had just settled back in our chairs for our
second cup of coffee and a cigarette, when Currie, answering
an impetuous ringing of the front-door bell, ushered the
District Attorney into the living-room.

"By all that's holy!" he exclaimed, raising his hands in
mock astonishment. "New York's leading *flâneur* and art
connoisseur is up and about!"

"And I am suffused with blushes at the disgrace of it,"
Vance replied.

It was evident, however, that the District Attorney was
not in a jovial mood. His face suddenly sobered.

"Vance, a serious thing has brought me here. I'm in a
great hurry, and merely dropped by to keep my promise.
. . . The fact is, Alvin Benson has been murdered."

Vance lifted his eyebrows languidly.

"Really, now," he drawled. "How messy! But he no
doubt deserved it. In any event, that's no reason why
you should repine. Take a chair and have a cup of Currie's
incomp'rable coffee." And before the other could protest,
he rose and pushed a bell-button.

Markham hesitated a second or two.

"Oh, well. A couple of minutes won't make any difference. But only a gulp." And he sank into a chair
facing us.

CHAPTER II

(Friday, June 14th ; 9 a.m.)

JOHN F.-X MARKHAM, as you remember, had been elected District Attorney of New York County on the Independent Reform Ticket during one of the city's periodical reactions against Tammany Hall. He served his four years, and would probably have been elected to a second term had not the ticket been hopelessly split by the political juggling of his opponents. He was an indefatigable worker, and projected the District Attorney's office into all manner of criminal and civil investigations. Being utterly incorruptible, he not only aroused the fervid admiration of his constituents, but produced an almost unprecedented sense of security in those who had opposed him on partisan lines.

He had been in office only a few months when one of the newspapers referred to him as the Watch Dog; and the sobriquet clung to him until the end of his administration. Indeed, his record as a successful prosecutor during the four years of his incumbency was such a remarkable one that even to-day it is not infrequently referred to in legal and political discussions.

Markham was a tall, strongly-built man in the middle forties, with a clean-shaven, somewhat youthful face which belied his uniformly grey hair. He was not handsome according to conventional standards, but he had an unmistakable air of distinction, and was possessed of an amount of social culture rarely found in our latter-day political office-holders. Withal he was a man of brusque and vindictive temperament; but his brusqueness was an incrustation on a solid foundation of good-breeding, not —as is usually the case—the roughness of substructure showing through an inadequately superimposed crust of gentility.

When his nature was relieved of the stress of duty and care, he was the most gracious of men. But early in my acquaintance with him I had seen his attitude of cordiality suddenly displaced by one of grim authority. It was as if a new personality—hard, indomitable, symbolic of eternal justice—had in that moment been born in Markham's body. I was to witness this transformation many times before our association ended. In fact, this very morning, as he sat opposite to me in Vance's living-room, there was more than a hint of it in the aggressive sternness of his expression and I knew that he was deeply troubled over Alvin Benson's murder.

He swallowed his coffee rapidly, and was setting down the cup, when Vance, who had been watching him with quizzical amusement, remarked:

"I say; why this sad preoccupation over the passing of one Benson? You weren't, by any chance, the murderer, what?"

Markham ignored Vance's levity.

"I'm on my way to Benson's. Do you care to come along? You asked for the experience, and I dropped in to keep my promise."

I then recalled that several weeks before at the Stuyvesant Club, when the subject of the prevalent homicides in New York was being discussed, Vance had expressed a desire to accompany the District Attorney on one of his investigations; and that Markham had promised to take him on his next important case. Vance's interest in the psychology of human behaviour had prompted the desire, and his friendship with Markham, which had been of long standing, had made the request possible.

"You remember everything, don't you?" Vance replied lazily. "An admirable gift, even if an uncomfortable one." He glanced at the clock on the mantel: it lacked a few minutes of nine. "But what an indecent hour! Suppose someone should see me."

Markham moved forward impatiently in his chair.

"Well, if you think the gratification of your curiosity would compensate you for the disgrace of being seen in public at nine o'clock in the morning, you'll have to hurry. I certainly won't take you in dressing-gown and bedroom slippers. And I most certainly won't wait over five minutes for you to get dressed."

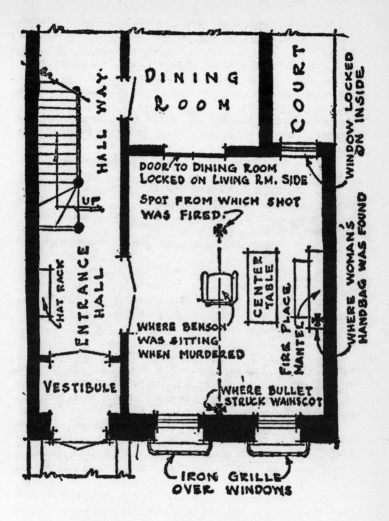

DINING ROOM

COURT

HALL WAY.

UP

ENTRANCE HALL

CHAT RACK

VESTIBULE

WINDOW LOCKED ON INSIDE

WHERE WOMAN'S HANDBAG WAS FOUND

DOOR TO DINING ROOM LOCKED ON LIVING RM. SIDE

SPOT FROM WHICH SHOT WAS FIRED.

CENTER TABLE

FIRE PLACE MANTEL

WHERE BENSON WAS SITTING WHEN MURDERED

WHERE BULLET STRUCK WAINSCOT

IRON GRILLE OVER WINDOWS

WEST 48TH. STREET

"Why the haste, old dear?" Vance asked, yawning. "The chap's dead, don't y' know; he can't possibly run away."

"Come, get a move on, you orchid," the other urged. "This affair is no joke. It's damned serious; and from the looks of it, it's going to cause an ungodly scandal. What are you going to do?"

"Do? I shall humbly follow the great avenger of the common people," returned Vance, rising and making an obsequious bow.

He rang for Currie, and ordered his clothes brought to him.

"I'm attending a levee which Mr. Markham is holding over a corpse, and I want something rather spiffy. Is it warm enough for a silk suit? . . . And a lavender tie, by all means."

"I trust you won't also wear your green carnation," grumbled Markham.

"Tut! Tut!" Vance chid him. "You've been reading Mr. Hichens. Such heresy in a District Attorney! Anyway, you know full well I never wear *boutonnières*. The decoration has fallen into disrepute. The only remaining devotees of the practice are *roués* and saxophone players. . . . But tell me about the departed Benson."

Vance was now dressing, with Currie's assistance, at a rate of speed I had rarely seen him display in such matters. Beneath his bantering pose I recognised the true eagerness of the man for a new experience and one that promised such dramatic possibilities for his alert and observing mind.

"You knew Alvin Benson casually, I believe," the District Attorney said. "Well, early this morning his house-keeper 'phoned the local precinct station that she had found him shot through the head, fully dressed and sitting in his favourite chair in his living-room. The message, of course, was put through at once to the Telegraph Bureau at Headquarters, and my assistant on duty notified me immediately. I was tempted to let the case follow the regular police routine. But half an hour later, Major Benson, Alvin's brother, 'phoned me and asked me, as a special favour, to take charge. I've known the Major for twenty years, and I couldn't very well refuse. So I took a hurried breakfast and started for Benson's house. He lives on West Forty-eighth Street; and as I passed your corner I remembered your request, and dropped in to see if you cared to go along."

"Most consid'rate," murmured Vance, adjusting his four-in-hand before a small polychrome mirror by the door. Then he turned to me. "Come, Van. We'll all gaze upon the defunct Benson. I'm sure some of Markham's sleuths will unearth the fact that I detested the bounder and accuse me of the crime; and I'll feel safer, don't y'know, with legal talent at hand. . . . No objections—eh, what, Markham?"

"Certainly not," the other agreed readily, although I felt that he would rather not have had me along. But I was too deeply interested in the affair to offer any ceremonious objections, and I followed Vance and Markham downstairs.

As we settled back in the waiting taxicab and started up Madison Avenue, I marvelled a little, as I had often done before, at the strange friendship of these two dissimilar men beside me—Markham, forthright, conventional, a trifle austere, and over-serious in his dealing with life; and Vance, casual, mercurial, debonair, and whimsically cynical in the face of the grimmest realities. And yet this temperamental diversity seemed, in some wise, the very cornerstone of their friendship: it was as if each saw in the other some unattainable field of experience and sensation that had been denied himself. Markham represented to Vance the solid and immutable realism of life, whereas Vance symbolised for Markham the care-free, exotic, gipsy spirit of intellectual adventure. Their intimacy, in fact, was even greater than showed on the surface: and despite Markham's exaggerated deprecations of the other's attitudes and opinions, I believe he respected Vance's intelligence more profoundly than that of any other man he knew.

As we rode up town that morning Markham appeared preoccupied and gloomy. No word had been spoken since we left the apartment; but as we turned west into Forty-eighth Street Vance asked:

"What is the social etiquette of these early-morning murder functions, aside from removing one's hat in the presence of the body?"

"You keep your hat on," growled Markham.

"My word! Like a synagogue, what? Most int'restin'!
Perhaps one takes off one's shoes so as not to confuse the
footprints."

"No," Markham told him. "The guests remain fully
clothed—in which the function differs from the ordinary
evening affairs of your smart set."

"My *dear* Markham!"—Vance's tone was one of melancholy reproof—"The horrified moralist in your nature is at
work again. That remark of yours was pos'tively Epworth
Leaguish."

Markham was too abstracted to follow up Vance's badinage.

"There are one or two things," he said soberly, "that
I think I'd better warn you about. From the looks of it,
this case is going to cause considerable noise, and there'll
be a lot of jealousy and battling for honours. I won't be
fallen upon and caressed affectionately by the police for
coming in at this stage of the game; so be careful not to
rub their bristles the wrong way. My assistant, who's
there now, tells me he thinks the Inspector has put Heath
in charge. Heath's a sergeant in the Homicide Bureau,
and is undoubtedly convinced at the present moment that
I'm taking hold in order to get the publicity."

"Aren't you his technical superior?" asked Vance.

"Of course; and that makes the situation just so much
more delicate. . . . I wish to God the Major hadn't called
me up."

"*Eheu!*" sighed Vance. "The world is full of Heaths.
Beastly nuisances."

"Don't misunderstand me," Markham hastened to assure
him. "Heath is a good man—in fact, as good a man as
we've got. The mere fact that he was assigned to the case
shows how seriously the affair is regarded at Headquarters.
There'll be no unpleasantness about my taking charge, you
understand; but I want the atmosphere to be as halcyon as
possible. Heath'll resent my bringing along you two chaps
as spectators, anyway; so I beg of you, Vance, emulate the
modest violet."

"I prefer the blushing rose, if you don't mind," Vance
protested. "However, I'll instantly give the hypersensitive
Heath one of my choicest *Régie* cigarettes with the rose-
petal tips."

"If you do," smiled Markham, "he'll probably arrest you as a suspicious character."

We had drawn up abruptly in front of an old brown-stone residence on the upper side of Forty-eighth Street, near Sixth Avenue. It was a house of the better class, built on a twenty-five foot lot in a day when permanency and beauty were still matters of consideration among the city's architects. The design was conventional, to accord with the other houses in the block, but a touch of luxury and individuality was to be seen in its decorative copings and in the stone carvings about the entrance and above the windows.

There was a shallow paved areaway between the street line and the front elevation of the house; but this was enclosed in a high iron railing, and the only entrance was by way of the front door, which was about six feet above the street level at the top of a flight of ten broad stone stairs. Between the entrance and the right-hand wall were two spacious windows covered with heavy iron grilles.

A considerable crowd of morbid onlookers had gathered in front of the house; and on the steps lounged several alert-looking young men whom I took to be newspaper reporters. The door of our taxicab was opened by a uniformed patrol man who saluted Markham with exaggerated respect and ostentatiously cleared a passage for us through the gaping throng of idlers. Another uniformed patrolman stood in the little vestibule, and on recognising Markham, held the outer door open for us and saluted with great dignity.

"*Ave, Cæsar, te salutamus,*" whispered Vance, grinning.

"Be quiet," Markham grumbled. "I've got troubles enough without your garbled quotations."

As we passed through the massive carved-oak front door into the main hallway, we were met by Assistant District Attorney Dinwiddie, a serious, swarthy young man with a prematurely lined face, whose appearance gave one the impression that most of the woes of humanity were resting upon his shoulders.

"Good morning, Chief," he greeted Markham, with eager relief. "I'm damned glad you've got here. This case'll rip things wide open. Cut-and-dried murder, and not a lead."

Markham nodded gloomily, and looked past him into the living-room.

"Who's here?" he asked.

"The whole works, from the Chief Inspector down," Dinwiddie told him, with a hopeless shrug, as if the fact boded ill for all concerned.

At that moment a tall, massive, middle-aged man with a pink complexion and a closely-cropped white moustache, appeared in the doorway of the living-room. On seeing Markham he came forward stiffly with outstretched hand. I recognised him at once as Chief Inspector O'Brien, who was in command of the entire Police Department. Dignified greetings were exchanged between him and Markham, and then Vance and I were introduced to him. Inspector O'Brien gave us each a curt, silent nod, and turned back to the living-room, with Markham, Dinwiddie, Vance and myself following.

The room, which was entered by a wide double door about ten feet down the hall, was a spacious one, almost square, and with high ceilings. Two windows gave on the street; and on the extreme right of the north wall, opposite to the front of the house, was another window opening on a paved court. To the left of this window were the sliding doors leading into the dining-room at the rear.

The room presented an appearance of garish opulence. About the walls hung several elaborately framed paintings of racehorses and a number of mounted hunting trophies. A highly coloured oriental rug covered nearly the entire floor. In the middle of the east wall, facing the door, was an ornate fireplace and carved marble mantel. Placed diagonally in the corner on the right stood a walnut upright piano with copper trimmings. Then there was a mahogany bookcase with glass doors and figured curtains, a sprawling tapestried davenport, a squat Venetian tabouret with inlaid mother-of-pearl, a teak-wood stand containing a large brass samovar, and a buhl-topped centre-table nearly six feet long. At the side of the table nearest the hallway, with its back to the front windows, stood a large wicker lounge chair with a high, fan-shaped back.

In this chair reposed the body of Alvin Benson.

Though I had served two years at the front in the World

War and had seen death in many terrible guises, I could not repress a strong sense of revulsion at the sight of this murdered man. In France, death had seemed an inevitable part of my daily routine, but here all the organisms of environment were opposed to the idea of fatal violence. The bright June sunshine was pouring into the room, and through the open windows came the continuous din of the city's noises, which, for all their cacophony, are associated with peace and security and the orderly social processes of life.

Benson's body was reclining in the chair in an attitude so natural that one almost expected him to turn to us and ask why we were intruding upon his privacy. His head was resting against the chair's back. His right leg was crossed over his left in a position of comfortable relaxation. His right arm was resting easily on the centre-table, and his left arm lay along the chair's arm. But that which most strikingly gave his attitude its appearance of naturalness, was a small book which he held in his right hand with his thumb still marking the place where he had evidently been reading.[1]

He had been shot—through the forehead—from the front; and the small circular bullet-mark was now almost black as a result of the coagulation of the blood. A large dark spot on the rug at the rear of the chair indicated the extent of the hæmorrhage caused by the grinding passage of the bullet through his brain. Had it not been for these grisly indications one might have thought that he had merely paused momentarily in his reading to lean back and rest.

He was attired in an old smoking-jacket and red felt bedroom slippers, but still wore his dress trousers and evening shirt, though he was collarless, and the neck band of the shirt had been unbuttoned as if for comfort. He was not an attractive man physically, being almost completely bald and more than a little stout. His face was flabby, and the puffiness of his neck was doubly conspicuous

---

[1] The book was O. Henry's "Strictly Business," and the place at which it was being held open was, curiously enough, the story entitled "A Municipal Report."

without its confining collar. With a slight shudder of distaste I ended my brief contemplation of him, and turned to the other occupants of the room.

Two burly fellows with large hands and feet, their black felt hats pushed far back on their heads, were minutely inspecting the grill-work over the front windows. They seemed to be giving particular attention to the points where the bars were cemented into the masonry; and one of them had just taken hold of a grille with both hands and was shaking it, simian-wise, as if to test its strength. Another man, of medium height and dapper appearance, with a small blond moustache, was bending over in front of the grate looking intently, so it seemed, at the dusty gas-logs. On the far side of the table a thick-set man in blue serge and a derby hat, stood with arms a-kimbo scrutinising the silent figure in the chair. His eyes, hard and pale blue, were narrowed, and his square prognathous jaw was rigidly set. He was gazing with rapt intensity at Benson's body, as though he hoped, by sheer power of concentration, to probe the secret of the murder.

Another man, of unusual mien, was standing before the rear window, with a jeweller's magnifying glass in his eye, inspecting a small object held in the palm of his hand. From pictures I had seen of him I knew he was Captain Carl Hagedorn, the most famous firearms expert in America. He was a large, cumbersome, broad-shouldered man of about fifty; and his black shiny clothes were several sizes too large for him. His coat hitched up behind, and in front hung half-way down to his knees; and his trousers were baggy and lay over his ankles in grotesquely comic folds. His head was round and abnormally large, and his ears seemed sunken into his skull. His mouth was entirely hidden by a scraggly, grey-shot moustache, all the hairs of which grew downwards, forming a kind of lambrequin to his lips. Captain Hagedorn had been connected with the New York Police Department for thirty years, and though his appearance and manner were ridiculed at Headquarters, he was profoundly respected. His word on any point pertaining to firearms and gunshot wounds was accepted as final by Headquarters men.

In the rear of the room, near the dining-room door,

stood two other men talking earnestly together. One was Inspector William M. Moran, Commanding Officer of the Detective Bureau; the other, Sergeant Ernest Heath of the Homicide Bureau, of whom Markham had already spoken to us.

As we entered the room in the wake of Chief Inspector O'Brien everyone ceased his occupation for a moment and looked at the District Attorney in a spirit of uneasy, but respectful, recognition. Only Captain Hagedorn, after a cursory squint at Markham, returned to the inspection of the tiny object in his hand, with an abstracted unconcern which brought a faint smile to Vance's lips.

Inspector Moran and Sergeant Heath came forward with stolid dignity; and after the ceremony of hand-shaking (which I later observed to be a kind of religious rite among the police and members of the District Attorney's Staff), Markham introduced Vance and me, and briefly explained our presence. The Inspector bowed pleasantly to indicate his acceptance of the intrusion, but I noted that Heath ignored Markham's explanation, and proceeded to treat us as if we were non-existent.

Inspector Moran was a man of different quality from the others in the room. He was about sixty, with white hair and a brown moustache, and was immaculately dressed. He looked more like a successful Wall Street broker of the better class than a police official.[1]

"I've assigned Sergeant Heath to the case, Mr. Markham," he explained in a low, well-modulated voice. "It looks as though we were in for a bit of trouble before it's finished. Even the Chief Inspector thought it warranted his lending the moral support of his presence to the preliminary rounds. He has been here since eight o'clock."

Inspector O'Brien had left us immediately upon entering the room, and now stood between the front windows, watching the proceedings with a grave, indecipherable face.

"Well, I think I'll be going," Moran added. "They had me out of bed at seven-thirty, and I haven't had any

---

[1] Inspector Moran (as I learned later) had once been the President of a large up-State bank that had failed during the panic of 1907, and during the Gaynor Administration had been seriously considered for the post of Police Commissioner.

breakfast yet. I won't be needed anyway now that you're here. . . . Good morning." And again he shook hands.

When he had gone Markham turned to the Assistant District Attorney.

"Look after these two gentlemen, will you, Dinwiddie? They're babes in the wood, and want to see how these affairs work. Explain things to them while I have a little confab with Sergeant Heath."

Dinwiddie accepted the assignment eagerly. I think he was glad of the opportunity to have someone to talk to by way of venting his pent-up excitement.

As the three of us turned rather instinctively towards the body of the murdered man—he was, after all, the hub of this tragic drama—I heard Heath say in a sullen voice:

"I suppose you'll take charge now, Mr. Markham."

Dinwiddie and Vance were talking together, and I watched Markham with interest after what he had told us of the rivalry between the Police Department and the District Attorney's office.

Markham looked at Heath with a slow gracious smile, and shook his head.

"No, Sergeant," he replied. "I'm here to work with you, and I want that relationship understood from the outset. In fact, I wouldn't be here now if Major Benson hadn't 'phoned me and asked me to lend a hand. And I particularly want my name kept out of it. It's pretty generally known—and if it isn't, it will be—that the Major is an old friend of mine; so it will be better all round if my connection with the case is kept quiet."

Heath murmured something I did not catch, but I could see that he had, in large measure, been placated. He, in common with all other men who were acquainted with Markham, knew his word was good; and he personally liked the District Attorney.

"If there's any credit coming from this affair," Markham went on, "the Police Department is to get it; therefore I think it best for you to see the reporters. . . . And, by the way," he added good-naturedly, "if there's any blame coming, you fellows will have to bear that, too."

"Fair enough," assented Heath.

"And now, Sergeant, let's get to work," said Markham.

CHAPTER III

A LADY'S HANDBAG

(*Friday, June 14th ;* 9.30 *a.m.*)

THE District Attorney and Heath walked up to the body, and stood regarding it.

"You see," Heath explained, "he was shot directly from the front. A pretty powerful shot, too; for the bullet passed through the head and struck the woodwork over there by the window." He pointed to the place on the wainscot a short distance from the floor near the drapery of the window nearest the hall-way. "We found the expelled shell, and Captain Hagedorn's got the bullet."

He turned to the firearms expert.

"How about it, Captain? Anything special?"

Hagedorn raised his head slowly, and gave Heath a myopic frown. Then, after a few awkward movements, he answered with unhurried precision:

"A ·45 army bullet—Colt automatic."

"Any idea how close to Benson the gun was held?" asked Markham.

"Yes, sir, I have," Hagedorn replied, in his ponderous monotone. "Between five and six feet—probably."

Heath snorted.

"'Probably,'" he repeated to Markham with good-natured contempt. "You can bank on it if the Captain says so. . . . You see, sir, nothing smaller than a ·44 or ·45 will stop a man and these steel-capped army bullets go through a human skull like it was cheese. But in order to carry straight to the woodwork the gun had to be held pretty close; and as there aren't any powder marks on the face, it's a safe bet to take the Captain's figures as to distance."

At this point we heard the front door open and close, and Dr. Doremus, the Chief Medical Examiner, accompanied by his assistant, bustled in. He shook hands with

Markham and Inspector O'Brien, and gave Heath a friendly salutation.

"Sorry I couldn't get here sooner," he apologised.

He was a nervous man with a heavily seamed face and the manner of a real-estate salesman.

"What have we got here?" he asked, in the same breath, making a wry face at the body in the chair.

"You tell us, Doc," retorted Heath.

Dr. Doremus approached the murdered man with a callous indifference indicative of a long process of hardening. He first inspected the face closely—he was, I imagine, looking for powder marks. Then he glanced at the bullet hole in the forehead and at the ragged wound in the back of the head. Next he moved the dead man's arm, bent the fingers, and pushed the head a little to the side. Having satisfied himself as to the state of *rigor mortis*, he turned to Heath.

"Can we get him on the settee there?"

Heath looked at Markham inquiringly.

"All through, sir?"

Markham nodded, and Heath beckoned to the two men at the front windows and ordered the body placed on the davenport. It retained its sitting posture, due to the hardening of the muscles after death, until the doctor and his assistant straightened out the limbs. The body was then undressed, and Dr. Doremus examined it carefully for other wounds. He paid particular attention to the arms; and he opened both hands wide and scrutinised the palms. At length he straightened up and wiped his hands on a large coloured silk handkerchief.

"Shot through the left frontal," he announced. "Direct angle of fire. Bullet passed completely through the skull. Exit wound in the left occipital region—base of skull—you found the bullet, didn't you? He was awake when shot, and death was immediate—probably never knew what hit him. . . . He's been dead about—well, I should judge, eight hours; maybe longer."

"How about twelve-thirty for the exact time?" asked Heath.

The doctor looked at his watch.

"Fits O.K. . . . Anything else?"

No one answered, and after a slight pause the Chief Inspector spoke.

"We'd like a post-mortem report to-day, doctor."

"That'll be all right," Dr. Doremus answered, snapping shut his medical case and handing it to his assistant. "But get the body to the mortuary as soon as you can."

After a brief hand-shaking ceremony, he went out hurriedly.

Heath turned to the detective who had been standing by the table when we entered.

"Burke, you 'phone to Headquarters to call for the body —and tell 'em to get a move on. Then go back to the office and wait for me."

Burke saluted and disappeared.

Heath then addressed one of the two men who had been inspecting the grilles of the front windows.

"How about that ironwork, Snitkin?"

"No chance, Sergeant," was the answer. "Strong as a jail—both of 'em. Nobody got in through those windows."

"Very good," Heath told him. "Now, you two fellows chase along with Burke."

When they had gone the dapper man in the blue serge suit and derby, whose sphere of activity had seemed to be the fireplace, laid two cigarette butts on the table.

"I found these under the gas-logs, Sergeant," he explained unenthusiastically. "Not much; but there's nothing else laying around."

"All right, Emery." Heath gave the butts a disgruntled look. "You needn't wait, either. I'll see you at the office later."

Hagedorn came ponderously forward.

"I guess I'll be getting along, too," he rumbled. "But I'm going to keep this bullet awhile. It's got some peculiar rifling marks on it. You don't want it specially, do you, Sergeant?"

Heath smiled tolerantly.

"What'll I do with it, Captain? You keep it. But don't you dare lose it."

"I won't lose it," Hagedorn assured him, with stodgy seriousness; and, without so much as a glance at either the District Attorney or the Chief Inspector, he waddled from the room with a slightly rolling movement which suggested that of some huge amphibious mammal.

Vance, who was standing beside me near the door, turned and followed Hagedorn into the hall. The two stood talking in low tones for several minutes. Vance appeared to be asking questions, and although I was not close enough to hear the conversation, I caught several words and phrases —"trajectory," "muzzle velocity," "angle of fire," "impetus," "impact," "deflection," and the like—and wondered what on earth had prompted this strange interrogation.

As Vance was thanking Hagedorn for his information Inspector O'Brien entered the hall.

"Learning fast?" he asked, smiling patronizingly at Vance. Then, without waiting for a reply: "Come along, Captain; I'll drive you down town."

Markham heard him.

"Have you got room for Dinwiddie, too, Inspector?"

"Plenty, Mr. Markham."

The three of them went out.

Vance and I were now left alone in the room with Heath and the District Attorney, and, as if by common impulse, we all settled ourselves in chairs, Vance taking one near the dining-room door directly facing the chair in which Benson had been murdered.

I had been keenly interested in Vance's manner and actions from the moment of his arrival at the house. When he had first entered the room he had adjusted his monocle carefully—an act which, despite his air of passivity, I recognised as an indication of interest. When his mind was alert and he wished to take on external impressions quickly, he invariably brought out his monocle. He could see adequately enough without it, and his use of it, I had observed, was largely the result of an intellectual dictate. The added clarity of vision it gave him seemed subtly to affect his clarity of mind.[1]

At first he had looked over the room incuriously and watched the proceedings with bored apathy; but during

---

[1] Vance's eyes were slightly bifocal. His right eye was 1·2 astigmatic, whereas his left eye was practically normal.

Heath's brief questioning of his subordinates, an expression of cynical amusement had appeared in his face. Following a few general queries to Assistant District Attorney Dinwiddie, he had sauntered, with apparent aimlessness, about the room, looking at the various articles and occasionally shifting his gaze back and forth between different pieces of furniture. At length he had stooped down and inspected the mark made by the bullet on the wainscot; and once he had gone to the door and looked up and down the hall.

The only thing that had seemed to hold his attention to any extent was the body itself. He had stood before it for several minutes, studying its position, and even bent over the outstretched arm on the table as if to see just how the dead man's hand was holding the book. The crossed position of the legs, however, had attracted him most, and he had stood studying them for a considerable time. Finally, he had returned his monocle to his waistcoat pocket, and joined Dinwiddie and me near the door, where he had stood, watching Heath and the other detectives with lazy indifference, until the departure of Captain Hagedorn.

The four of us had no more than taken seats when the patrolman stationed in the vestibule appeared at the door.

"There's a man from the local precinct station here, sir," he announced, "who wants to see the officer in charge, Shall I sent him in?"

Heath nodded curtly, and a moment later a large red-faced Irishman, in civilian clothes, stood before us. He saluted Heath, but on recognizing the District Attorney, made Markham the recipient of his report.

"I'm Officer McLaughlin, sir—West Forty-seventh Street station," he informed us, "and I was on duty on this beat last night. Around midnight, I guess it was, there was a big grey Cadillac standing in front of this house—I noticed it particular, because it had a lot of fishing-tackle sticking out the back, and all its lights were on. When I heard of the crime this morning I reported the car to the station-sergeant, and he sent me around to tell you about it."

"Excellent," Markham commented; and then, with a nod, referred the matter to Heath.

"May be something in it," the latter admitted dubiously. "How long would you say the car was here, officer?"

"A good half-hour, anyway. It was here before twelve, and when I come back at twelve-thirty or thereabouts it was still here. But the next time I come by, it was gone."

"You saw nothing else? Nobody in the car, or anyone hanging around who might have been the owner?"

"No, sir, I did not."

Several other questions of a similar nature were asked him; but nothing more could be learned, and he was dismissed.

"Anyway," remarked Heath, "the car story will be good stuff to hand the reporters."

Vance had sat through the questioning of McLaughlin with drowsy inattention—I doubt if he even heard more than the first few words of the officer's report—and now, with a stifled yawn, he rose and, sauntering to the centre-table, picked up one of the cigarette butts that had been found in the fireplace. After rolling it between his thumb and forefinger and scrutinising the tip, he ripped the paper open with his thumb-nail, and held the exposed tobacco to his nose.

Heath, who had been watching him gloweringly, leaned suddenly forward in his chair.

"What are you doing there?" he demanded, in a tone of surly truculence.

Vance lifted his eyes in decorous astonishment.

"Merely smelling of the tobacco," he replied, with condescending unconcern. "It's rather mild, y'know, but delicately blended."

The muscles in Heath's cheeks worked angrily. "Well, you'd better put it down, sir," he advised. Then he looked Vance up and down. "Tobacco expert?" he asked, with ill-disguised sarcasm.

"Oh, dear no." Vance's voice was dulcet. "My speciality is scarab-cartouches of the Ptolemaic dynasties."

Markham interposed diplomatically.

"You really shouldn't touch anything around here, Vance, at this stage of the game. You never know what'll turn out to be important. Those cigarette stubs may quite possibly be significant evidence."

"Evidence?" repeated Vance sweetly. "My word! You don't say, really! Most amusin'!"

Markham was plainly annoyed; and Heath was boiling inwardly, but made no further comment: he even forced a mirthless smile. He evidently felt that he had been a little too abrupt with this friend of the District Attorney, however much the friend might have deserved being reprimanded.

Heath, however, was no sycophant in the presence of his superiors. He knew his worth and lived up to it with his whole energy, discharging the tasks to which he was assigned with a dogged indifference to his own political well-being. This stubbornness of spirit, and the solidity of character it implied, were respected and valued by the men over him.

He was a large, powerful man, but agile and graceful in his movements, like a highly trained boxer. He had hard, blue eyes, remarkably bright and penetrating, a small nose, a broad oval chin, and a stern, straight mouth with lips that appeared always compressed. His hair, which, though he was well along in his forties, was without a trace of greyness, was cropped about the edges, and stood upright in a short bristly pompadour. His voice had an aggressive resonance, but he rarely blustered. In many ways he accorded with the conventional notion of what a detective is like. But there was something more to the man's personality, an added capability and strength, as it were; and as I sat watching him that morning, I felt myself unconsciously admiring him, despite his very obvious limitations.

"What's the exact situation, Sergeant?" Markham asked. "Dinwiddie gave me only the barest facts."

Heath cleared his throat.

"We got the word a little before seven. Benson's housekeeper, a Mrs. Platz, called up the local station and reported that she'd found him dead, and asked that somebody be sent over at once. The message, of course, was relayed to Headquarters. I wasn't there at the time, but Burke and Emery were on duty, and after notifying Inspector Moran, they came on up here. Several of the men from the local station were already on the job doing the usual nosing about. When the Inspector had got here and looked the situation over, he telephoned me to hurry along. When I arrived the local men had gone, and three more men from the Homicide Bureau had joined Burke and Emery. The Inspector also 'phoned Captain Hagedorn—he thought the case big enough to call him in on it at once—and the Captain had just got here when you arrived. Mr. Dinwiddie had come in right after the Inspector, and 'phoned you at once. Chief Inspector O'Brien came along a little ahead of me. I questioned the Platz woman right off; and my men were looking the place over when you showed up."

"Where's this Mrs. Platz now?" asked Markham.

"Upstairs, being watched by one of the local men. She lives in the house."

"Why did you mention the specific hour of twelve-thirty to the doctor?"

"Platz told me she heard a report at that time, which I thought might have been the shot. I guess now it *was* the shot—it checks up with a number of things."

"I think we'd better have another talk with Mrs. Platz," Markham suggested. "But first: did you find anything suggestive in the room here—anything to go on?"

Heath hesitated almost imperceptibly; then he drew from his coat pocket a woman's handbag and a pair of long white kid gloves, and tossed them on the table in front of the District Attorney.

"Only these," he said. "One of the local men found them on the end of the mantel over there."

After a casual inspection of the gloves, Markham opened the handbag and turned its contents out on to the table. I came forward and looked on, but Vance remained in his chair, placidly smoking a cigarette.

The handbag was of fine gold mesh with a catch set with small sapphires. It was unusually small, and obviously designed only for evening wear. The objects which it had held, and which Markham was now inspecting, consisted of a flat watered-silk cigarette-case, a small gold phial of Roger and Gallet's *Fleurs d'Amour* perfume, a *cloisonné* vanity-compact, a short delicate cigarette-holder of inlaid amber, a gold-cased lipstick, a small embroidered French linen handkerchief with "M. St.C." monogrammed in the corner, and a Yale latch-key.

"This ought to give us a good lead," said Markham, indicating the handkerchief. "I suppose you went over the articles carefully, Sergeant?"

Heath nodded.

"Yes; and I imagine the bag belongs to the woman Benson was out with last night. The housekeeper told me he had an appointment and went out to dinner in his dress clothes. She didn't hear Benson when he came back, though. Anyway, we ought to be able to run down Miss 'M. St.C.' without much trouble."

Markham had taken up the cigarette case again, and as he held it upside down a little shower of loose dried tobacco fell on the table.

Heath stood up suddenly.

"Maybe those cigarettes came out of that case," he suggested. He picked up the intact butt and looked at it. "It's a lady's cigarette, all right. It looks as though it might have been smoked in a holder, too."

"I beg to differ with you, Sergeant," drawled Vance. "You'll forgive me, I'm sure. But there's a bit of lip-rouge on the end of the cigarette. It's hard to see, on account of the gold tip."

Heath looked at Vance sharply; he was too much surprised to be resentful. After a closer inspection of the cigarette, he turned again to Vance.

"Perhaps you could also tell us from these tobacco grains, if the cigarettes came from this case," he suggested, with gruff irony.

"One never knows, does one?" Vance replied, indolently rising.

Picking up the case, he pressed it wide open, and tapped it on the table. Then he looked into it closely, and a humorous smile twitched the corners of his mouth. Putting his forefinger deep into the case, he drew out a small cigarette which had evidently been wedged flat along the bottom of, of the pocket.

"My olfact'ry gifts won't be necess'ry now," he said. "It is apparent even to the naked eye that the cigarettes are, to speak loosely, identical—eh what, Sergeant?"

Heath grinned good-naturedly.

"That's one on us, Mr. Markham." And he carefully

put the cigarette and the stub in an envelope, which he marked and pocketed.

"You see now, Vance," observed Markham, "the importance of those cigarette butts."

"Can't say that I do," responded the other. "Of what possible value is a cigarette butt? You can't smoke it, y'know."

"It's evidence, my dear fellow," explained Markham patiently. "One knows that the owner of this bag returned with Benson last night, and remained long enough to smoke two cigarettes."

Vance lifted his eyebrows in mock astonishment.

"One does, does one? Fancy that, now."

"It only remains to locate her," interjected Heath.

"She's a rather decided brunette, at any rate—if that fact will facilitate your quest any," said Vance easily; "though why you should desire to annoy the lady, I can't for the life of me imagine—really I can't, don't y'know."

"Why do you say she's a brunette?" asked Markham.

"Well, if she isn't," Vance told him, sinking listlessly back in his chair, "then she should consult a cosmetician as to the proper way to make up. I see she uses 'Rachel' powder and Guerlain's dark lipstick. And it simply isn't done among blondes, old dear."

"I defer, of course, to your expert opinion," smiled Markham. Then, to Heath: "I guess we'll have to look for a brunette, Sergeant."

"It's all right with me," agreed Heath, jocularly. By this time, I think, he had entirely forgiven Vance for destroying the cigarette butt.

CHAPTER IV

THE HOUSEKEEPER'S STORY

(Friday, June 14th; 11 a.m.)

"Now," suggested Markham, "suppose we take a look over the house. I imagine you've done that pretty thoroughly already, Sergeant, but I'd like to see the layout. Anyway,

I don't want to question the housekeeper until the body has been removed."

Heath rose.

"Very good, sir. I'd like another look myself."

The four of us went into the hall and walked down the passageway to the rear of the house. At the extreme end, on the left, was a door leading downstairs to the basement; but it was locked and bolted.

"The basement is only used for storage now," Heath explained, "and the door which opens from it into the street areaway is boarded up. The Platz woman sleeps upstairs—Benson lived here alone, and there's plenty of spare room in the house—and the kitchen is on this floor."

He opened a door on the opposite side of the passageway, and we stepped into a small modern kitchen. Its two high windows, which gave into the paved rear yard at a height of about eight feet from the ground, were securely guarded with iron bars, and, in addition, the sashes were closed and locked. Passing through a swinging door we entered the dining-room, which was directly behind the living-room. The two windows here looked upon a small stone court—really no more than a deep air-well between Benson's house and the adjoining one—and these also were iron-barred and locked.

We now re-entered the hallway and stood for a moment at the foot of the stairs leading above.

"You can see, Mr. Markham," Heath pointed out, "that whoever shot Benson must have gotten in by the front door. There's no other way he could have entered. Living alone, I guess Benson was a little touchy on the subject of burglars. The only window that wasn't barred was the rear one in the living-room; and that was shut and locked. Anyway, it only leads into the inside court. The front windows of the living-room have that ironwork over them; so they couldn't have been used even to shoot through, for Benson was shot from the opposite direction. . . . It's pretty clear the gunman got in the front door."

"Looks that way," said Markham.

"And pardon me for saying so," remarked Vance, "but Benson let him in."

"Yes?" retorted Heath unenthusiastically. "Well, we'll find all that out later, I hope."

"Oh, doubtless," Vance drily agreed.

We ascended the stairs, and entered Benson's bedroom, which was directly over the living-room. It was severely but well furnished, and in excellent order. The bed was made, showing it had not been slept in that night; and the window-shades were drawn. Benson's dinner-jacket and white piqué waistcoat were hanging over a chair. A winged collar and a black bow-tie were on the bed, where they had evidently been thrown when Benson had taken them off on returning home. A pair of low evening shoes were standing by the bench at the foot of the bed. In a glass of water on the night-table was a platinum plate of four false teeth; and a toupee of beautiful workmanship was lying on the chiffonier.

This last item aroused Vance's special interest. He walked up to it and regarded it closely.

"Most int'restin'," he commented. "Our departed friend seems to have worn false hair; did you know that, Markham?"

"I always suspected it," was the indifferent answer.

Heath, who had remained standing on the threshold, seemed a little impatient.

"There's only one other room on this floor," he said, leading the way down the hall. "It's also a bedroom—for guests, so the housekeeper explained."

Markham and I looked in through the door, but Vance remained lounging against the balustrade at the head of the stairs. He was manifestly uninterested in Alvin Benson's domestic arrangements; and when Markham and Heath and I went up to the third floor, he sauntered down into the main hallway. When at length we descended from our tour of inspection he was casually looking over the titles in Benson's bookcase.

We had just reached the foot of the stairs when the front door opened and two men with a stretcher entered. The ambulance from the Department of Welfare had arrived to take the corpse to the morgue; and the brutal, businesslike way in which Benson's body was covered up, lifted on to the stretcher, carried out, and shoved into the wagon, made me shudder. Vance, on the other hand, after the merest fleeting glance at the two men, paid no attention to them. He had found a volume with a beautiful Humphrey-Milford binding, and was absorbed in its Roger Payne tooling and powdering.

"I think an interview with Mrs. Platz is indicated now," said Markham; and Heath went to the foot of the stairs and gave a loud, brisk order.

Presently, a grey-haired, middle-aged woman entered the living-room, accompanied by a plain-clothes man smoking a large cigar. Mrs. Platz was of the simple, old-fashioned, motherly type, with a calm, benevolent countenance. She impressed me as highly capable, and as a woman given little to hysteria—an impression strengthened by her attitude of passive resignation. She seemed, however, to possess that taciturn shrewdness that is so often found among the ignorant.

"Sit down, Mrs. Platz," Markham greeted her kindly. "I'm the District Attorney, and there are some questions I want to ask you."

She took a straight chair by the door and waited, gazing nervously from one to the other of us. Markham's gentle persuasive voice, though, appeared to encourage her, and her answers became more and more fluent.

The main facts that transpired from a quarter-of-an-hour's examination may be summed up as follows:

Mrs. Platz had been Benson's housekeeper for four years and was the only servant employed. She lived in the house, and her room was on the third, or top, floor in the rear.

On the afternoon of the preceding day Benson had returned from his office at an unusually early hour—around four o'clock—announcing to Mrs. Platz that he would not be home for dinner that evening. He had remained in the living-room, with the hall door closed, until half-past six, and had then gone upstairs to dress.

He had left the house about seven o'clock, but had not said where he was going. He had remarked casually that he would return in fairly good season, but had told Mrs. Platz she need not wait up for him—which was her custom whenever he intended bringing guests home. This was the last she had seen him alive. She had not heard him when he returned that night.

She had retired about half-past ten, and, because of the heat, had left the door ajar. She had been awakened some time later by a loud detonation. It had startled her, and she had turned on the light by her bed, noting that it was just half-past twelve by the small alarm-clock she used for rising. It was, in fact, the early hour which had reassured her. Benson, whenever he went out for the evening, rarely returned home before two; and this fact, coupled with the stillness of the house, had made her conclude that the noise which had aroused her had been merely the backfiring of an automobile in Forty-ninth Street. Consequently, she had dismissed the matter from her mind, and gone back to sleep.

At seven o'clock the next morning she came downstairs as usual to begin her day's duties, and, on her way to the front door to bring in the milk and cream, had discovered Benson's body. All the shades in the living-room were down.

At first she thought Benson had fallen asleep in his chair, but when she saw the bullet hole and noticed that the electric lights had been switched off, she knew he was dead. She had gone at once to the telephone in the hall and, asking the operator for the Police Station, had reported the murder. She had then remembered Benson's brother, Major Anthony Benson, and had telephoned him also. He had arrived at the house almost simultaneously with the detectives from the West Forty-seventh Street station. He had questioned her a little, talked with the plain-clothes men, and gone away before the men from Headquarters arrived.

"And now, Mrs. Platz," said Markham, glancing at the notes he had been making, "one or two more questions, and we won't trouble you further. . . . Have you noticed anything in Mr. Benson's actions lately that might lead you to suspect that he was worried—or, let us say, in fear of anything happening to him?"

"No, sir," the woman answered readily. "It looked like he was in special good humour for the last week or so."

"I notice that most of the windows on this floor are barred. Was he particularly afraid of burglars, or of people breaking in?"

"Well—not exactly," was the hesitant reply. "But he did use to say as how the police were no good—begging your pardon, sir—and how a man in this city had to look out for himself if he didn't want to get held up."

Markham turned to Heath with a chuckle.

"You might make a special note of that for your files, Sergeant." Then to Mrs. Platz: "Do you know of anyone who had a grudge against Mr. Benson?"

"Not a soul, sir," the housekeeper answered emphatically. "He was a queer man in many ways, but everybody seemed to like him. He was all the time going to parties or giving parties. I just can't see why anybody'd want to kill him."

Markham looked over his notes again.

"I don't think there's anything else for the present. . . . How about it, Sergeant? Anything further you want to ask?"

Heath pondered a moment.

"No, I can't think of anything more just now. . . . But you, Mrs. Platz," he added, turning a cold glance on the woman, "will stay here in this house till you're given permission to leave. We'll want to question you later. But you're not to talk to anyone else—understand? Two of my men will be here for a while yet."

Vance, during the interview, had been jotting down something on the fly-leaf of a small pocket address-book, and as Heath was speaking, he tore out the page and handed it to Markham. Markham glanced at it frowningly and pursed his lips. Then after a few minutes' hesitation, he addressed himself again to the housekeeper.

"You mentioned, Mrs. Platz, that Mr. Benson was liked by everyone. Did you yourself like him?"

The woman shifted her eyes to her lap.

"Well, sir," she replied reluctantly, "I was only working for him, and I haven't got any complaint about the way he treated me."

Despite her words, she gave the impression that she either disliked Benson extremely or greatly disapproved of him. Markham, however, did not push the point.

"And by the way, Mrs. Platz," he said next, "did Mr. Benson keep any firearms about the house? For instance, do you know if he owned a revolver?"

For the first time during the interview, the woman appeared agitated, even frightened.

"Yes, sir, I—think he did," she admitted, in an unsteady voice.

"Where did he keep it?"

The woman glanced up apprehensively, and rolled her eyes slightly as if weighing the advisability of speaking frankly. Then she replied in a low voice:

"In that hidden drawer there in the centre-table. You—you use that little brass button to open it with."

Heath jumped up, and pressed the button she had indicated. A tiny, shallow drawer shot out; and in it lay a Smith and Wesson thirty-eight revolver with an inlaid pearl handle. He picked it up, broke the carriage, and looked at the head of the cylinder.

"Full," he announced laconically.

An expression of tremendous relief spread over the woman's features, and she sighed audibly.

Markham had risen and was looking at the revolver over Heath's shoulder.

"You'd better take charge of it, Sergeant," he said; "though I don't see exactly how it fits in with the case."

He resumed his seat, and glancing at the notation Vance had given him, turned again to the housekeeper.

"One more question, Mrs. Platz. You said Mr. Benson came home early and spent his time before dinner in this room. Did he have any callers during that time?"

I was watching the woman closely, and it seemed to me that she quickly compressed her lips. At any rate, she sat up a little straighter in her chair before answering.

"There wasn't no one, so far as I know."

"But surely you would have known if the bell rang," insisted Markham. "You would have answered the door, wouldn't you?"

"There wasn't no one," she repeated, with a trace of sullenness.

"And last night: did the door-bell ring at all after you had retired?"

"No, sir."

"You would have heard it, even if you'd been asleep?"

"Yes, sir. There's a bell just outside my door, the same as in the kitchen. It rings in both places. Mr. Benson had it fixed that way."

Markham thanked her and dismissed her. When she had gone, he looked at Vance questioningly.

"What idea did you have in your mind when you handed me those questions?"

"I might have been a bit presumptuous, y'know," said Vance; "but when the lady was extolling the deceased's popularity, I rather felt she was overdoing it a bit. There was an unconscious implication of antithesis in her eulogy, which suggested to me that she herself was not ardently enamoured of the gentleman."

"And what put the notion of firearms into your mind?"

"That query," explained Vance, "was a corollary of your own question about barred windows and Benson's fear of burglars. If he was in a funk about house-breakers or enemies, he'd be likely to have weapons at hand—eh, what?"

"Well, anyway, Mr. Vance," put in Heath, "your curiosity unearthed a nice little revolver that's probably never been used."

"By the bye, Sergeant," returned Vance, ignoring the other's good humoured sarcasm, "just what do you make of that nice little revolver?"

"Well, now," Heath replied, with ponderous facetiousness, "I deduct that Mr. Benson kept a pearl-handled Smith and Wesson in a secret drawer of his centre-table."

"You don't say so—really!" exclaimed Vance in mock admiration. "Pos'tively illuminatin'!"

Markham broke up this raillery.

"Why did you want to know about visitors, Vance? There obviously hadn't been anyone here."

"Oh, just a whim of mine. I was assailed by an impulsive yearning to hear what La Platz would say."

Heath was studying Vance curiously. His first impressions of the man were being dispelled, and he had begun to suspect that beneath the other's casual and debonair exterior there was something of a more solid nature than he had at first imagined. He was not altogether satisfied with Vance's explanations to Markham, and seemed to be endeavouring to penetrate to his real reasons for supplementing the District Attorney's interrogation of the housekeeper. Heath was astute, and he had the worldly man's ability to read people;

but Vance, being different from the men with whom he usually came in contact, was an enigma to him.

At length he relinquished his scrutiny, and drew up his chair to the table with a spirited air.

"And now, Mr. Markham," he said crisply, "we'd better outline our activities so as not to duplicate our efforts. The sooner I get my men started, the better."

Markham assented readily.

"The investigation is entirely up t⁻ you, Sergean   I'm here to help wherever I'm needed."

"That's very kind of you, sir," Heath returned. "But it looks to me as though there'd be enough work for all parties. . . . Suppose I get to work on running down the owner of the handbag, and send some men out scouting among Benson's night-life cronies—I can pick up some names from the housekeeper, and they'll be a good starting point. And I'll get after that Cadillac, too. . . . Then we ought to look into his lady friends—I guess he had enough of 'em."

"I may get something out of the Major along that line," supplied Markham. "He'll tell me anything I want to know. And I can also look into Benson's business associates through the same channel."

"I was going to suggest that you could do that better than I could," Heath rejoined. "We ought to run into something pretty quick that'll give us a line to go on. And I've got an idea that when we locate the lady he took to dinner last night and brought back here, we'll know a lot more than we do now."

"Or a lot less," murmured Vance.

Heath looked up quickly, and grunted with an air of massive petulance.

"Let me tell you something, Mr. Vance," he said, "since I understand you want to learn something about these affairs: when anything goes seriously wrong in this world, it's pretty safe to look for a woman in the case."

"Ah, yes," smiled Vance. "*Cherchez la femme*—an aged notion. Even the Romans laboured under the superstition —they expressed it with *Dux femina facti*."

"However they expressed it," retorted Heath, "they had the right idea. And don't let 'em tell you different."

Again Markham diplomatically intervened.

"That point will be settled very soon, I hope. . . . And now, Sergeant, if you've nothing else to suggest, I'll be getting along. I told Major Benson I'd see him at lunch-time; and I may have some news for you by to-night."

"Right," assented Heath. "I'm going to stick around here for a while and see if there's anything I overlooked. I'll arrange for a guard outside and also for a man inside to keep an eye on the Platz woman. Then I'll see the reporters, and let them in on the disappearing Cadillac and Mr. Vance's mysterious revolver in the secret drawer. I guess that ought to hold 'em. If I find out anything, I'll 'phone you."

When he had shaken hands with the District Attorney, he turned to Vance.

"Good-bye, sir," he said pleasantly, much to my surprise, and to Markham's, too, I imagine. "I hope you learned something this morning."

"You'd be positively dumbfounded, Sergeant, at all I did learn," Vance answered carelessly.

Again I noted the look of shrewd scrutiny in Heath's eyes; but in a second it was gone.

"Well, I'm glad of that," was his perfunctory reply.

Markham, Vance and I went out, and the patrolman on duty hailed a taxicab for us.

"So that's the way our lofty *gendarmerie* approaches the mysterious wherefores of criminal enterprise—eh?" mused Vance, as we started on our way across town. "Markham, old dear, how do these robust lads ever succeed in running down a culprit?"

"You have witnessed only the barest preliminaries," Markham explained. "There are certain things that must be done as a matter of routine—*ex abundanti cautelæ*, as we lawyers say."

"But, my word!—such technique!" sighed Vance. "Ah, well, *quantum est in rebus inane!* as we laymen say."

"You don't think much of Heath's capacity, I know "—Markham's voice was patient—"but he's a clever man, and one that it's very easy to underestimate."

"I dare say," murmured Vance. "Anyway, I'm deuced grateful to you, and all that, for letting me behold the solemn proceedings. I've been vastly amused, even if not uplifted. Your official Æsculapius rather appealed to me, y'know—such a brisk, unemotional chap, and utterly unimpressed with the corpse. He really should have taken up crime in a serious way, instead of studying medicine."

Markham lapsed into gloomy silence, and sat looking out of the window in troubled meditation until we reached Vance's house.

"I don't like the look of things," he remarked, as we drew up to the kerb. "I have a curious feeling about this case."

Vance regarded him a moment from the corner of his eye.

"See here, Markham," he said with unwonted seriousness; "haven't you any idea who shot Benson?"

Markham forced a faint smile.

"I wish I had. Crimes of wilful murder are not so easily solved. And this case strikes me as a particularly complex one."

"Fancy, now!" said Vance, as he stepped out of the machine. "And I thought it extr'ordin'rily simple."

CHAPTER V

GATHERING INFORMATION

(Saturday, June 15th; forenoon)

You will remember the sensation caused by Alvin Benson's murder. It was one of those crimes that appeal irresistibly to the popular imagination. Mystery is the basis of all romance, and about the Benson case there hung an impenetrable aura of mystery. It was many days before any definite light was shed on the circumstances surrounding the shooting; but numerous *ignes fatui* arose to beguile the public's imagination, and wild speculations were heard on all sides.

Alvin Benson, while not a romantic figure in any respect—had been well known; and his personality had been a colourful and spectacular one. He had been a member of New York's wealthy bohemian set—an avid sportsman, a rash gambler, and professional man-about-town; and his life, led on the borderland of the *demi-monde*, had contained many high-lights. His exploits in the night clubs and cabarets had long supplied the subject-matter for exaggerated stories and comments in the various local papers and magazines which batten on Broadway's scandalmongers.

Benson and his brother Anthony, had, at the time of the former's sudden death, been running a brokerage office at 21 Wall Street, under the name of Benson and Benson. Both were regarded by the other brokers of the Street as shrewd business men, though perhaps a shade unethical when gauged by the constitution and by-laws of the New York Stock Exchange. They were markedly contrasted as to temperament and taste, and saw little of each other outside the office. Alvin Benson devoted his entire leisure to pleasure-seeking and was a regular patron of the city's leading cafés; whereas Anthony Benson, who was the older and had served as a major in the late War, followed a sedate and conventional existence, spending most of his evenings quietly at his clubs. Both, however, were popular in their respective circles, and between them they had built up a large clientele.

The glamour of the financial district had much to do with the manner in which the crime was handled by the newspapers. Moreover, the murder had been committed at a time when the metropolitan press was experiencing a temporary lull in sensationalism; and the story was spread over the front pages of the papers with a prodigality rarely encountered in such cases.[1] Eminent detectives throughout the country were interviewed by enterprising reporters. Histories of famous unsolved murder cases were revived; and clairvoyants and astrologers were engaged by the Sunday editors to solve the mystery by various metaphysical devices. Photographs and detailed diagrams were the daily accompaniments of these journalistic outpourings.

[1] Even the famous Elwell case, which came several years later and bore certain points of similarity to the Benson case, created no greater sensation, despite the fact that Elwell was more widely known than Benson, and the persons involved were more prominent socially. Indeed, the Benson case was referred to several times in descriptions of the Elwell case; and one anti-administration paper regretted editorially that John F.-X. Markham was no longer District Attorney of New York.

In all the news stories the grey Cadillac and the pearl-handled Smith and Wesson were featured. There were pictures of Cadillac cars, "touched-up," and reconstructed to accord with Patrolman McLaughlin's description, some of them even showing the fishing-tackle protruding from the tonneau. A photograph of Benson's centre-table had been taken, with the secret drawer enlarged and reproduced in an "inset." One Sunday magazine went so far as to hire an expert cabinet-maker to write a dissertation on secret compartments in furniture.

The Benson case from the outset had proved a trying and difficult one from the police standpoint. Within an hour of the time that Vance and I had left the scene of the crime a systematic investigation had been launched by the men of the Homicide Bureau in charge of Sergeant Heath. Benson's house was again gone over thoroughly, and all his private correspondence read; but nothing was brought forth that could throw any light on the tragedy. No weapon was found aside from Benson's own Smith and Wesson; and though all the window grilles were again inspected, they were found to be secure, indicating that the murderer had either let himself in with a key, or else been admitted by Benson. Heath, by the way, was unwilling to admit the latter possibility despite Mrs. Platz's positive assertion that no other person besides herself and Benson had a key.

Because of the absence of any definite clue, other than the handbag and the gloves, the only proceeding possible was the interrogating of Benson's friends and associates in the hope of uncovering some fact which would furnish a trail. It was by this process also that Heath hoped to establish the identity of the owner of the handbag. A special effort was therefore made to ascertain where Benson had spent the evening; but though many of his acquaintances were questioned, and the cafés where he habitually dined were visited, no one could at once be found who had seen him that night; nor, as far as it was possible to learn, had he mentioned to anyone his plans for the evening. Furthermore, no general information of a helpful nature came to light immediately, although the police pushed their inquiry with the utmost thoroughness. Benson apparently had no

enemies; he had not quarrelled seriously with anyone; and
his affairs were reported in their usual orderly shape.

Major Anthony Benson was naturally the principal person looked to for information, because of his intimate
knowledge of his brother's affairs; and it was in this connection that the District Attorney's office did its chief function-
ing at the beginning of the case. Markham had lunched
with Major Benson the day the crime was discovered, and
though the latter had shown a willingness to co-operate—
even to the detriment of his brother's character—his suggestions were of little value. He explained to Markham
that, though he knew most of his brother's associates, he
could not name anyone who would have any reason for
committing such a crime, or anyone who, in his opinion,
would be able to help in leading the police to the guilty person.
He admitted frankly, however, that there was a side to his
brother's life with which he was unacquainted, and regretted
that he was unable to suggest any specific way of ascertaining the hidden facts. But he intimated that his brother's
relations with women were of a somewhat unconventional
nature; and he ventured the opinion that there was a bare
possibility of a motive being found in that direction.

Pursuant of the few indefinite and unsatisfactory suggestions of Major Benson, Markham had immediately
put to work two good men from the Detective Division
assigned to the District Attorney's office, with instructions
to confine their investigations to Benson's women acquaintances so as not to appear in any way to be encroaching
upon the activities of the Central Office men. Also, as a
result of Vance's apparent interest in the housekeeper at the
time of the interrogation, he had sent a man to look into the
woman's antecedents and relationships.

Mrs. Platz, it was learned, had been born in a small
Pennsylvania town, of German parents, both of whom
were dead; and had been a widow for over sixteen years.
Before coming to Benson, she had been with one family
for twelve years, and had left the position only because
her mistress had given up housekeeping and moved into a
hotel. Her former employer, when questioned, said she
thought there had been a daughter, but had never seen
the child, and knew nothing of it. In these facts there

was nothing to take hold of, and Markham had merely filed
the report as a matter of form.

Heath had instigated a city-wide search for the grey
Cadillac, although he had little faith in its direct connection with the crime; and in this the newspapers helped
considerably by the extensive advertising given the car.
One curious fact developed that fired the police with the
hope that the Cadillac might indeed hold some clue to the
mystery. A street-cleaner, having read or heard about
the fishing-tackle in the machine, reported the finding of
two jointed fishing-rods, in good condition, at the side of
one of the drives in Central Park near Columbus Circle.
The question was: were these rods part of the equipment
Patrolman McLaughlin had seen in the Cadillac? The
owner of the car might conceivably have thrown them
away in his flight; but, on the other hand, they might have
been lost by someone else while driving through the park.
No further information was forthcoming, and on the morning of the day following the discovery of the crime the case,
so far as any definite progress towards a solution was concerned,
had taken no perceptible forward step.

That morning Vance had sent Currie out to buy him
every available newspaper; and he had spent over an hour
perusing the various accounts of the crime. It was unusual
for him to glance at a newspaper, even casually, and I could
not refrain from expressing my amazement at his sudden
interest in a subject so entirely outside his normal routine.

"No, Van, old dear," he explained languidly, "I am not
becoming sentimen'al or even human, as that word is
erroneously used to-day. I cannot say with Terence,
'Homo sum, humani nihil a me alienum puto,' because I
regard most things that are called human as decidedly
alien to myself. But, y'know, this little flurry in crime
has proved rather int'restin', or, as the magazine writers
say, intriguing—beastly word! . . . Van, you really should
read this precious interview with Sergeant Heath. He
takes an entire column to say, 'I know nothin'. A priceless
lad! I'm becoming pos'tively fond of him."

"It may be," I suggested, "that Heath is keeping his
true knowledge from the papers, as a bit of tactical diplo-
macy."

"No," Vance returned, with a sad wag of the head; "no man has so little vanity that he would delib'rately reveal himself to the world as a creature with no perceptible powers of human reasoning—as he does in all these morning journals—for the mere sake of bringing one murderer to justice. That would be martyrdom gone mad."

"Markham, at any rate, may know or suspect something that hasn't been revealed," I said.

Vance pondered a moment.

"That's not impossible," he admitted. "He has kept himself modestly in the background in all this journalistic palaver. Suppose we look into the matter more thoroughly—eh, what?"

Going to the telephone he called the District Attorney's office, and I heard him make an appointment with Markham for lunch at the Stuyvesant Club.

"What about that Nadelmann statuette at Stieglitz's," I asked, remembering the reason for my presence at Vance's that morning.

"I ain't[1] in the mood for Greek simplifications to-day," he answered, turning again to his newspapers.

To say that I was surprised at his attitude is to express it mildly. In all my association with him I had never known him to forgo his enthusiasm for art in favour of any other divertisement; and heretofore anything pertaining to the law and its operations had failed to interest him. I realised, therefore, that something of an unusual nature was at work in his brain, and I refrained from further comment.

Markham was a little late for the appointment at the Club, and Vance and I were already at our favourite corner-table when he arrived.

"Well, my good Lycurgus," Vance greeted him, "aside from the fact that several new and significant clues have been unearthed and that the public may expect important

[1] Vance, who had lived many years in England, frequently said "ain't"—a contraction which is regarded there more leniently than in this country. He also pronounced *ate* as if it were spelled *et*; and I cannot remember his ever using the word "stomach" or "bug," both of which are under the social ban in England.

developments in the very near future, and all that sort of tosh, how are things really going?"

Markham smiled.

"I see you have been reading the newspapers. What do you think of the accounts?"

"Typical, no doubt," replied Vance. "They carefully and painstakingly omit nothing but the essentials."

"Indeed?" Markham's tone was jocular. "And what, may I ask, do you regard as the essentials of the case?"

"In my foolish amateur way," said Vance, "I looked upon dear Alvin's toupee as a rather conspicuous essential, don't y'know."

"Benson, at any rate, regarded it in that light, I imagine. ¡ . . Anything else?"

"Well, there was the collar and tie on the chiffonier."

"And," added Markham chaffingly, "don't overlook the false teeth in the tumbler."

"You're pos'tively coruscatin'!" Vance exclaimed. "Yes, they, too, were an essential of the situation. And I'll warrant the imcomp'rable Heath didn't even notice them. But the other Aristotles present were equally sketchy in their observations."

"You weren't particularly impressed by the investigation yesterday, I take it," said Markham.

"On the contrary," Vance assured him, "I was impressed to the point of stupefaction. The whole proceedings constituted a masterpiece of absurdity. Everything relevant was sublimely ignored. There were at least a dozen *points de départ*, all leading in the same direction, but not one of them apparently was even noticed by any of the officiating *pourparleurs*. Everybody was too busy at such silly occupations as looking for cigarette-ends and inspecting the ironwork at the windows—those grilles, by the way, were rather attractive—Florentine design."

Markham was both amused and ruffled.

"One's pretty safe with the police, Vance," he said. "They get there eventually."

"I simply adore your trusting nature," murmured Vance. "But confide in me: what do you know regarding Benson's murder?"

Markham hesitated.

"This is, of course, in confidence," he said at length; "but this morning, right after you 'phoned, one of the men I had put to work on the amatory end of Benson's life, reported that he had found the woman who left her handbag and gloves at the house that night—the initials on the handkerchief gave him the clue. And he dug up some interesting facts about her. As I suspected, she was Benson's dinner companion that evening. She's an actress—musical comedy, I believe. Muriel St. Clair by name."

"Most unfortunate," breathed Vance. "I was hoping, y'know, your myrmidons wouldn't discover the lady. I haven't the pleasure of her acquaintance, or I'd send her a note of commiseration. . . . Now, I presume, you'll play the *juge d'instruction* and chivvy her most horribly, what?"

"I shall certainly question her, if that's what you mean."

Markham's manner was preoccupied, and during the rest of the lunch we spoke but little.

As we sat in the Club's lounge-room later, having our smoke, Major Benson, who had been standing dejectedly at a window close by, caught sight of Markham and came over to us. He was a full-faced man of about fifty, with grave kindly features and a sturdy, erect body.

He greeted Vance and me with a casual bow, and turned at once to the District Attorney.

"Markham, I've been thinking things over constantly since our lunch yesterday," he said, "and there's one other suggestion I think I might make. There's a man named Leander Pfyfe who was very close to Alvin; and it's possible he could give you some helpful information. His name didn't occur to me yesterday, for he doesn't live in the city; he's on Long Island somewhere—Port Washington, I think. It's just an idea. The truth is, I can't seem to figure out anything that makes sense in this terrible affair."

He drew a quick, resolute breath, as if to check some involuntary sign of emotion. It was evident that the man, for all his habitual passivity of nature, was deeply moved.

"That's a good suggestion, Major," Markham said, making a notation on the back of a letter. "I'll get after it immediately."

Vance, who, during this brief interchange, had been

gazing unconcernedly out of the window, turned and addressed himself to the Major.

"How about Colonel Ostrander? I've seen him several
times in the company of your brother."

Major Benson made a slight gesture of deprecation.

"Only an acquaintance. He'd be of no value."

Then he turned to Markham.

"I don't imagine it's time even to hope that you've run
across anything?"

Markham took his cigar from his mouth, and turning it
about in his fingers, contemplated it thoughtfully.

"I wouldn't say that," he remarked after a moment.
"I've managed to find out whom your brother dined with
Thursday night; and I know that this person returned
home with him shortly after midnight." He paused as if
deliberating the wisdom of saying more. Then: "The fact
is, I don't need a great deal more evidence than I've got
already to go before the Grand Jury and ask for an indictment."

A look of surprised admiration flashed in the Major's
sombre face.

"Thank God for that, Markham!" he said. Then, setting
his heavy jaw, he placed his hand on the District Attorney's
shoulder. "Go the limit—for my sake!" he urged. "If
you want me for anything, I'll be here at the Club till late."

With this he turned and walked from the room.

"It seems a bit cold-blooded to bother the Major with
questions so soon after his brother's death," commented
Markham. "Still, the world has got to go on."

Vance stifled a yawn.

"Why—in heaven's name?" he murmured listlessly.

CHAPTER VI

VANCE OFFERS AN OPINION

(*Saturday, June 15th; 2 p.m.*)

WE sat for a while smoking in silence, Vance gazing lazily
out into Madison Square, Markham frowning deeply at the

faded oil portrait of old Peter Stuyvesant that hung over the fireplace.

Presently Vance turned and contemplated the District Attorney with a faintly sardonic smile.

"I say, Markham," he drawled; "it has always been a source of amazement to me how easily you investigators of crime are misled by what you call clues. You find a footprint, or a parked motor-car, or a monogrammed hand-kerchief, and then dash off on a wild chase with your eternal *Ecce signum !* 'Pon my word, it's as if you chaps were all under the spell of shillin' shockers. Won't you ever learn that crimes can't be solved by deductions based merely on material clues and circumst'ntial evidence?"

I think Markham was as much surprised as I at this sudden criticism; yet we both knew Vance well enough to realise that, despite his placid and almost flippant tone, there was a serious purpose behind his words.

"Would you advocate ignoring all the tangible evidence of a crime?" asked Markham, a bit patronisingly.

"Most emphatically," Vance declared calmly. "It's not only worthless, but dangerous. . . . The great trouble with you chaps, d'ye see, is that you approach every crime with a fixed and unshakable assumption that the criminal is either half-witted or a colossal bungler. I say, has it never by any chance occurred to you that if a detective could see a clue, the criminal would also have seen it, and would either have concealed it or disguised it, if he had not wanted it found? And have you never paused to consider that anyone clever enough to plan and execute a successful crime these days, is, *ipso facto,* clever enough to manufacture whatever clues suit his purpose? Your detective seems wholly unwilling to admit that the surface appearance of a crime may be delib'r-ately deceptive, or that the clues may have been planted for the def'nite purpose of misleading him."

"I'm afraid," Markham pointed out, with an air of in-dulgent irony, "that we'd convict very few criminals if we were to ignore all indicatory evidence, cogent circumstances and irresistible inferences. . . . As a rule, you know, crimes are not witnessed by outsiders."

"That's your fundamental error, don't y'know," Vance observed impassively. "Every crime is witnessed by out-

siders, just as is every work of art.   The fact that no one sees
the criminal, or the artist, actu'lly at work, is wholly incon-
s'quential.   The modern investigator of crime would doubtless refuse to believe that Rubens painted the "Descent from
the Cross" in the Cathedral at Antwerp if there was sufficient
circumst'ntial evidence to indicate that he had been away on
diplomatic business, for instance, at the time it was painted.
And yet, my dear fellow, such a conclusion would be prepost'rous.   Even if the inf'rences to the contr'ry were so
irresistible as to be legally overpowering, the picture itself
would prove conclusively that Rubens did paint it.   Why?
For the simple reason, d'ye see, that no one but Rubens could
have painted it.   It bears the indelible imprint of his personality and genius—and his alone."

"I'm not an æsthetician," Markham reminded him, a
trifle testily.   "I'm merely a practical lawyer, and when
it comes to determining the authorship of a crime, I prefer
tangible evidence to metaphysical hypotheses."

"Your pref'rence, my dear fellow," Vance returned
blandly, "will inev'tably involve you in all manner of em-
barrassing errors."

He slowly lit another cigarette, and blew a wreath of
smoke towards the ceiling.

"Consider, for example, your conclusions in the present
murder case," he went on in his emotionless drawl.   "You
are labouring under the grave misconception that you
know the person who prob'bly killed the unspeakable
Benson.   You admitted as much to the Major; and you
told him you had nearly enough evidence to ask for an
indictment.   No doubt, you do possess a number of what
the learned Solons of to-day regard as convincing clues.
But the truth is, don't y'know, you haven't your eye on
the guilty person at all.   You're about to bedevil some poor
girl who had nothing whatever to do with the crime."

Markham swung about sharply.

"So!" he retorted.   "I'm about to bedevil an innocent
person, eh?   Since my assistants and I are the only ones
who happen to know what evidence we hold against her,
perhaps you will explain by what occult process you acquired
your knowledge of this person's innocence."

"It's quite simple, y'know," Vance replied, with a quizzical twitch of the lips. "You haven't your eye on the murderer for the reason that the person who committed this particular crime was sufficiently shrewd and perspicacious to see to it that no evidence which you or the police were likely to find, would even remotely indicate his guilt."

He had spoken with easy assurance of one who enunciates an obvious fact—a fact which permits of no argument.

Markham gave a disdainful laugh.

"No law-breaker," he asserted oracularly, "is shrewd enough to see all contingencies. Even the most trivial event has so many intimately related and serrated points of contact with other events which precede and follow, that it is a known fact that every criminal—however long and carefully he may plan—leaves some loose end to his preparations, which in the end betrays him."

"A known fact?" Vance repeated. "No, my dear fellow —merely a conventional superstition, based on the childish idea of an implacable, avenging Nemesis. I can see how this esoteric notion of the inev'tability of divine punishment would appeal to the popular imagination, like fortune-telling and Ouija boards, don't y'know; but—my word—it desolates me to think that you, old chap, would give credence to such mystical moonshine!"

"Don't let it spoil your entire day," said Markham acridly.

"Regard the unsolved or successful crimes that are taking place every day," Vance continued, disregarding the other's irony, "crimes which completely baffle the best detectives in the business, what? The fact is, the only crimes that are ever solved are those planned by stupid people. That's why, whenever a man of even mod'rate sagacity decides to commit a crime, he accomplishes it with but little diff'culty, and fortified with the positive assurance of his immunity to discovery."

"Undetected crimes," scornfully submitted Markham, "result, in the main, from official bad luck—not from superior criminal cleverness."

"Bad luck"—Vance's voice was almost dulcet—"is merely a defensive and self-consoling synonym for inefficiency. A man with ingenuity and brains is not harassed by bad luck. . . . No, Markham, old dear; unsolved crimes are simply crimes which have been intelligently planned and executed. And, d'ye see, it happens that the Benson murder falls into that categ'ry. Therefore, when, after a few hours' investigation, you say you're pretty sure who committed it, you must pardon me if I take issue with you."

He paused and took a few meditative puffs on his cigarette.

"The factitious and casuistic methods of deduction you chaps pursue are apt to lead almost anywhere. In proof of which assertion I point triumphantly to the unfortunate young lady whose liberty you are now plotting to take away."

Markham, who had been hiding his resentment behind a smile of tolerant contempt, now turned on Vance and fairly glowered.

"It so happens—and I'm speaking *ex cathedra*," he proclaimed defiantly, "that I come pretty near having the goods on your 'unfortunate young lady.'"

Vance was unmoved.

"And yet, y'know," he observed drily, "no woman could possibly have done it."

I could see that Markham was furious. When he spoke he almost spluttered.

"A woman couldn't have done it, eh—no matter what the evidence?"

"Quite so," Vance rejoined placidly: "not if she herself swore to it and produced a tome of what you scions of the law term, rather pompously, incontrovertible evidence."

"Ah!" There was no mistaking the sarcasm of Markham's tone. "I am to understand then that you even regard confessions as valueless?"

"Yes, my dear Justinian," the other responded with an air of complacency; "I would have you understand precisely that. Indeed, they are worse than valueless—they're downright misleading. The fact that occasionally they may prove to be correct—like woman's prepost'rously overrated intuition—renders them just so much more unreliable."

Markham grunted disdainfully.

"Why should any person confess something to his detriment unless he felt that the truth had been found out, or was likely to be found out?"

"'Pon my word, Markham, you astound me! Permit me to murmur, *privatissime et gratis*, into your innocent ear that there are many other presumable motives for confessing. A confession may be the result of fear, or duress, or expediency, or mother-love, or chivalry, or what the psycho-analysts call the inferiority complex, or delusions, or a mistaken sense of duty, or a perverted egotism, or sheer vanity, or any other of a hundred causes. Confessions are the most treach'rous and unreliable of all forms of evidence; and even the silly and unscientific law repudiates them in murder cases unless substantiated by other evidence."

"You are eloquent; you wring me," said Markham. "But if the law threw out all confessions and ignored all material clues, as you appear to advise, then society might as well close down all its courts and scrap all its jails."

"A typical *non sequitur* of legal logic," Vance replied.

"But how would you convict the guilty, may I ask?"

"There is one infallible method of determining human guilt and responsibility," Vance explained; "but as yet the police are as blissfully unaware of its possibilities as they are ignorant of its operations. The truth can be learned only by an analysis of the pyschological factors of a crime and an application of them to the individual. The only real clues are psychological—not material. Your truly profound art expert, for instance, does not judge and authenticate pictures by an inspection of the underpainting and a chemical analysis of the pigments, but by studying the creative personality revealed in the picture's conception and execution. He asks himself: Does this work of art embody the qualities of form and technique and mental attitude that made up the genius —namely, the personality—of Rubens, or Michelangelo, or Veronese, or Titian, or Tintoretto, or whoever may be the artist to whom the work was tentatively credited."

"My mind is, I fear," Markham confessed, "still sufficiently primitive to be impressed by vulgar facts; and in the present instance—unfortunately for your most original and artistic analogy—I possess quite an array of such facts, all of which indicate that a certain young woman is the—shall we say—creator of the criminal *opus* entitled *The Murder of Alvin Benson.*"

Vance shrugged his shoulders almost imperceptibly.

"Would you mind telling me—in confidence, of course —what these facts are?"

"Certainly not," Markham acceded. "*Imprimis:* the lady was in the house at the time the shot was fired."

Vance affected incredibility.

"Eh—my word! She was actu'lly there? Most extr'-ordin'ry!"

"The evidence of her presence is unassailable," pursued Markham. "As you know, the gloves she wore at dinner, and the handbag she carried with her, were both found on the mantel in Benson's living-room."

"Oh!" murmured Vance, with a faintly deprecating smile. "It was not the lady, then, but her gloves and bag which were present—a minute and unimportant distinction, no doubt, from the legal point of view. . . . Still," he added, "I deplore the inability of my layman's untutored mind to accept the two conditions as identical. My trousers are at the dry-cleaners; therefore, I am at the dry-cleaners, what?"

Markham turned on him with considerable warmth.

"Does it mean nothing in the way of evidence, even to your layman's mind, that a woman's intimate and necessary articles, which she has carried throughout the evening, are found in her escort's quarters the following morning?"

"In admitting that it does not." Vance acknowledged quietly, "I no doubt expose a legal perception lamentably inefficient."

"But since the lady certainly wouldn't have carried these particular objects during the afternoon, and since she couldn't have called at the house that evening during Benson's absence without the housekeeper knowing it, how, may one ask, did these articles happen to be there the next morning if she herself did not take them there late that night?"

"'Pon my word, I haven't the slightest notion," Vance rejoined. "The lady herself could doubtless appease your curiosity. But there are any number of possible explanations, y'know. Our departed Chesterfield might have brought them home in his coat pocket—women are eternally handing men all manner of gewgaws and bundles to carry for 'em. with the cooing request: 'Can you put this in your pocket for me?' . . . Then again, there is the possibility that the real murderer secured them in some way, and placed them on the mantel delib'rately to mislead the *polizei*. Women, don't y'know, never put their belongings in such neat, out-of-the-way places as mantels and hat racks. They invariably throw them down on your fav'rite chair or your centre-table."

"And, I suppose," Markham interjected, "Benson also brought the lady's cigarette butts home in his pocket?"

"Stranger things have happened," returned Vance equably; "though I shan't accuse him of it in this instance. . . . The cigarette butts may, y'know, be evidence of a previous *conversazione*."

"Even your despised Heath," Markham informed him, "had sufficient intelligence to ascertain from the house-keeper that she sweeps out the grate every morning."

Vance smiled admiringly.

"You're *so* thorough, aren't you? . . . But, I say, that can't be, by any chance, your only evidence against the lady?"

"By no means," Markham assured him. "But, despite your superior distrust it's good corroboratory evidence, nevertheless."

"I dare say," Vance agreed, "seeing with what frequency innocent persons are condemned in our courts. . . . But tell me more."

Markham proceeded with an air of quiet self-assurance.

"My man learned, first, that Benson dined alone with this woman at the 'Marseilles,' a little bohemian restaurant in West Fortieth Street; secondly, that they quarrelled, and thirdly, that they departed at midnight, entering a taxicab together. . . . Now, the murder was committed at twelve-thirty; but since the lady lives on Riverside Drive, in the Eighties, Benson couldn't possibly have accompanied her home—which obviously he would have done had he not taken her to his own house—and returned by the time the shot was fired. But we have further proof pointing to her being at Benson's. My man learned, at the woman's apartment-house, that actually she did not get home until shortly after one. Moreover, she was without her gloves and hand-bag, and had to be let in to her rooms with a pass-key, because, as she explained, she had lost hers. As you remember, we found the key in her bag. And—to clinch the whole matter—the smoked cigarettes in the grate corresponded to the one you found in her case."

Markham paused to relight his cigar.

"So much for that particular evening," he resumed. "As soon as I learned the woman's identity this morning, I put two more men to work on her private life. Just as I was leaving the office this noon the men 'phoned in their reports. They had learned that the woman has a fiancé, a chap named Leacock, who was a captain in the army, and who would be likely to own just such a gun as Benson was killed with. Furthermore, this Captain Leacock lunched with the woman the day of the murder and also called on her at her apartment the morning after."

Markham leaned slightly forward, and his next words were emphasised by the tapping of his fingers on the arm of the chair.

"As you see, we have the motive, the opportunity and the means. . . . Perhaps you will tell me now that I possess no incriminating evidence."

"My dear Markham," Vance affirmed calmly, "you haven't brought out a single point which could not easily be explained away by any bright schoolboy." He shook his head lugubriously. "And on such evidence people are deprived of their life and liberty! 'Pon my word, you alarm me. I tremble for my personal safety."

Markham was nettled.

Would you be so good as to point out, from your dizzy pinnacle of sapience, the errors in my reasoning?"

"As far as I can see," returned Vance evenly, "your particularisation concerning the lady is innocent of reasoning. You've simply taken several unaffined facts, and jumped to a false conclusion. I happen to know the conclusion is false because all the psychological indications of the crime contradict it—that is to say, the only real evidence in the case points unmistakably in another direction."

He made a gesture of emphasis, and his tone assumed an unwonted gravity.

"And if you arrest any woman for killing Alvin Benson, you will simply be adding another crime—a crime of delib'rate and unpardonable stupidity—to the one already committed. And between shooting a bounder like Benson and ruining an innocent woman's reputation, I'm inclined to regard the latter as the more reprehensible."

I could see a flash of resentment leap into Markham's eyes; but he did not take offence. Remember: these two.

men were close friends; and, for all their divergency of nature, they understood and respected each other. Their frankness —severe and even mordant at times—was, indeed, a result of that respect.

There was a moment's silence; then Markham forced a smile.

"You fill me with misgivings," he averred mockingly; but, despite the lightness of his tone, I felt that he was half in earnest. "However, I hadn't exactly planned to arrest the lady just yet."

"You reveal commendable restraint," Vance complimented him. "But I'm sure you've already arranged to bullyrag the lady and perhaps trick her into one or two of those contradictions so dear to every lawyer's heart—just as if any nervous or high-strung person could help indulging in apparent contradictions while being cross-questioned as a suspect in a crime they had nothing to do with. . . . To 'put 'em on the grill'—a most accurate designation. So reminiscent of burning people at the stake, what?"

"Well, I'm most certainly going to question her," replied Markham firmly, glancing at his watch. "And one of my men is escorting her to the office in half an hour; so I must break up this most delightful and edifying chat."

"You really expect to learn something incriminating by interrogating her?" asked Vance. "Y'know, I'd jolly well like to witness your humiliation. But I presume your heckling of suspects is a part of the legal arcana."

Markham had risen and turned towards the door, but at Vance's words he paused and appeared to deliberate.

"I can't see any particular objection to your being present," he said, "if you really care to come."

I think he had an idea that the humiliation of which the other had spoken would prove to be Vance's own; and soon we were in a taxicab headed for the Criminal Courts Building.

CHAPTER VII

REPORTS AND AN INTERVIEW

(Saturday, June 15th; 3 p.m.)

WE entered the ancient building, with its discoloured marble pillars and balustrades and its old-fashioned iron scroll-work, by the Franklin Street door, and went directly to the District Attorney's office on the fourth floor. The office, like the building, breathed an air of former days. Its high ceilings, its massive golden-oak woodwork, its elaborate low-hung chandelier of bronze and china, its dingy bay walls of painted plaster, and its four high narrow windows to the south—all bespoke a departed era in architecture and decoration.

On the floor was a large velvet carpet-rug of dingy brown; and the windows were hung with velour draperies of the same colour. Several large comfortable chairs stood about the walls and before the long oak table in front of the District Attorney's desk. This desk, directly under the windows and facing the room, was broad and flat, with carved uprights and two rows of drawers extending to the floor. To the right of the high-backed swivel desk-chair, was another table of carved oak. There were also several filing cabinets in the room, and a large safe. In the centre of the east wall a leather-covered door, decorated with large brass nail-heads, led into a long narrow room, between the office and the waiting-room, where the District Attorney's secretary and several clerks had their desks. Opposite to this door was another one opening into the District Attorney's inner sanctum; and still another door, facing the windows, gave on the main corridor.

Vance glanced over the room casually.

"So this is the matrix of municipal justice—eh, what?" He walked to one of the windows and looked out upon the grey circular tower of the Tombs opposite. "And there, I take it, are the oubliettes where the victims of our law are incarc'rated so as to reduce the competition of criminal activity among the remaining citizenry. A most distressin' sight, Markham."

The District Attorney had sat down at his desk and was glancing at several notations on his blotter.

"There are a couple of my men waiting to see me," he remarked without looking up; "so, if you'll be good enough to take a chair over here, I'll proceed with my humble efforts to undermine society still further."

He pressed a button under the edge of his desk, and an alert young man with thick-lensed glasses appeared at the door.

"Swacker, tell Phelps to come in," Markham ordered. "And also tell Springer, if he's back from lunch, that I want to see him in a few minutes."

The secretary disappeared, and a moment later a tall, hawk-faced man, with stoop-shoulders and an awkward angular gait, entered.

"What news?" asked Markham.

"Well, Chief," the detective replied in a low, grating voice, "I just found out something I thought you could use right away. After I reported this noon, I ambled round to this Captain Leacock's house, thinking I might learn something from the house-boys, and ran into the Captain coming out. I tailed along; and he went straight up to the lady's house on the ,Drive, and stayed there over an hour. Then he went back home, looking worried."

Markham considered a moment.

"It may mean nothing at all, but I'm glad to know it, anyway. St. Clair'll be here in a few minutes, and I'll find out what she has to say. There's nothing else for to-day. . . . . Tell Swacker to send Tracy in."

Tracy was the antithesis of Phelps. He was short, a trifle stout, and exuded an atmosphere of studied suavity. His face was rotund and genial; he wore a *pince-nez;* and his clothes were modish and fitted him well.

"Good morning, Chief," he greeted Markham in a quiet, ingratiating tone. "I understand the St. Clair woman is to call here this afternoon, and there are a few things I've found out that may assist in your questioning."

He opened a small note-book and adjusted his *pince-nez.*

"I thought I might learn something from her singing teacher, an Italian formerly connected with the Metropolitan, but now running a sort of choral society of his own. He trains aspiring *prima donnas* in their rôles with a chorus and settings, and Miss St. Clair is one of his pet students. He talked to me, without any trouble; and it seems he knew Benson well. Benson attended several of St. Clair's rehearsals, and sometimes called for her in a taxicab. Rinaldo—that's the man's name—thinks he had a bad crush on the girl. Last winter, when she sang at the Criterion in a small part, Rinaldo was back stage, coaching, and Benson sent her enough hot-house flowers to fill the star's dressing-room and have some left over. I tried to find out if Benson was playing the 'angel' for her, but Rinaldo either didn't know or pretended he didn't." Tracy closed his note-book and looked up. "That any good to you, Chief?"

"First-rate," Markham told him. "Keep at work along that line, and let me hear from you again about this time Monday."

Tracy bowed, and as he went out the secretary again appeared at the door.

"Springer's here now, sir," he said. "Shall I send him in?"

Springer proved to be a type of detective quite different from either Phelps or Tracy. He was older, and had the gloomy capable air of a hard-working book-keeper in a bank. There was no initiative in his bearing, but one felt that he could discharge a delicate task with extreme competency.

Markham took from his pocket the envelope on which he had noted the name given him by Major Benson.

"Springer, there's a man down on Long Island that I want to interview as soon as possible. It's in connection with the Benson case, and I wish you'd locate him and get him up here as soon as possible. If you can find him in the telephone-book you needn't go down personally. His name is Leander Pfyfe, and he lives, I think, at Port Washington."

Markham jotted down the name on a card and handed it to the detective.

"This is Saturday, so if he comes to town to-morrow, have him ask for me at the Stuyvesant Club. I'll be there in the afternoon."

When Springer had gone, Markham again rang for his secretary and gave instructions that the moment Miss St. Clair arrived she was to be shown in.

"Sergeant Heath is here," Swacker informed him, "and wants to see you if you're not too busy."

Markham glanced at the clock over the door.

"I guess I'll have time. Send him in."

Heath was surprised to see Vance and me in the District Attorney's office, but after greeting Markham with the customary handshake, he turned to Vance with a good-natured smile.

"Still acquiring knowledge, Mr. Vance?"

"Can't say that I am, Sergeant," returned Vance lightly. "But I'm learning a number of most int'restin' errors. . . . How goes the sleuthin'?"

Heath's face became suddenly serious.

"That's what I'm here to tell the Chief about." He addressed himself to Markham. "This case is a jaw-breaker, sir. My men and myself have talked to a dozen of Benson's cronies, and we can't worm a single fact of any value out of 'em. They either don't know anything, or they're giving a swell imitation of a lot of clams. They all appear to be greatly shocked—bowled over, floored, flabbergasted—by the news of the shooting. And have they got any idea as to why or how it happened? They'll tell the world they haven't. You know the line of talk: Who'd want to shoot good old Al? Nobody could've done it but a burglar who didn't know good old Al? If he'd known good old Al, even the burglar wouldn't have done it. . . . Hell! I felt like killing off a few of those birds myself so they could go and join their good old Al."

"Any news of the car?" asked Markham.

Heath grunted his disgust.

"Not a word. And that's funny, too, seeing all the advertising it got. Those fishing-rods are the only thing we've got. . . . The Inspector, by the way, sent me the post-mortem report this morning; but it didn't tell us anything we didn't know. Translated into human language, it said Benson died from a shot in the head, with all his organs sound. It's a wonder, though, they didn't discover that he'd been poisoned with a Mexican bean or bit by an African snake, or something, so's to make the case a little more intricate than it already is."

"Cheer up, Sergeant," Markham exhorted him. "I've had a little better luck. Tracy ran down the owner of the handbag and found out she'd been to dinner with Benson that night. He and Phelps also learned a few other supplementary facts that fit in well; and I'm expecting the lady here at any minute. I'm going to find out what she has to say for herself."

An expression of resentment came into Heath's eyes as the District Attorney was speaking, but he erased it at once and began asking questions. Markham gave him every detail, and also informed him of Leander Pfyfe.

"I'll let you know immediately how the interview comes out," he concluded.

As the door closed on Heath, Vance looked up at Markham with a sly smile.

"Not exactly one of Nietzsche's *Uebermenschen*—eh, what? I fear the subtleties of this complex world bemuse him a bit, y'know. . . . And he's so disappointin'. I felt pos'tively elated when the bustling lad with the thick glasses announced his presence. I thought surely he wanted to tell you he had jailed at least six of Benson's murderers."

"Your hopes run too high, I fear," commented Markham.

"And yet, that's the usual procedure—if the headlines in our great moral dailies are to be credited. I always thought that the moment a crime was committed the police began arresting people promiscuously—to maintain the excitement, don't y'know. Another illusion gone! . . . Sad, sad," he murmured. "I shan't forgive our Heath: he has betrayed my faith in him."

At this point, Markham's secretary came to the door and announced the arrival of Miss St. Clair.

I think we were all taken a little aback at the spectacle presented by this young woman as she came slowly into the room with a firm, graceful step, and with her head held slightly to one side in an attitude of supercilious inquiry. She was small and strikingly pretty, although "pretty" is not exactly the word with which to describe her. She possessed that faintly exotic beauty that we find in the portraits of the Carracci, who sweetened the severity of Leonardo and made it at once intimate and decadent. Her eyes were dark and widely spaced; her nose was delicate and straight, and her forehead broad. Her full, sensuous lips were almost sculpturesque in their linear precision, and her mouth wore an enigmatic smile, or hint of a smile. Her rounded firm chin was a bit heavy when examined apart from the other features, but not in the *ensemble*. There was poise and a certain strength of character in her bearing; but one sensed the potentialities of powerful emotions beneath her exterior calm. Her clothes harmonised with her personality; they were quiet and apparently in the conventional style, but a touch of colour and originality here and there conferred on them a fascinating distinction.

Markham rose and, bowing with formal courtesy, indicated a comfortable upholstered chair directly in front of his desk. With a barely perceptible nod, she glanced at the chair, and then seated herself in a straight armless chair standing next to it.

"You won't mind, I'm sure," she said, "if I choose my own chair for the inquisition."

Her voice was low and resonant—the speaking voice of the highly-trained singer. She smiled as she spoke, but it was not a cordial smile: it was cold and distant, yet somehow indicative of levity.

"Miss St. Clair," began Markham, in a tone of polite severity, "the murder of Mr. Alvin Benson has intimately involved yourself. Before taking any definite steps, I have invited you here to ask you a few questions, I can, therefore, advise you quite honestly that frankness will best serve your interests."

He paused, and the woman looked at him with an ironically questioning gaze.

"Am I supposed to thank you for your generous advice?"

Markham's scowl deepened as he glanced down at a typewritten page on his desk.

"You are probably aware that your gloves and handbag were found in Mr. Benson's house the morning after he was shot?"

"I can understand how you might have traced the handbag to me," she said: "but how did you arrive at the conclusion that the gloves were mine?"

Markham looked up sharply.

"Do you mean to say the gloves are not yours?"

"Oh, no." She gave him another wintry smile. "I merely wondered how you knew they belonged to me, since you couldn't have known either my taste in gloves or the size I wore."

"They're your gloves, then?"

"If they are Tréfousse, size five-and-three-quarters, of white kid and elbow length, they are certainly mine. And I'd so like to have them back, if you don't mind."

"I'm sorry," said Markham, "but it is necessary that I keep them for the present."

She dismissed the matter with a slight shrug of the shoulders.

"Do you mind if I smoke?" she asked.

Markham instantly opened a drawer of his desk, and took out a box of Benson and Hedges cigarettes.

"I have my own, thank you," she informed him. "But I would so appreciate my holder. I've missed it horribly."

Markham hesitated. He was manifestly annoyed by the woman's attitude.

"I'll be glad to lend it to you," he compromised; and reaching into another drawer of his desk, he laid the holder on the table before her.

"Now, Miss St. Clair," he said, resuming his gravity of manner, "will you tell me how these personal articles of yours happened to be in Mr. Benson's living-room?"

"No, Mr. Markham, I will not," she answered.

"Do you realise the serious construction your refusal places upon the circumstances?"

"I really hadn't given it much thought." Her tone was indifferent.

"It would be well if you did," Markham advised her. "Your position is not an enviable one; and the presence of your belongings in Mr. Benson's room is, by no means, the only thing that connects you directly with the crime."

The woman raised her eyes inquiringly, and again the enigmatic smile appeared at the corners of her mouth.

"Perhaps you have sufficient evidence to accuse me of the murder?"

Markham ignored this question.

"You were well acquainted with Mr. Benson, I believe?"

"The finding of my handbag and gloves in his apartment might lead one to assume as much, mightn't it?" she parried.

"He was, in fact, much interested in you?" persisted Markham.

She made a *moue*, and sighed.

"Alas, yes! Too much for my peace of mind. . . . Have I been brought here to discuss the attentions this gentleman paid me?"

Again Markham ignored her query.

"Where were you, Miss St. Clair, between the time you left the 'Marseilles' at midnight and the time you arrived home —which, I understand, was after one o'clock?"

"You are simply wonderful!" she exclaimed. "You seem

to know everything. . . . Well, I can only say that during that time I was on my way home."

"Did it take you an hour to go from Fortieth Street to Eighty-first and Riverside Drive?"

"Just about that, I should say—a few minutes more or less, perhaps."

"How do you account for that?" Markham was becoming impatient.

"I can't account for it," she said, "except by the passage of time. Time does fly, doesn't it, Mr. Markham?"

"By your attitude you are only working detriment to yourself," Markham warned her, with a show of irritation. "Can you not see the seriousness of your position? You are known to have dined with Mr. Benson, to have left the restaurant at midnight, and to have arrived at your own apartment after one o'clock. At twelve-thirty, Mr. Benson was shot; and your personal articles were found in the same room the morning after."

"It looks terribly suspicious, I know," she admitted, with whimsical seriousness. "And I'll tell you this, Mr. Markham, if my thoughts could have killed Mr. Benson, he would have died long ago. I know I shouldn't speak ill of the dead—there's a saying about it beginning '*de mortuis*,' isn't there?—but the truth is, I had reason to dislike Mr. Benson exceedingly."

"Then why did you go to dinner with him?"

"I've asked myself the same question a dozen times since," she confessed dolefully. "We women are such impulsive creatures—always doing things we shouldn't. . . . But I know what you're thinking: if I had intended to shoot him, that would have been a natural preliminary. Isn't that what's in your mind? I suppose all murderesses do go to dinner with their victims first."

While she spoke she opened her vanity-case and looked at her reflection in its mirror. She daintily adjusted several imaginary stray ends of her abundant dark-brown hair, and touched her arched eye-brows gently with her little finger as if to rectify some infinitesimal disturbance in their pencilled contour. Then she tilted her head, regarded herself appraisingly, and returned her gaze to the District Attorney only as she came to the end of her speech. Her actions had perfectly conveyed to her listeners the impression that the subject of the conversation was, in her scheme of things, of secondary importance to her personal appearance. No words could have expressed her indifference so convincingly as had her little pantomime.

Markham was becoming exasperated. A different type of district attorney would no doubt have attempted to use the pressure of his office to force her into a more amenable frame of mind. But Markham shrank instinctively from the bludgeoning, threatening methods of the ordinary Public Prosecutor, especially in his dealings with women. In the present case, however, had it not been for Vance's strictures at the Club, he would no doubt have taken a more aggressive stand. But it was evident he was labouring under a burden of uncertainty superinduced by Vance's words and augmented by the evasive deportment of the woman herself.

After a moment's silence he asked grimly:

"You did considerable speculating through the firm of Benson and Benson, did you not?"

A faint ring of musical laughter greeted this question.

"I see that the dear Major has been telling tales. . . . Yes, I've been gambling most extravagantly. And I had no business to do it. I'm afraid I'm avaricious."

"And is it not true that you've lost heavily of late—that, in fact, Mr. Alvin Benson called upon you for additional margin and finally sold out your securities?"

"I wish to Heaven it were not true," she lamented, with a look of simulated tragedy. Then: "Am I supposed to have done away with Mr. Benson out of sordid revenge, or as an act of just retribution?" She smiled archly and waited expectantly, as if her question had been part of a guessing game.

Markham's eyes hardened as he coldly enunciated his next words.

"Is it not a fact that Captain Philip Leacock owned just such a pistol as Mr. Benson was killed with—a forty-five army Colt automatic?"

At the mention of her fiancé's name she stiffened perceptibly and caught her breath. The part she had been playing fell from her, and a faint flush suffused her cheeks

and extended to her forehead. But almost immediately she
had reassumed her rôle of playful indifference.

"I never inquired into the make or calibre of Captain
Leacock's firearms," she returned carelessly.

"And is it not a fact," pursued Markham's imperturbable
voice, "that Captain Leacock lent you his pistol when he
called at your apartment on the morning before the
murder?"

"It's most ungallant of you, Mr. Markham," she reprimanded him coyly, "to inquire into the personal relations
of an engaged couple; for I am betrothed to Captain Leacock
—though you probably know it already."

Markham stood up, controlling himself with effort.

"Am I to understand that you refuse to answer any of
my questions or to endeavour to extricate yourself from
the very serious position you are in?"

She appeared to consider.

"Yes," she said slowly, "I haven't anything I care especially
to say just now."

Markham leaned over and rested both hands on the
desk.

"Do you realise the possible consequences of your attitude?" he asked ominously. "The facts I know regarding
your connection with the case, coupled with your refusal to
offer a single extenuating explanation, give me more grounds
than I actually need to order your being held."

I was watching her closely as he spoke, and it seemed to
me that her eyelids drooped involuntarily the merest fraction
of an inch. But she gave no other indication of being affected
by the pronouncement, and merely looked at the District
Attorney with an air of defiant amusement.

Markham with a sudden contraction of the jaw, turned and
reached towards a bell-button beneath the edge of his desk.
But, in doing so, his glance fell upon Vance; and he paused
indecisively. The look he had encountered on the other's
face was one of reproachful amazement: not only did it express complete surprise at his apparent decision, but it stated,
more eloquently than words could have done, that he was
about to commit an act of irreparable folly.

There were several moments of tense silence in the room.
Then calmly and unhurriedly Miss St. Clair opened her vanity-

case and powdered her nose. When she had finished, she turned a serene gaze upon the District Attorney.

"Well, do you want to arrest me now?" she asked.

Markham regarded her for a moment, deliberating. Instead of answering at once, he went to the window and stood for a full minute looking down upon the Bridge of Sighs which connects the Criminal Courts Building with the Tombs.

"No, I think not to-day," he said slowly.

He stood a while longer in absorbed contemplation; then, as if shaking off his mood of irresolution, he swung about and confronted the woman.

"I'm not going to arrest you—yet," he reiterated a bit harshly. "But I'm going to order you to remain in New York for the present. And if you attempt to leave, you *will* be arrested. I hope that is clear."

He pressed a button, and his secretary entered.

"Swacker, please escort Miss St. Clair downstairs and call a taxicab for her. . . . Then you can go home yourself."

She rose and gave Markham a little nod.

"You were very kind to lend me my cigarette holder," she said pleasantly, laying it on his desk.

Without another word, she walked calmly from the room.

The door had no more than closed behind her when Markham pressed another button. In a few moments the door leading into the outer corridor opened, and a white-haired, middle-aged man appeared.

"Ben," ordered Markham hurriedly, "have that woman that Swacker's taking downstairs followed. Keep her under surveillance, and don't let her get lost. She's not to leave the city—understand? It's the St. Clair woman Tracy dug up."

When the man had gone, Markham turned and stood glowering at Vance.

"What do you think of your innocent young lady now?" he asked, with an air of belligerent triumph.

"Nice gel—eh, what?" replied Vance blandly. "Extr'-ordin'ry control. And she's about to marry a professional milit'ry man! Ah well. *De gustibus.* . . . Y'know, I was afraid for a moment you were actu'lly going to send for the manacles. And if you had, Markham, old dear, you'd have regretted it to your dying day."

Markham studied him for a few seconds. He knew there was something more than a mere whim beneath Vance's certitude of manner; and it was this knowledge that had stayed his hand when he was about to have the woman placed in custody.

"Her attitude was certainly not conducive to one's belief in her innocence," Markham objected. "She played her part damned cleverly, though. But it was just the part a shrewd woman knowing herself guilty, would have played."

"I say, didn't it occur to you," asked Vance, "that perhaps she didn't care a farthing whether you thought her guilty or not?—that, in fact, she was a bit disappointed when you let her go."

"That's hardly the way I read the situation," returned Markham. "Whether guilty or innocent, a person doesn't ordinarily invite arrest."

"By the bye," asked Vance, "where was the fortunate swain during the hour of Alvin's passing?"

"Do you think we didn't check up on that point?" Markham spoke with disdain. "Captain Leacock was at his own apartment that night from eight o'clock on."

"Was he, really?" airily retorted Vance. "A most model young fella!"

Again Markham looked at him sharply.

"I'd like to know what weird theory has been struggling in your brain to-day," he mused. "Now that I've let the lady go temporarily—which is what you obviously wanted me to do—and have stultified my own better judgment in so doing, why not tell me frankly what you've got up your sleeve?"

"'Up my sleeve?' Such an inelegant metaphor! One would think I was a prestidig'tator, what?"

Whenever Vance answered in this fashion it was a sign that he wished to avoid making a direct reply; and Markham dropped the matter.

"Anyway," he submitted, "you didn't have the pleasure of witnessing my humiliation as you prophesied."

Vance looked up in simulated surprise.

"Didn't I, now?" Then he added sorrowfully: "Life is so full of disappointments, y'know."

CHAPTER VIII

VANCE ACCEPTS A CHALLENGE

(Saturday, June 15th; 4 p.m.)

AFTER Markham had telephoned Heath the details of the interview we returned to the Stuyvesant Club. Ordinarily the District Attorney's office shuts down at one o'clock on Saturdays; but to-day the hour had been extended because of the importance attaching to Miss St. Clair's visit. Markham had lapsed into an introspective silence which lasted until we were again seated in the alcove of the Club's lounge-room. Then he spoke irritably.

"Damn it! I shouldn't have let her go. . . . I still have a feeling she's guilty."

Vance assumed an air of gushing credulousness.

"Oh, really! I dare say you're *so* psychic. Been that way all your life, no doubt. And haven't you had lots and lots of dreams that come true? I'm sure you've often had a 'phone call from someone you were thinking about at the moment. A delectable gift. Do you read palms, also? . . . Why not have the lady's horoscope cast?"

"I have no evidence as yet," Markham retorted, "that your belief in her innocence is founded on anything more substantial that your impressions."

"Ah, but it is," averred Vance. "I *know* she's innocent. Furthermore, I know that no woman could possibly have fired the shot."

"Don't get the erroneous idea in your head that a woman couldn't have manipulated a forty-five army Colt."

"Oh, that?" Vance dismissed the notion with a shrug. "The material indications of the crime don't enter into my calculations, y'know—I leave 'em entirely to you lawyers and the lads with the bulging deltoids. I have other, and surer, ways of reaching conclusions. That's why I told you that if you arrested any woman for shooting Benson you'd be blundering most shamefully."

Markham grunted indignantly.

"And yet you seem to have repudiated all processes of deduction whereby the truth may be arrived at. Have you, by any chance, entirely renounced your faith in the operations of the human mind?"

"Ah, there speaks the voice of God's great common people!" exclaimed Vance. "Your mind is so typical, Markham. It works on the principle that what you don't know isn't knowledge, and that, since you don't understand a thing, there is no explanation. A comfortable point of view. It relieves one from all care and uncertainty. Don't you find the world a very sweet and wonderful place?"

Markham adopted an attitude of affable forbearance.

"You spoke at lunch-time, I believe, of one infallible method of detecting crime. Would you care to divulge this profound and priceless secret to a mere district attorney?"

Vance bowed with exaggerated courtesy.[1]

"Delighted, I'm sure," he returned. "I referred to the science of individual character and the psychology of human nature. We all do things, d'ye see, in a certain individual way, according to our temp'raments. Every human act— no matter how large or how small—is a direct expression of a man's personality, and bears the inev'table impress of his nature. Thus, a musician, by looking at a sheet of music, is able to tell at once whether it was composed, for example, by Beethoven, or Schubert, or Debussy, or Chopin. And an artist, by looking at a canvas knows immediately whether it is a Corot, a Harpignies, a Rembrandt, or a Franz Hals. And just as no two faces are exactly alike, so no two natures are exactly alike; the combination of ingredients which go to make up our personalities, varies in each individual. That is why, when twenty artists, let us say, sit down to paint the same subject, each one conceives and executes in a different manner. The result in each case is a distinct and unmistak-

[1] The following conversation in which Vance explains his psychological methods of criminal analysis is, of course, set down from memory. However, a proof of this passage was sent to him with a request that he revise and alter it in whatever manner he chose; so that, as it now stands, it describes Vance's theory in practically his own words.

able expression of the personality of the painter who did it.
. . . It's really rather simple, don't y'know."

"Your theory, doubtless, would be comprehensible to an
artist," said Markham, in a tone of indulgent irony. "But
its metaphysical refinements are, I admit, considerably beyond the grasp of a vulgar worldling like myself."

" 'The mind inclined to what is false rejects the nobler
course,'" murmured Vance with a sigh.

"There is," argued Markham, "a slight difference between
art and crime."

"Psychologically, old chap, there's none," Vance amended
evenly. "Crimes possess all the basic factors of a work of
art—approach, conception, technique, imagination, attack,
method and organisation. Moreover, crimes vary fully as
much in their manner, their aspects, and their general nature,
as do works of art. Indeed, a carefully planned crime is
just as direct an expression of the individual as is a painting,
for instance. And therein lies the one great possibility of
detection. Just as an expert æsthetician can analyse a picture
and tell you who painted it, or the personality and temperament of the person who painted it, so can the expert
psychologist analyse a crime and tell you who committed it
—that is, if he happens to be acquainted with the person, or
else can describe to you, with almost mathematical surety,
the criminal's nature and character. . . . And that, my
dear Markham, is the only sure and inev'table means of determining human guilt. All others are mere guess-work,
unscientific, uncertain, and—perilous."

Throughout this explanation Vance's manner had been
almost casual; yet the very serenity and assurance of his
attitude conferred upon his words a curious sense of authority.
Markham had listened with interest, though it could be seen
that he did not regard Vance's theorising seriously.

"Your system ignores motive altogether," he objected.

"Naturally," Vance replied, "since it's an irrelevant factor
in most crimes. Every one of us, my dear chap, has just as
good a motive for killing at least a score of men, as the motives
which actuate ninety-nine crimes out of a hundred. And,
when anyone is murdered, there are dozens of innocent people
who had just as strong a motive for doing it as had the actual
murderer. Really, y'know, the fact that a man has a motive

is no evidence whatever that he's guilty—such motives are too universal a possession of the human race. Suspecting a man of murder because he has a motive is like suspecting a man of running away with another man's wife because he has two legs. The reason that some people kill and others don't is a matter of temp'rament—of individual psychology. It all comes back to that. . . . And another thing: when a person does possess a real motive—something tremendous and overpowering—he's pretty apt to keep it to himself, to hide it and guard it carefully—eh, what? He may even have disguised the motive through years of preparation; or the motive may have been born within five minutes of the crime through the unexpected discovery of facts a decade old. . . . So, d'ye see, the absence of any apparent motive in a crime might be regarded as more incriminating than the presence of one."

"You are going to have some difficulty in eliminating the idea of *cui bono* from the consideration of crime."

"I dare say," agreed Vance. "The idea of *cui bono* is just silly enough to be impregnable. And yet, many persons would be benefited by almost anyone's death. Kill Sumner, and, on that theory, you could arrest the entire membership of the Authors' League."

"Opportunity, at any rate," persisted Markham, "is an insuperable factor in crime—and by opportunity I mean that affinity of circumstances and conditions which make a particular crime possible, feasible and convenient for a particular person."

"Another irrelevant factor," asserted Vance. "Think of the opportunities we have every day to murder people we dislike! Only the other night I had ten insuff'rable bores to dinner in my apartment—a social devoir. But I refrained —with consid'rable effort, I admit—from putting arsenic in the Pontet Canet. The Borgias and I, y'see, merely belong to different psychological categ'ries. On the other hand, had I been resolved to do murder, I would—like those resourceful *cinquecento* patricians—have created by own opportunity. . . . And there's the rub—one can either make an opportunity or disguise the fact that he had it, with false alibis and various other tricks. You remember the case of the murderer who called the police to break into his victim's house before the latter had been killed, saying he suspected foul play, and who then preceded the policemen indoors and stabbed the man as they were trailing up the stairs."[1]

"Well, what of actual proximity or presence—the proof of a person being on the scene of the crime at the time it was committed?"

"Again misleading," Vance declared. "An innocent person's presence is too often used as a shield by the real murderer who is actu'lly absent. A clever criminal can commit a crime from a distance through an agency that is present. Also, a clever criminal can arrange an alibi and then go to the scene of the crime disguised and unrecognised. There are far too many convincing ways of being present when one is believed to be absent—and *vice versa*. . . . But we can never part from our individualities and our natures. And that is why all crime inev'tably comes back to human psychology—the one fixed undisguisable basis of deduction."

"It's a wonder to me," said Markham, "in view of your theories, that you don't advocate dismissing nine-tenths of the police force and installing a gross or two of those psychological machines so popular with the Sunday Supplement editor."

Vance smoked a minute meditatively.

"I've read about 'em. Int'restin' toys. They can no doubt indicate a certain augmented emotional stress when the patient transfers his attention from the pious platitudes of Dr. Frank Crane to a problem in spherical trigonometry. But if an innocent person were harnessed up to the various tubes, galvanometers, electro-magnets, glass plates, and brass knobs of one of these apparatuses, and then quizzed about some recent crime, your indicat'ry needle would cavort about like a Russian dancer as a result of sheer nervous panic on the patient's part."

Markham smiled patronisingly.

"And I suppose the needle would remain static with a guilty person in contact?"

[1] I don't know what case Vance was referring to; but there are several instances of this device on record, and writers of detective fiction have often used it. The latest instance is to be found in G. K. Chesterton's "The Innocence of Father Brown," in the story entitled "The Wrong Shape."

"Oh, on the contr'ry," Vance's tone was unruffled. "The needle would bob up and down just the same—but not *because* he was guilty. If he was stupid, for instance, the needle would jump as a result of his resentment at a seemingly newfangled third-degree torture. And if he was intelligent, the needle would jump because of his suppressed mirth at the puerility of the legal mind for indulging in such nonsense."

"You move me deeply," said Markham. "My head is spinning like a turbine. But there are those of us poor worldlings who believe that criminality is a defect of the brain."

"So it is," Vance readily agreed. "But unfortunately the entire human race possesses the defect. The virtuous ones haven't, so to speak, the courage of their defects. . . . However, if you were referring to a criminal type, then, alas! we must part company. It was Lombroso, that darling of the yellow journals, who invented the idea of the congenital criminal. Real scientists like DuBois, Karl Pearson and Goring have shot his idiotic theories full of holes."[1]

"I am floored by your erudition," declared Markham, as he signalled to a passing attendant and ordered another cigar. "I console myself, however, with the fact that, as a rule, murder will leak out."

Vance smoked his cigarette in silence, looking thoughtfully out through the window up at the hazy June sky.

"Markham," he said at length, "the number of fantastic ideas extant about criminals is pos'tively amazing. How a sane person can subscribe to that ancient hallucination that 'murder will out' is beyond me. It rarely 'outs,' old dear. And, if it did 'out,' why a Homicide Bureau? Why all this whirlin'-dervish activity by the police whenever a body is found? . . . The poets are to blame for this bit of lunacy. Chaucer probably started it with his 'Mordre wol

[1] It was Pearson and Goring who, about twenty years ago, made an extensive investigation and tabulation of professional criminals in England, the results of which showed (1) that criminal careers began mostly between the ages of 16 and 21; (2) that over ninety per cent. of criminals were mentally normal; (3) and that more criminals had criminal older brothers than criminal fathers.

out,' and Shakespeare helped it along by attributing to
murder a miraculous organ that speaks in lieu of a tongue.
It was some poet, too, no doubt, who conceived the fancy that
carcasses bleed at the sight of the murderer. . . . Would
you, as the great Protector of the Faithful, dare tell the
police to wait calmly in their offices, or clubs, or favourite
beauty-parlours—or wherever policemen do their waiting—
until a murder 'outs'? Poor dear!—if you did, they'd ask
the Governor for your detention as _particeps criminis_, or
apply for a _de lunatico inquirendo_."[1]

Markham grunted good-naturedly. He was busy cutting
and lighting his cigar.

"I believe you chaps have another hallucination about
crime," continued Vance, "namely, that the criminal always
returns to the scene of the crime. This weird notion is even
explained on some recondite and misty psychological ground.
But, I assure you, psychology teaches no such prepost'rous
doctrine. If ever a murderer returned to the body of his
victim for any reason other than to rectify some blunder he
had made, then he is a subject for Broadmoor—or Blooming-
dale. . . . How easy it would be for the police if this fanciful
notion were true! They'd merely have to sit down at the
scene of the crime, play bezique or Mah Jongg until the
murderer returned, and then escort him to the _bastille_, what?
The true psychological instinct in anyone having committed
a punishable act is to get as far away from the scene of it as
the limits of this world will permit." [2]

[1] Sir Basil Thomson, K.C.B., former Assistant Commissioner
of Metropolitan Police, London, writing in _The Saturday Evening
Post_ several years after this conversation, said: "Take, for
example, the proverb that murder will out, which is employed
whenever one out of many thousands of undiscovered murderers
is caught through a chance coincidence that captures the popular
imagination. It is because murder will not out that the pleasant
shock of surprise when it does out, calls for a proverb to enshrine
the phenomenon. The poisoner who is brought to justice has
almost invariably proved to have killed other victims without
exciting suspicion until he has grown careless."

[2] In "Popular Fallacies About Crime" (_Saturday Evening Post_,
April 21, 1923, p. 8) Sir Basil Thomson also upheld this point of
view.

"In the present case, at any rate," Markham reminded him, "we are neither waiting inactively for the murder to out, nor sitting in Benson's living-room trusting to the voluntary return of the criminal."

"Either course would achieve success as quickly as the one you are now pursuing," Vance said.

"Not being gifted with your singular insight," retorted Markham, "I can only follow the inadequate processes of human reasoning."

"No doubt," Vance agreed commiseratingly. "And the results of your activities thus far force me to the conclusion that a man with a handful of legalistic logic can successfully withstand the most obst'nate and heroic assaults of ordin'ry common sense."

Markham was piqued.

"Still harping on the St. Clair woman's innocence, eh? However, in view of the complete absence of any tangible evidence pointing elsewhere, you must admit I have no choice of courses."

"I admit nothing of the kind," Vance told him; "for, I assure you, there is an abundance of evidence pointing elsewhere. You simply failed to see it."

"You think so!" Vance's nonchalant cocksureness had at last overthrown Markham's equanimity. "Very well, old man; I hereby enter an emphatic denial to all your fine theories; and I challenge you to produce a single piece of this evidence which you say exists."

He threw his words out with asperity, and gave a curt, aggressive gesture with his extended fingers, to indicate that, as far as he was concerned, the subject was closed.

Vance, too, I think, was pricked a little.

"Y'know, Markham, old dear, I'm no avenger of blood, or vindicator of the honour of society. The rôle would bore me."

Markham smiled loftily, but made no reply.

Vance smoked meditatively for a while. Then, to my amazement, he turned calmly and deliberately to Markham, and said in a quiet, matter-of-fact voice:

"I'm going to accept your challenge. It's a bit alien to my tastes; but the problem, y'know, rather appeals to me; it presents the same diff'culties as the *Concert*

Champêtre affair—a question of disputed authorship, as it were."[1]

Markham abruptly suspended the motion of lifting his cigar to his lips. He had scarcely intended his challenge literally: it had been uttered more in the nature of a verbal defiance: and he scrutinised Vance a bit uncertainly. Little did he realise that the other's casual acceptance of his unthinking and but half-serious challenge was to alter the entire criminal history of New York.

"Just how do you intend to proceed?" he asked.

Vance waved his hand carelessly.

"Like Napoleon, *je m'en gage, et puis je vois.* However, I must have your word that you'll give me every possible assistance, and will refrain from all profound legal objections."

Markham pursed his lips. He was frankly perplexed by the unexpected manner in which Vance had met his defiance. But immediately he gave a good-natured laugh, as if, after all, the matter was of no serious consequence.

"Very well," he assented. "You have my word. . . . And now what?"

After a moment Vance lit a fresh cigarette, and rose languidly.

"First," he announced, "I shall determine the exact height of the guilty person. Such a fact will, no doubt, come under the head of indicat'ry evidence—eh, what?"

Markham stared at him incredulously.

"How, in heaven's name, are you going to do that?"

"By those primitive deductive methods to which you so touchingly pin your faith," he answered easily. "But come; let us repair to the scene of the crime."

He moved towards the door, Markham reluctantly following in a state of perplexed irritation.

"But you know the body was removed," the latter protested; "and the place by now has no doubt been straightened up."

"Thank heaven for that!" murmured Vance. "I'm not

---

[1] For years the famous *Concert Champêtre* in the Louvre was officially attributed to Titian. Vance, however, took it upon himself to convince the Curator, M. Lepelletier, that it was a Giorgione, with the result that the painting is now credited to that artist.

particularly fond of corpses; and untidiness, y'know, annoys me frightfully."

As we emerged into Madison Avenue he signalled to the commissionaire for a taxicab, and without a word urged us into it.

"This is all nonsense," Markham declared ill-naturedly, as we started on our journey up town. "How do you expect to find any clues now? By this time everything has been obliterated."

"Alas, my dear Markham," lamented Vance, in a tone of mock solicitude, "how woefully deficient you are in philosophic theory! If anything, no matter how inf'nitesimal, could really be obliterated, the universe, y'know, would cease to exist—the cosmic problem would be solved, and the Creator would write Q.E.D. across an empty firmament. Our only chance of going on with this illusion we call Life, d'ye see, lies in the fact that consciousness is like an inf'nite decimal point. Did you, as a child, ever try to complete the decimal, one-third, by filling a whole sheet of paper with the numeral three? You always had the fraction, one-third, left don't y'know. If you could have eliminated the smallest one-third, after having set down ten thousand threes, the problem would have ended. So with life, my dear fellow. It's only because we can't erase or obliterate anything that we go on existing."

He made a movement with his fingers, putting a sort of tangible period to his remarks, and looked dreamily out of the window up at the fiery film of sky.

Markham had settled back into his corner, and was chewing morosely at his cigar. I could see he was fairly simmering with impotent anger at having let himself be goaded into issuing his challenge. But there was no retreating now. As he told me afterwards, he was fully convinced he had been dragged forth out of a comfortable chair, on a patent and ridiculous fool's errand.

CHAPTER IX

THE HEIGHT OF THE MURDERER

(Saturday, June 15th : 5 p.m.)

WHEN we arrived at Benson's house a patrolman leaning somnolently against the iron paling of the areaway came suddenly to attention and saluted. He eyed Vance and me hopefully, regarding us no doubt as suspects being taken to the scene of the crime for questioning by the District Attorney. We were admitted by one of the men from the Homicide Bureau who had been in the house on the morning of the investigation.

Markham greeted him with a nod.

"Everything going all right?"

"Sure," the man replied good-naturedly. "The old lady's as meek as a cat—and a swell cook."

"We want to be alone for a while, Sniffin," said Markham, as we passed into the living-room.

"The gastronome's name is Snitkin—not Sniffin," Vance corrected him, when the door had closed on us.

"Wonderful memory," muttered Markham churlishly.

"A failing of mine," said Vance. "I suppose you are one of those rare persons who never forget a face, but just can't recall names, what?"

But Markham was in no mood to be twitted.

"Now that you've dragged me here, what are you going to do?" He waved his hand deprecatingly and sank into a chair with an air of contemptuous abdication.

The living-room looked much the same as when we saw it last, except that it had been put neatly in order. The shades were up, and the late afternoon light was flooding in profusely. The ornateness of the room's furnishings seemed intensified by the glare.

Vance glanced about him and gave a shudder.

"I'm half inclined to turn back," he drawled. "It's a clear case of justifiable homicide by an outraged interior decorator."

"My dear æsthete," Markham urged impatiently, "be good enough to bury your artistic prejudices, and to proceed with your problem. . . . Of course," he added with a malicious smile, "if you fear the result, you may still withdraw, and thereby preserve your charming theories in their present virgin state."

"And permit you to send an innocent maiden to the chair!" exclaimed Vance, in mock indignation. "Fie, fie! *La politesse* alone forbids my withdrawal. May I never have to lament, with Prince Henry, that 'to my shame I have a truant been to chivalry.'"

Markham set his jaw, and gave Vance a ferocious look.

"I'm beginning to think that, after all, there is something in your theory that every man has some motive for murdering another."

"Well," replied Vance cheerfully, "now that you have begun to come round to my way of thinking do you mind if I send Mr. Snitkin on an errand?"

Markham sighed audibly and shrugged his shoulders.

"I'll smoke during the *opéra bouffe*, if it won't interfere with your performance."

Vance went to the door and called Snitkin.

"I say, would you mind going to Mrs. Platz and borrowing a long tape-measure and a ball of string. . . . The District Attorney wants them," he added, giving Markham a sycophantic bow.

"I can't hope that you're going to hang yourself, can I?" asked Markham.

Vance gazed at him reprovingly.

"Permit me," he said sweetly, "to commend *Othello* to your attention:

> 'How poor are they that have not patience!
> What wound did ever heal but by degrees?'

Or—to descend from a poet to a platitudinarian—let me present for your consid'ration a pentameter from Longfellow: 'All things come round to him who will but wait.' Untrue, of course, but consolin'. Milton said it much better in his 'They also serve——.' But Cervantes said it best: 'Patience and shuffle the cards.' Sound advice, Markham—and advice expressed rakishly, as all good advice should be. . . . **To** be sure, patience is a sort of last resort—a practice to adopt when there's nothing else to do. Still, like virtue, it occasionally rewards the practitioner; although I'll admit that, as a rule, it is—again like virtue—bootless. That is to say, it is its own reward. It has, however, been swathed in many verbal robes. It is 'sorrow's slave,' and the 'sov'reign o'er transmuted ills,' as well as 'all the passion of great hearts.' Rousseau wrote *La patience est amère, mais son fruit est doux.* But perhaps your legal taste runs to Latin. *Superanda omnis fortuna erenlo est,* quoth Virgil. And Horace also spoke on the subject. *Durum!* said he, *sed levius fit patientia*——"

"Why the hell doesn't Snitkin come?" growled Markham.

Almost as he spoke the door opened, and the detective handed Vance the tape-measure and string.

"And now, Markham, for your reward!"

Bending over the rug Vance moved the large wicker chair into the exact position it had occupied when Benson had been shot. The position was easily determined, for the impressions of the chair's castors on the deep nap of the rug were plainly visible. He then ran the string through the bullet hole in the back of the chair, and directed me to hold one end of it against the place where the bullet had struck the wainscot. Next he took up the tape-measure and, extending the string through the hole measured a distance of five feet and six inches along it, starting at the point which corresponded to the location of Benson's forehead as he sat in the chair. Tying a knot in the string to indicate the measurement, he drew the string taut, so that it extended in a straight line from the mark on the wainscot, through the hole in the back of the chair, to a point five feet and six inches in front of where Benson's head had rested.

"This knot in the string," he explained, "now represents the exact location of the muzzle of the gun that ended Benson's career. You see the reasoning—eh, what? Having two points in the bullet's course—namely, the hole in the chair and the mark on the wainscot—and also knowing the approximate vertical line of explosion, which was between five and six feet from the gentleman's skull, it was merely necess'ry to extend the straight line of the bullet's course to the vertical line of explosion in order to ascertain the exact point at which the shot was fired."

"Theoretically very pretty," commented Markham; "though why you should go to so much trouble to ascertain this point in space I can't imagine. . . . Not that it matters, for you have overlooked the possibility of the bullet's deflection."

"Forgive me for contradicting you," smiled Vance; "but yesterday morning I questioned Captain Hagedorn at some length, and learned that there had been no deflection of the bullet. Hagedorn had inspected the wound before we arrived; and he was really pos'tive on that point. In the first place, the bullet struck the frontal bone at such an angle as to make deflection practically impossible even had the pistol been of smaller calibre. And in the second place, the pistol with which Benson was shot was of so large a bore—a ·45—and the muzzle velocity was so great, that the bullet would have taken a straight course even had it been held at a greater distance from the gentleman's brow."

"And how," asked Markham, "did Hagedorn know what the muzzle velocity was?"

"I was inquis'tive on that point myself," answered Vance; "and he explained that the size and character of the bullet and the expelled shell told him the whole tale. That's how he knew the gun was an army Colt automatic—I believe he called it a U.S. Government Colt—and not the ordinary Colt automatic. The weight of the bullets ·of these two pistols is slightly different: the ordinary Colt bullet weighs 200 grains, whereas the army Colt bullet weighs 230 grains. Hagedorn, having a hypersensitive tactile sense, was able, I presume, to distinguish the diff'rence at once, though I didn't go into his physiological gifts with him—my reticent nature, you understand. . . . However, he could tell it was a ·45 army Colt automatic bullet; and knowing this, he knew that the muzzle velocity was 809 feet, and that the striking energy was 329—which gives a six-inch penetration in white pine at a distance of twenty-five yards. . . . . An amazin' creature, this Hagedorn. Imagine having one's head full of such entrancing information! The old mysteries of why a man should take up the bass-fiddle as a life work and where all the pins go, are babes' conundrums compared with the one of why a human being should devote his years to the idiosyncrasies of bullets."

"The subject is not exactly an enthralling one," said Markham wearily; "so, for the sake of argument, let us admit that you have now found the precise point of the gun's explosion. Where do we go from there?"

"While I hold the string on a straight line," directed Vance, "be good enough to measure the exact distance from the floor to the knot. Then my secret will be known."

"This game doesn't enthral me, either," Markham protested. "I'd much prefer 'London Bridge.'"

Nevertheless he made the measurement.

"Four feet, eight-and-a-half inches," he announced indifferently.

Vance laid a cigarette on the rug at a point directly beneath the knot.

"We now know the exact height at which the pistol was held when it was fired. . . . You grasp the process by which this conclusion was reached, I'm sure."

"It seems rather obvious," answered Markham.

Vance again went to the door and called Snitkin.

"The District Attorney desires the loan of your gun for a moment," he said. "He wishes to make a test."

Snitkin stepped up to Markham and held out his pistol wonderingly.

"The safety's on, sir: shall I shift it?"

Markham was about to refuse the weapon when Vance interposed.

"That's quite all right. Mr. Markham doesn't intend to fire it—I hope."

When the man had gone Vance seated himself in the wicker chair, and placed his head in juxtaposition with the bullet-hole.

"Now, Markham," he requested, "will you please stand on the spot where the murderer stood, holding the gun directly above that cigarette on the floor, and aim delib'rately at my left temple. . . . Take care," he cautioned, with an engaging smile, "not to pull the trigger, or you will never learn who killed Benson."

Reluctantly Markham complied. As he stood taking aim, Vance asked me to measure the height of the gun's muzzle from the floor.

The distance was four feet and nine inches.

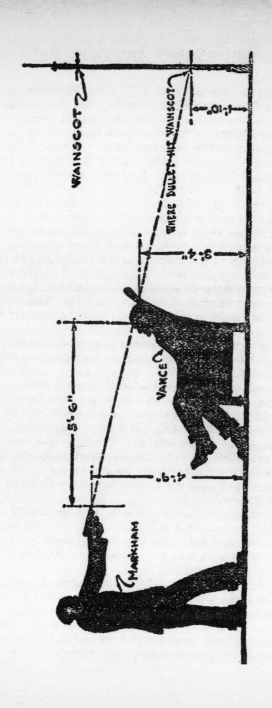

"Quite so," he said, rising. "Y'see, Markham, you are five feet eleven inches tall; therefore the person who shot Benson was very nearly your own height—certainly not under five feet ten. . . . That, too, is rather obvious, what?"

His demonstration had been simple and clear. Markham was frankly impressed; his manner had become serious, He regarded Vance for a moment with a meditative frown; then he said:

"That's all very well; but the person who fired the shot might have held the pistol relatively higher than I did."

"Not tenable," returned Vance. "I've done too much shooting myself not to know that when an expert takes delib'rate aim with a revolver at a small target, he does it with a stiff arm and with a slightly raised shoulder, so as to bring the sight on a straight line between his eye and the object at which he aims. The height at which one holds a revolver, under such conditions, pretty accurately determines his own height."

"Your argument is based on the assumption that the person who killed Benson was an expert taking deliberate aim at a small target?"

"Not an assumption, but a fact," declared Vance. "Consider: had the person not been an expert shot, he would not —at a distance of five or six feet—have selected the forehead, but a larger target—namely the breast. And having selected the forehead, he most certainly took delib'rate aim, what? Furthermore had he not been an expert shot, and had he pointed the gun at the breast without taking delib'rate aim he would, in all prob'bility, have fired more than one shot."

Markham pondered.

"I'll grant that, on the face of it, your theory sounds plausible," he conceded at length. "On the other hand, the guilty man could have been almost any height over five feet, ten; for certainly a man may crouch as much as he likes and still take deliberate aim."

"True," agreed Vance. "But don't overlook the fact that the murderer's position, in this instance, was a perfectly natural one. Otherwise, Benson's attention would have been attracted, and he would not have been taken unawares. That he was shot unawares was indicated by his attitude. Of course, the assassin might have stooped a little without causing Benson to look up. . . . Let us say, therefore, that the guilty person's height was somewhere between five feet ten and six feet two. Does that appeal to you?"

Markham was silent.

"The delightful Miss St. Clair, y'know," remarked Vance, with a japish smile, "can't possibly be over five feet five or six."

Markham grunted, and continued to smoke abstractedly.

"This Captain Leacock, I take it," said Vance, "is over six feet—eh, what?"

Markham's eyes narrowed.

"What makes you think so?"

"You just told me, don't y'know."

"I told you!"

"Not in so many words," Vance pointed out. "But after I had shown you the approximate height of the murderer, and it didn't correspond at all to that of the young lady you suspected, I knew your active mind was busy looking around for another possibility. And, as the lady's *inamorato* was the only other possibility on the horizon, I concluded that you were permitting your thoughts to play about the Captain. Had he, therefore, been the stipulated height, you would have said nothing; but when you argued that the murderer might have stooped to fire the shot, I decided that the Captain was inord'nately tall. . . . Thus, in the pregnant silence that emanated from you, old dear, your spirit held sweet communion with mine, and told me that the gentleman was a six-footer, no less."

"I see that you include mind-reading among your gifts," said Markham. "I now await an exhibition of slate-writing."

His tone was irritable, but his irritation was that of a man reluctant to admit the alteration of his beliefs. He felt himself yielding to Vance's guiding rein, but he still held stubbornly to the course of his own previous convictions.

"Surely you don't question my demonstration of the guilty person's height?" asked Vance mellifluously.

"Not altogether," Markham replied. "It seems colourable enough. . . . But why, I wonder, didn't Hagedorn work the thing out, if it was so simple?"

"Anaxagoras said that those who have occasion for a

lamp, supply it with oil. A profound remark, Markham—one of those seemingly simple quips that contain a great truth. A lamp without oil, y'know, is useless. The police always have plenty of lamps—every variety in fact—but no oil, as it were. That's why they never find anyone unless it's broad daylight."

Markham's mind was now busy in another direction, and he rose and began to pace the floor.

"Until now I hadn't thought of Captain Leacock as the actual agent of the crime."

"Why hadn't you thought of him? Was it because one of your sleuths told you he was at home like a good boy that night?"

"I suppose so." Markham continued pacing thoughtfully. Then suddenly he swung about. "That wasn't it, either. It was the amount of damning circumstantial evidence against the St. Clair woman. . . . And, Vance, despite your demonstration here to-day, you haven't explained away any of the evidence against her. Where was she between twelve and one? Why did she go with Benson to dinner? How did her handbag get here? And what about those burned cigarettes of hers in the grate?—they're the obstacle, those cigarette butts; and I can't admit that your demonstration wholly convinces me—despite the fact that it *is* convincing—as long as I've got the evidence of those cigarettes to contend with, for that evidence is also convincing."

"My word!" sighed Vance. "You're in a pos'tively ghastly predic'ment. However, maybe I can cast illumination on those disquietin' cigarette butts."

Once more he went to the door, and summoning Snitkin, returned the pistol.

"The District Attorney thanks you," he said. "And will you be good enough to fetch Mrs. Platz. We wish to chat with her."

Turning back to the room, he smiled amiably at Markham.

"I desire to do all the conversing with the lady this time, if you don't mind. There are potentialities in Mrs. Platz which you entirely overlooked when you questioned her yesterday."

Markham was interested, though sceptical.

"You have the floor," he said.

CHAPTER X

ELIMINATING A SUSPECT

(Saturday, June 15th ; 5.30 p.m.)

WHEN the housekeeper entered she appeared even more composed than when Markham had first questioned her. There was something at once sullen and indomitable in her manner, and she looked at me with a slightly challenging expression. Markham merely nodded to her, but Vance stood up and indicated a low, tufted Morris chair near the fireplace, facing the front windows. She sat down on the edge of it, resting her elbows on its broad arms.

"I have some questions to ask you, Mrs. Platz," Vance began, fixing her sharply with his gaze; "and it will be best for everyone if you tell the whole truth. You understand me—eh, what?"

The easy-going, half whimsical manner he had taken with Markham had disappeared. He stood before the woman, stern and implacable.

At his words she lifted her head. Her face was blank, but her mouth was set stubbornly, and a smouldering look in her eyes told of a suppressed anxiety.

Vance waited a moment and then went on, enunciating each word with distinctness.

"At what time, on the day Mr. Benson was killed, did the lady call here?"

The woman's gaze did not falter, but the pupils of her eyes dilated.

"There was nobody here."

"Oh, yes, there was, Mrs. Platz." Vance's tone was assured. "What time did she call?"

"Nobody was here, I tell you," she persisted.

Vance lit a cigarette with interminable deliberation, his eyes resting steadily on hers. He smoked placidly until her gaze dropped. Then he stepped nearer to her, and said firmly:

"If you tell the truth no harm will come to you. But if you refuse any information you will find yourself in trouble.

The withholding of evidence is a crime, y'know, and the law will show you no mercy."

He made a sly grimace at Markham, who was watching the proceedings with interest.

The woman now began to show signs of agitation. She drew in her elbows and her breathing quickened.

"In God's name, I swear it!—there wasn't anybody here." A slight hoarseness gave evidence of her emotion.

"Let us not invoke the deity," suggested Vance carelessly. "What time was the lady here?"

She set her lips stubbornly, and for a whole minute there was silence in the room. Vance smoked quietly, but Markham held his cigar motionless between his thumb and forefinger in an attitude of expectancy.

Again Vance's impassive voice demanded: "What time was she here?"

The woman clinched her hands with a spasmodic gesture, and thrust her head forward.

"I tell you—I swear it——"

Vance made a peremptory movement of his hand, and smiled coldly.

"It's no go," he told her. "You're acting stupidly. We're here to get the truth—and you're going to tell us."

"I've told you the truth."

"Is it going to be necess'ry for the District Attorney here to order you placed in custody?"

"I've told you the truth," she repeated.

Vance crushed out his cigarette decisively in an ash-receiver on the table.

"Righto, Mrs. Platz. Since you refuse to tell me about the young woman who was here that afternoon, I'm going to tell you about her."

His manner was easy and cynical, and the woman watched him suspiciously.

"Late in the afternoon of the day your employer was shot the door bell rang. Perhaps you had been informed by Mr. Benson that he was expecting a caller, what? Anyhow, you answered the door and admitted a charming young lady. You showed her into this room . . . and—what do you think, my dear madam!—she took that very chair on which you are resting so uncomfortably."

He paused and smiled tantalisingly.

"Then," he continued, "you served tea to the young lady and Mr. Benson. After a bit she departed, and Mr. Benson went upstairs to dress for dinner. . . . Y'see, Mrs. Platz, I happen to know."

He lit another cigarette.

"Did you notice the young lady particularly? If not, I'll describe her to you. She was rather short—*petite* is the word. She had dark hair and dark eyes, and she was dressed quietly."

A change had come over the woman. Her eyes stared; her cheeks were now grey; and her breathing had become audible.

"Now, Mrs. Platz," demanded Vance sharply, "what have you to say?"

She drew a deep breath.

"There wasn't anybody here," she said doggedly. There was something almost admirable in her obstinacy.

Vance considered a moment. Markham was about to speak, but evidently thought better of it, and sat watching the woman fixedly.

"Your attitude is understandable." Vance observed finally. "The young lady, of course, was well known to you, and you had a personal reason for not wanting it known she was here."

At these words she sat up straight, a look of terror to her face.

"I never saw her before," she cried: then stopped abruptly.

"Ah!" Vance gave her an amused leer. "You had never seen the young lady before—eh, what? . . . That's quite possible. But it's immaterial. She's a nice girl, though, I'm sure—even if she did have a dish of tea with your employer alone in his home."

"Did she tell you she was here?" The woman's voice was listless. The reaction to her tense obduracy had left her apathetic.

"Not exactly," Vance replied. "But it wasn't necess'ry: I knew without her informing me. . . . Just when did she arrive, Mrs. Platz?"

"About a half-hour after Mr. Benson got here from the office." She had at last given over all denials and evasions. "But he didn't expect her—that is, he didn't say anything to me about her coming; and he didn't order tea until after she came."

Markham thrust himself forward.

"Why didn't you tell me she'd been here, when I asked you yesterday morning?"

The woman cast an uneasy glance about the room.

"I rather fancy," Vance intervened pleasantly, "that Mrs. Platz was afraid you might unjustly suspect the young lady."

She grasped eagerly at his words.

"Yes, sir—that was all. I was afraid you might think she —did it. And she was such a quiet, sweet-looking girl. . . . That was the only reason, sir."

"Quite so," agreed Vance consolingly. "But tell me; did it not shock you to see such a quiet, sweet-looking young lady smoking cigarettes?"

Her apprehension gave way to astonishment.

"Why—yes, sir, it did. . . . . But she wasn't a bad girl —I could tell that. And most girls smoke nowadays. They don't think anything of it, like they used to."

"You're quite right," Vance assured her. "Still young ladies really shouldn't throw their cigarettes in tiled, gas-log fireplaces, should they, now?"

The woman regarded him uncertainly; she suspected him of jesting.

"Did she do that?" She leaned over and looked into the fireplace. "I didn't see any cigarettes there this morning."

"No, you wouldn't have," Vance informed her. "One of the District Attorney's sleuths, d'ye see, cleaned it all up nicely for you yesterday."

She shot Markham a questioning glance. She was not sure whether Vance's remark was to be taken seriously; but his casualness of manner and pleasantness of voice tended to put her at ease.

"Now that we understand each other, Mrs. Platz," he was saying, "was there anything else you particularly noticed when the young lady was here? You will be doing her a good service by telling us, because both the District Attorney and I happen to know she is innocent."

She gave Vance a long, shrewd look, as if appraising his sincerity. Evidently the results of her scrutiny were favourable, for her answer left no doubt as to her complete frankness.

"I don't know if it'll help, but when I came in with the toast, Mr. Benson looked like he was arguing with her. She seemed worried about something that was going to happen, and asked him not to hold her to some promise she'd made. I was only in the room a minute, and I didn't hear much. But just as I was going out, he laughed and said it was only a bluff, and that nothing was going to happen."

She stopped, and waited anxiously. She seemed to fear that her revelation might, after all, prove injurious rather than helpful to the girl.

"Was that all?" Vance's tone indicated that the matter was of no consequence.

The woman demurred.

"That was all I heard; but . . . there was a small blue box of jewellery sitting on the table."

"My word—a box of jewellery! Do you know whose it was?"

"No, sir, I don't. The lady hadn't brought it, and I never saw it in the house before."

"How did you know it was jewellery?"

"When Mr. Benson went upstairs to dress, I came in to clear the tea things away, and it was still sitting on the table."

Vance smiled.

"And you played Pandora and took a peep—eh, what? Most natural—I'd have done it myself."

He stepped back and bowed politely.

"That will be all, Mrs. Platz. . . . And you needn't worry about the young lady. Nothing is going to happen to her.'

When she had left us, Markham leaned forward and shook his cigar at Vance.

"Why didn't you tell me you had information about the case unknown to me?"

"My dear chap!" Vance lifted his eyebrows in protestation. "To what do you refer specifically?"

"How did you know this St. Clair woman had been here, in the afternoon?"

"I didn't; but I surmised it. There were cigarette butts of hers in the grate; and, as I knew she hadn't been here on the night Benson was shot. I thought it rather likely she had been here earlier in the day. And since Benson didn't arrive from his office until four, I whispered into my ear that she had called some time between four and the hour of his departure for dinner. . . . An element'ry syllogism, what?"

"How did you know she wasn't here that night?"

"The psychological aspects of the crime left me in no doubt. As I told you, no woman committed it—my metaphysical hypotheses again; but never mind. . . . Furthermore, yesterday morning I stood on the spot where the murderer stood, and sighted with my eye along the line of fire, using Benson's head and the mark on the wainscot as my points of coinc'dence. It was evident to me then, even without measurements, that the guilty person was rather tall."

"Very well. . . . But how did you know she left here that afternoon before Benson did?" persisted Markham.

"How else could she have changed into an evening gown? Really, y'know, ladies don't go about *décolletées* in the afternoon."

"You assume, then, that Benson himself brought her gloves and handbag back here that night?"

"Someone did—and it certainly wasn't Miss St. Clair."

"All right," conceded Markham. "And what about this Morris chair—how did you know she sat in it?"

"What other chair could she have sat in, and still thrown her cigarettes into the fireplace? Women are notoriously poor shots, even if they were given to hurling their cigarette stubs across the room."

"That deduction is simple enough," admitted Markham. "But suppose you tell me how you know she had tea here unless you were privy to some information on the point?"

"It pos'tively shames me to explain it. But the humiliating truth is that I inferred the fact from the condition of your samovar. I noted yesterday that it had been used, and had not been emptied or wiped off."

Markham nodded with contemptuous elation.

"You seem to have sunk to the despised legal level of material clues."

"That's why I'm blushing so furiously. . . . However, psychological deductions alone do not determine facts *in esse*, but only *in posse*. Other conditions must, of course, be considered. In the present instance the indications of the samovar served merely as the basis for an assumption, or guess, with which to draw out the housekeeper."

"Well, I won't deny that you succeeded," said Markham. "I'd like to know, though, what you had in mind when you accused the woman of a personal interest in the girl. That remark certainly indicated some pre-knowledge of the situation."

Vance's face became serious.

"Markham, I give you my word," he said earnestly, "I had nothing in mind. I made the accusation, thinking it was false, merely to trap her into a denial. And she fell into the trap. But—deuce take it!—I seemed to hit some nail squarely on the head, what? I can't for the life of me imagine why she was frightened. But it really doesn't matter."

"Perhaps not," agreed Markham, but his tone was dubious. "What do you make of the box of jewellery and the disagreement between Benson and the girl?"

"Nothing yet. They don't fit in, do they?"

He was silent a moment. Then he spoke with unusual seriousness.

"Markham, take my advice and don't bother with these side-issues. I'm telling you the girl had no part in the murder. Let her alone—you'll be happier in your old age, if you do."

Markham sat scowling, his eyes in space.

"I'm convinced that you *think* you know something."

"*Cogito, ergo sum*," murmured Vance. "Y'know, the naturalistic philosophy of Descartes has always rather appealed to me. It was a departure from universal doubt and a seeking for positive knowledge in self-consciousness. Spinoza, in his pantheism, and Berkeley, in his idealism, quite misunderstood the significance of their precursor's favourite enthymeme. Even Descartes' errors were brilliant. His method of reasoning, for all its scientific inaccuracies, gave new signif'cation to the symbols of the analyst. The mind, after all, if it is to function effectively, must combine the mathematical precision of a natural science with such pure speculations as astronomy. For instance, Descartes' doctrines of Vortices——"

"Oh, be quiet," growled Markham. "I'm not insisting

that you reveal your precious information. So why burden me with a dissertation on seventeenth-century philosophy?"

"Anyhow, you'll admit, won't you," asked Vance lightly, "that, in eliminating those disturbing cigarette butts, so to speak, I've elim'nated Miss St. Clair as a suspect?"

Markham did not answer at once. There was no doubt that the developments of the past hour had made a decided impression upon him. He did not underestimate Vance, despite his persistent opposition; and he knew that, for all his flippancy, Vance was fundamentally serious. Furthermore, Markham had a finely developed sense of justice. He was not narrow, even though obstinate at times; and I have never known him to close his mind to the possibilities of truth, however opposed to his own interests. It did not, therefore, surprise me in the least when, at last, he looked up with a gracious smile of surrender.

"You've made your point," he said; "and I accept it with proper humility. I'm most grateful to you."

Vance walked indifferently to the window and looked out.

"I am happy to learn that you are capable of accepting such evidence as the human mind could not possibly deny."

I had always noticed, in the relationship of these two men, that whenever either made a remark that bordered on generosity, the other answered in a manner which ended all outward show of sentiment. It was as if they wished to keep this more intimate side of their mutual regard hidden from the world.

Markham, therefore, ignored Vance's thrust.

"Have you perhaps any enlightening suggestions, other than negative ones, to offer as to Benson's murderer?" he asked.

"Rather!" said Vance. "No end of suggestions."

"Could you spare me a good one?" Markham imitated the other's playful tone.

Vance appeared to reflect.

"Well, I should advise that, as a beginning, you look for a rather tall man, cool-headed, familiar with firearms, a good shot, and fairly well known to the deceased—a man who was aware that Benson was going to dinner with Miss St. Clair, or who had reason to suspect the fact."

Markham looked narrowly at Vance for several moments.

"I think I understand. . . . Not a bad theory, either.

You know, I'm going to suggest immediately to Heath that he investigates more thoroughly Captain Leacock's activities on the night of the murder."

"Oh, by all means," said Vance carelessly, going to the piano.

Markham watched him with an expression of puzzled interrogation. He was about to speak when Vance began playing a rollicking French café song which opens, I believe, with

"*Ils sont dans les vignes, les moineaux.*"

CHAPTER XI

A MOTIVE AND A THREAT

(Sunday, June 16; afternoon)

THE following day, which was Sunday, we lunched with Markham at the Stuyvesant Club. Vance had suggested the appointment the evening before; for, as he explained to me, he wished to be present in case Leander Pfyfe should arrive from Long Island.

"It amuses me tremendously," he had said, "the way human beings delib'rately complicate the most ordin'ry issues. They have a downright horror of anything simple and direct. The whole modern commercial system is nothing but a colossal mechanism for doing things in the most involved and roundabout way. If one makes a recent purchase at a department store nowadays, a complete history of the transaction is written out in triplicate, checked by a dozen floor-walkers and clerks, signed and countersigned, entered into innum'rable ledgers with various coloured inks, and then elab'rately secreted in steel filing cabinets. And not content with all this superfluous *chinoiserie*, our business men have created a large and expensive army of efficiency experts whose sole duty is to complicate and befuddle this system still further. . . . It's the same with everything else in modern life. Regard that insup'rable mania called golf. It consists merely of knocking a ball into a hole with a stick. But the devotees of this pastime have developed a unique and distinctive livery in which to play it.   They concentrate for twenty years on the correct angulation of their feet and the proper method of entwining their fingers about the stick. Moreover, in order to discuss the pseudo-intr'cacies of this idiotic sport, they've invented an outlandish vocabulary which is unintelligible even to an English scholar."

He pointed disgustedly at a pile of Sunday newspapers.

"Then here's this Benson murder—a simple and incons'-quential affair.   Yet the entire machinery of the law is going at high pressure and blowing off jets of steam all over the community, when the matter could be settled quietly in five minutes with a bit of intelligent thinking."

At lunch, however, he did not refer to the crime; and, as if by tacit agreement, the subject was avoided.   Markham had merely mentioned casually to us as we went into the dining-room that he was expecting Heath a little later.

The Sergeant was waiting for us when we retired to the lounge-room for our smoke, and by his expression it was evident he was not pleased with the way things were going.

"I told you, Mr. Markham," he said, when we had drawn up our chairs, "that this case was going to be a tough one. . . . Could you get any kind of a lead from the St. Clair woman?"

Markham shook his head.

"She's out of it."   And he recounted briefly the happenings at Benson's house the preceding afternoon.

"Well, if you're satisfied," was Heath's somewhat dubious comment, "that's good enough for me.   But what about this Captain Leacock?"

"That's what I asked you here to talk about," Markham told him.   "There's no direct evidence against him, but there are several suspicious circumstances that tend to connect him with the murder.   He seems to meet the specification as to height; and we mustn't overlook the fact that Benson was shot with just such a gun as Leacock would be likely to possess.   He was engaged to the girl, and a motive might be found in Benson's attentions to her."

"And ever since the big scrap," supplemented Heath, "these army boys don't think anything of shooting people. They got used to blood on the other side."

"The only hitch," resumed Markham, "is that Phelps,

who had the job of checking up on the Captain, reported to me that he was home that night from eight o'clock on. Of course, there may be a loop-hole somewhere, and I was going to suggest that you have one of your men go into the matter thoroughly and see just what the situation is. Phelps got his information from one of the hall-boys; and I think it might be well to get hold of the boy again and apply a little pressure. If it was found that Leacock was not at home at twelve-thirty that night, we might have the lead you've been looking for."

"I'll attend to it myself," said Heath. "I'll go round there to-night, and if this boy knows anything he'll spill it before I'm through with him."

We had talked but a few minutes longer when a uniformed attendant bowed deferentially at the District Attorney's elbow and announced that Mr. Pfyfe was calling.

Markham requested that his visitor be shown into the lounge-room, and then added to Heath:

"You'd better remain, and hear what he has to say."

Leander Pfyfe was an immaculate and exquisite personage. He approached us with a mincing gait of self-approbation. His legs, which were very long and thin, with knees which seemed to bend slightly inward, supported a short bulging torso; and his chest curved outward in a generous arc, like that of a pouter-pigeon. His face was rotund, and his jowls hung in two loops over a collar too tight for comfort. His blond sparse hair was brushed back sleekly; and the ends of his narrow, silken moustache were waxed into needle-points. He was dressed in light-grey summer flannels, and wore a pale turquoise-green silk shirt, a vivid foulard tie, and grey suède Oxfords. A strong odour of oriental perfume was given off by the carefully arranged batiste handkerchief in his breast pocket.

He greeted Markham with viscid urbanity, and acknowledged his introduction to us with a patronising bow. After posing himself in a chair the attendant placed for him, he began polishing a gold-rimmed eyeglass which he wore on a ribbon, and fixed Markham with a melancholy gaze.

"A very sad occasion, this," he sighed.

"Realising your friendship for Mr. Benson," said Markham, "I deplore the necessity of appealing to you at this time. It was very good of you, by the way, to come to the city to-day."

Pfyfe made a mildly deprecating movement with his carefully manicured fingers. He was, he explained with an air of ineffable self-complacency, only too glad to discommode himself to give aid to servants of the public. A distressing necessity, to be sure; but his manner conveyed unmistakably that he knew and recognised the obligations attaching to the dictum of *noblesse oblige*, and was prepared to meet them.

He looked at Markham with a self-congratulatory air, and his eyebrows queried: "What can I do for you?" though his lips did not move.

"I understand from Major Anthony Benson," Markham said, "that you were very close to his brother, and therefore might be able to tell us something of his personal affairs, or private social relationships, that would indicate a line of investigation."

Pfyfe gazed sadly at the floor.

"Ah, yes. Alvin and I were very close—we were, in fact, the most intimate of friends. You cannot imagine how broken up I was at hearing of the dear fellow's tragic end." He gave the impression that here was a modern instance of Æneas and Achates. "And I was deeply grieved at not being able to come at once to New York to put myself at the service of those that needed me."

"I'm sure it would have been a comfort to his other friends," remarked Vance, with cool politeness. "But in the circumst'nces you will be forgiven."

Pfyfe blinked regretfully.

"Ah, but I shall never forgive myself—though I cannot hold myself altogether blameworthy. Only the day before the tragedy I had started on a trip to the Catskills. I had even asked dear Alvin to go along; but he was too busy." Pfyfe shook his head as if lamenting the incomprehensible irony of life. "How much better—ah, how infinitely much better —if only——"

"You were gone a very short time," commented Markham, interrupting what promised to be a homily on perverse providence.

"True," Pfyfe indulgently admitted. "But I met with a nost unfortunate accident." He polished his eyeglass a moment. "My car broke down, and I was necessitated to return."

"What road did you take?" asked Heath.

Pfyfe delicately adjusted his eyeglass, and regarded the Sergeant with an intimation of boredom.

"My advice, Mr.—ah—Sneed——"

"Heath," the other corrected him surlily.

"Ah, yes—Heath. . . . My advice, Mr. Heath, is, that if you are contemplating a motor trip to the Catskills, you apply to the Automobile Club of America for a road-map. My choice of itinerary might very possibly not suit you."

He turned back to the District Attorney with an air that implied he preferred talking to an equal.

"Tell me, Mr. Pfyfe," Markham asked: "did Mr. Benson have any enemies?"

The other appeared to think the matter over.

"No-o. Not one, I should say, who would actually have killed him as a result of animosity."

"You imply nevertheless that he had enemies. Could you not tell us a little more?"

Pfyfe passed his hand gracefully over the tips of his golden moustache, and then permitted his index-finger to linger on his cheek in an attitude of meditative indecision.

"Your request, Mr. Markham"—he spoke with pained reluctance—"brings up a matter which I hesitate to discuss. But perhaps it is best that I confide in you—as one gentleman to another. Alvin, in common with many other admirable fellows, had a—what shall I say?—a weakness—let me put it that way—for the fair sex."

He looked at Markham, seeking approbation for his extreme tact in stating an indelicate truth.

"You understand," he continued, in answer to the other's sympathetic nod, "Alvin was not a man who possessed the personal characteristics that women hold attractive." (I somehow got the impression that Pfyfe considered himself as differing radically from Benson in this respect.) "Alvin was aware of his physical deficiency, and the result was—I trust you will understand my hesitancy in mentioning this distressing fact—but the result was that Alvin used certain—ah, methods in his dealings with women, which you and I could never bring ourselves to adopt. Indeed—though it pains me to say it—he often took unfair advantage of women. He used underhand methods, as it were."

He paused, apparently shocked by this heinous imperfection of his friend, and by the necessity of his own seemingly disloyal revelation.

"Was it one of these women whom Benson had dealt with unfairly, that you had in mind?" asked Markham.

"No—not the woman herself," Pfyfe replied; "but a man who was interested in her. In fact, this man threatened Alvin's life. You will appreciate my reluctance in telling you this; but my excuse is that the threat was made quite openly. There were several others besides myself who heard it."

"That, of course, relieves you from any technical breach of confidence," Markham observed.

Pfyfe acknowledged the other's understanding with a slight bow.

"It happened at a little party of which I was the unfortunate host," he confessed modestly.

"Who was the man?" Markham's tone was polite but firm.

"You will comprehend my reticence. . . ." Pfyfe began. Then, with an air of righteous frankness, he leaned forward. "It might prove unfair to Alvin to withhold the gentleman's name. . . . He was Captain Philip Leacock."

He allowed himself the emotional outlet of a sigh.

"I trust you won't ask me for the lady's name."

"It won't be necessary," Markham assured him. "But I'd appreciate your telling us a little more of the episode."

Pfyfe complied with an expression of patient resignation.

"Alvin was considerably taken with the lady in question, and showed her many attentions which were, I am forced to admit, unwelcome. Captain Leacock resented these attentions; and at the little affair to which I had invited him and Alvin, some unpleasant and, I must say, unrefined words passed between them. I fear the wine had been flowing too freely, for Alvin was always punctilious—he was a man, indeed, skilled in the niceties of social intercourse; and the Captain, in an outburst of temper, told Alvin that, unless he left the lady strictly alone in the future, he would pay with his life. The Captain even went so far as to draw a revolver half-way out of his pocket."

"Was it a revolver, or an automatic pistol?" asked Heath.

Pfyfe gave the District Attorney a faint smile of annoyance, without deigning even to glance at the Sergeant.

"I mis-spoke myself; forgive me. It was not a revolver. It was, I believe, an automatic army pistol—though, you understand, I didn't see it in its entirety."

"You say there were others who witnessed the altercation?"

"Several of my guests were standing about," Pfyfe explained; "but, on my word, I couldn't name them. The fact is, I attached little importance to the threat—indeed, it had entirely slipped my memory until I read the account of poor Alvin's death. Then I thought at once of the unfortunate incident, and said to myself: Why not tell the District Attorney . . . ?"

"Thoughts that breathe and words that burn," murmured Vance, who had been sitting through the interview in oppressive boredom.

Pfyfe once more adjusted his eye-glass, and gave Vance a withering look.

"I beg your pardon, sir?"

Vance smiled disarmingly.

"Merely a quotation from Gray. Poetry appeals to me in certain moods, don't y'know. . . . Do you, by any chance, know Colonel Ostrander?"

Pfyfe looked at him coldly, but only a vacuous countenance met his gaze.

"I am acquainted with the gentleman," he replied haughtily.

"Was Colonel Ostrander present at this delightful little social affair of yours?" Vance's tone was artlessly innocent.

"Now that you mention it, I believe he was," admitted Pfyfe, and lifted his eyebrows inquisitively.

But Vance was again staring disinterestedly out of the window.

Markham, annoyed at the interruption, attempted to reestablish the conversation on a more amiable and practical basis. But Pfyfe, though loquacious, had little more information to give. He insisted constantly on bringing the talk back to Captain Leacock, and, despite his eloquent protestations, it was obvious he attached more importance to the threat than he chose to admit. Markham questioned him for fully an hour, but could learn nothing else of a suggestive nature.

When Pfyfe rose to go Vance turned from his contemplation of the outside world and, bowing affably, let his eyes rest on the other with ingenuous good-nature.

"Now that you are in New York, Mr. Pfyfe, and were so unfortunate as to be unable to arrive earlier, I assume that you will remain until after the investigation."

Pfyfe's studied and habitual calm gave way to a look of oily astonishment.

"I hadn't contemplated doing so."

"It would be most desirable—if you could arrange it," urged Markham; though I am sure he had no intention of making the request until Vance suggested it.

Pfyfe hesitated, and then made an elegant gesture of resignation.

"Certainly I shall remain. When you have further need of my services, you will find me at the Ansonia."

He spoke with exalted condescension, and magnanimously conferred upon Markham a parting smile. But the smile did not spring from within. It appeared to have been adjusted upon his features by the unseen hands of a sculptor; and it affected only the muscles about his mouth.

When he had gone Vance gave Markham a look of suppressed mirth.

"'Elegancy, facility and golden cadence.' . . . But put not your faith in poesy, old dear. Our Ciceronian friend is an unmitigated fashioner of deceptions."

"If you're trying to say that he's a smooth liar," remarked Heath, "I don't agree with you. I think that story about the Captain's threat is straight goods."

"Oh, that! Of course, it's true. . . . And, y'know, Markham, the knightly Mr. Pfyfe was frightfully disappointed when you didn't insist on his revealing Miss St. Clair's name. This Leander, I fear, would never have swum the Hellespont for a lady's sake."

"Whether he's a swimmer or not," said Heath impatiently, "he's given us something to go on."

Markham agreed that Pfyfe's recital had added materially to the case against Leacock.

"I think I'll have the Captain down to my office to-morrow, and question him," he said.

A moment later Major Benson entered the room, and Markham invited him to join us.

"I just saw Pfyfe get into a taxi," he said, when he had sat down. "I suppose you've been asking him about Alvin's affairs. . . . Did he help you any?"

"I hope so, for all our sakes," returned Markham kindly. "By the way, Major, what do you know about a Captain Philip Leacock?"

Major Benson lifted his eyes to Markham's in surprise.

"Didn't you know? Leacock was one of the captains in my regiment—a first-rate man. He knew Alvin pretty well, I think; but my impression is they didn't hit it off very chummily. . . . Surely you didn't connect him with this affair?"

Markham ignored the question.

"Did you happen to attend a party of Pfyfe's the night the Captain threatened your brother?"

"I went, I remember, to one or two of Pfyfe's parties," said the Major. "I don't as a rule, care for such gatherings, but Alvin convinced me it was a good business policy."

He lifted his head, and frowned fixedly into space, like one searching for an elusive memory.

"However, I don't recall—— By George! Yes, I believe I do. . . . But if the instance I am thinking of is what you have in mind, you can dismiss it. We were all a little moist that night."

"Did Captain Leacock draw a gun?" asked Heath.

The Major pursed his lips.

"Now that you mention it, I think he did make some motion of the kind."

"Did you see the gun?" pursued Heath.

"No, I can't say that I did."

Markham put the next question.

"Do you think Captain Leacock capable of the act of murder?"

"Hardly," Major Benson answered with emphasis. "Leacock isn't cold-blooded. The woman over whom the tiff occurred is more capable of such an act than he is."

A short silence followed, broken by Vance.

"What do you know, Major about this glass of fashion and mould of form, Pfyfe? He appears a rare bird. Has he a history, or is his presence his life's document?"

"Leander Pfyfe," said the Major, "is a typical specimen of the modern young do-nothing—I say young, though I imagine he's around forty. He was pampered in his up-bringing—had everything he wanted, I believe; but he became restless, and followed several different fads till he tired of them. He was two years in South Africa hunting big game, and, I think, wrote a book recounting his adventures. Since then he has done nothing that I know of. He married a wealthy shrew some years ago—for her money, I imagine. But the woman's father controls the purse-strings, and holds him down to a rigid allowance. . . . Pfyfe's a waster and an idler, but Alvin seemed to find some attraction in the man."

The Major's words had been careless in inflection and un-deliberated, like those of a man discussing a neutral matter; but all of us, I think, received the impression that he had a strong personal dislike for Pfyfe.

"Not a ravishing personality, what?" remarked Vance. "And he uses far too much *Jicky*."

"Still," supplied Heath, with a puzzled frown, "a fellow's got to have a lot of nerve to shoot big game. . . . And, speaking of nerve, I've been thinking that the guy who shot your brother, Major, was a mighty cool-headed proposition. He did it from the front when his man was wide awake, and with a servant upstairs. That takes nerve."

"Sergeant, you're pos'tively brilliant!" exclaimed Vance.

CHAPTER XII

THE OWNER OF A COLT ·45

(*Monday, June 17th; forenoon*)

THOUGH Vance and I arrived at the District Attorney's office the following morning a little after nine, the Captain had been waiting twenty minutes; and Markham directed Swacker to send him in at once.

Captain Philip Leacock was a typical army officer, very tall—fully six feet two inches—clean-shaven, straight and slender. His face was grave and immobile; and he stood before the District Attorney in the erect, earnest attitude of a soldier awaiting orders from his superior officer.

"Take a seat, Captain," said Markham, with a formal bow. "I have asked you here, as you probably know, to put a few questions to you concerning Mr. Alvin Benson. There are several points regarding your relationship with him, which I want you to explain."

"Am I suspected of complicity in the crime?" Leacock spoke with a slight Southern accent.

"That remains to be seen," Markham told him coldly. "It is to determine that point that I wish to question you."

The other sat rigidly in his chair and waited.

Markham fixed him with a direct gaze.

"You recently made a threat on Mr. Alvin Benson's life, I believe."

Leacock started, and his fingers tightened over his knees. But before he could answer, Markham continued:

"I can tell you the occasion on which the threat was made —it was at a party given by Mr. Leander Pfyfe."

Leacock hesitated; then thrust forward his jaw.

"Very well, sir; I admit I made the threat. Benson was a cad—he deserved shooting. . . . That night he had become more obnoxious than usual. He'd been drinking too much—and so had I, I reckon."

He gave a twisted smile, and looked nervously past the District Attorney out of the window.

"But I didn't shoot him, sir. I didn't even know he'd been shot until I read the paper next day."

"He was shot with an army Colt—the kind you fellows carried in the war," said Markham, keeping his eyes on the man.

"I know it," Leacock replied. "The papers said so."

"You have such a gun, haven't you, Captain?"

Again the other hesitated.

"No, sir." His voice was barely audible.

"What became of it?"

The man glanced at Markham, and then quickly shifted his eyes.

"I—I lost it . . . in France."

Markham smiled faintly.

"Then how do you account for the fact that Mr. Pfyfe saw the gun the night you made the threat?"

"Saw the gun?" He looked blankly at the District Attorney.

"Yes, saw it, and recognised it as an army gun," persisted Markham, in a level voice. "Also, Major Benson saw you make a motion as if to draw a gun."

Leacock drew a deep breath, and set his mouth doggedly.

"I tell you, sir, I haven't a gun . . . I lost it in France."

"Perhaps you didn't lose it, Captain. Perhaps you lent it to someone."

"I didn't, sir!" the words burst from his lips.

"Think a minute, Captain. . . . Didn't you lend it to someone?"

"No—I did not!"

"You paid a visit—yesterday—to Riverside Drive. . . . Perhaps you took it there with you?"

Vance had been listening closely.

"Oh—deuced clever!" he now murmured in my ear.

Captain Leacock moved uneasily. His face, even with its deep coat of tan, seemed to pale, and he sought to avoid the implacable glance of his questioner by concentrating his attention upon some object on the table. When he spoke, his voice, heretofore truculent, was coloured by anxiety. "I didn't have it with me. . . . And I didn't lend it to anyone."

Markham sat leaning forward over the desk, his chin on his hand, like a minatory graven image.

"It may be you lent it to someone prior to that morning."

"Prior to . . .?" Leacock looked up quickly and paused, as if analysing the other's remark.

Markham took advantage of his perplexity.

"Have you lent your gun to anyone since you returned from France?"

"No, I've never lent it——" he began, but suddenly halted and flushed. Then he added hastily: "How could I lend it? I just told you, sir——"

"Never mind that!" Markham cut in. "So you had a gun, did you, Captain? . . . Have you still got it?"

Leacock opened his lips to speak, but closed them again tightly.

Markham relaxed, and leaned back in his chair.

"You were aware, of course, that Benson had been annoying Miss St. Clair with his attentions?"

At the mention of the girl's name the Captain's body became rigid; his face turned a dull red, and he glanced menacingly at the District Attorney. At the end of a slow, deep inhalation he spoke through clenched teeth.

"Suppose we leave Miss St. Clair out of this." He looked as though he might spring at Markham.

"Unfortunately, we can't." Markham's words were sympathetic but firm. "Too many facts connect her with the case. Her handbag, for instance, was found in Benson's living-room the morning after the murder."

"That's a lie, sir!"

Markham ignored the insult.

"Miss St. Clair herself admits the circumstance." He held up his hand, as the other was about to answer. "Don't misinterpret my mentioning the fact. I am not accusing Miss St. Clair of having anything to do with the affair. I'm merely endeavouring to get some light on your own connection with it."

The Captain studied Markham with an expression that clearly indicated he doubted these assurances. Finally he set his mouth and announced with determination:

"I haven't anything more to say on the subject, sir."

"You knew, didn't you," continued Markham, "that Miss St. Clair dined with Benson at the Marseilles on the night he was shot?"

"What of it?" retorted Leacock sullenly.

"And you knew, didn't you, that they left the restaurant at midnight, and that Miss St. Clair did not reach home until after one?"

A strange look came into the man's eyes. The ligaments of his neck tightened, and he took a deep, resolute breath. But he neither glanced at the District Attorney nor spoke.

"You know, of course," pursued Markham's monotonous voice, "that Benson was shot at half-past twelve?"

He waited; and for a whole minute there was silence in the room.

"You have nothing more to say, Captain?" he asked at length; "no further explanations to give me?"

Leacock did not answer. He sat gazing imperturbably ahead of him; and it was evident he had sealed his lips for the time being.

Markham rose.

"In that case, let us consider the interview at an end."

The moment Captain Leacock had gone, Markham rang for one of his clerks.

"Tell Ben to have that man followed. Find out where he goes and what he does. I want a report at the Stuyvesant Club to-night."

When we were alone Vance gave Markham a look of half-bantering admiration.

"Ingenious—not to say artful. . . . But, y'know, your questions about the lady were shocking bad form."

"No doubt," Markham agreed. "But it looks now as if we were on the right track. Leacock didn't create an impression of unassailable innocence."

"Didn't he?" asked Vance. "Just what were the signs of his assailable guilt?"

"You saw him turn white when I questioned him about the weapon. His nerves were on edge—he was genuinely frightened."

Vance signed.

"What a perfect ready-made set of notions you have, Markham! Don't you know that an innocent man, when he comes under suspicion, is apt to be more nervous than a guilty one, who, to begin with, had enough nerve to commit the crime, and, secondly, realises that any show of nervousness is regarded as guilt by you lawyer chaps? 'My strength is as the strength of ten because my heart is pure' is a mere Sunday school pleasantry. Touch almost any innocent man on the shoulder and say 'You're arrested,' and his pupils will dilate, he'll break out in a cold sweat, the blood will rush from his face, and he'll have tremors and dyspnœa. If he's a *hystérique*, or a cardiac neurotic, he'll probably collapse completely. It's the guilty person, who when thus accosted, lifts his eyebrows in bored surprise and says 'You don't mean it, really—here, have a cigar.'"

"The hardened criminal may act as you say," Markham conceded; "but an honest man who's innocent doesn't go to pieces, even when accused."

Vance shook his head hopelessly.

"My dear fellow, Crile and Voronoff might have lived in vain for all of you. Manifestations of fear are the result of glandular secretions—nothing more. All they prove is that the person's thyroid is undeveloped or that his adrenals are subnormal. A man accused of a crime, or shown the bloody weapon with which it was committed, will either smile serenely, or scream, or have hysterics, or faint, or appear disint'rested —according to his hormones and irrespective of his guilt. Your theory, d'ye see, would be quite all right if everyone had the same amount of the various internal secretions. But they haven't. . . . Really, y'know, you shouldn't send a man to the electric chair simply because he's deficient in endocrines. It isn't cricket."

Before Markham could reply, Swacker appeared at the door and said Heath had arrived.

The Sergeant, beaming with satisfaction, fairly burst into the room. For once, he forgot to shake hands.

"Well, it looks like we'd got hold of something workable. I went to this Captain Leacock's apartment house last night, and here's the straight of it: Leacock was at home the night of the thirteenth all right; but shortly after midnight he went out, headed west—get that!—and he didn't return till about quarter of one!"

"What about the hall-boy's original story?" asked Markham.

"That's the best part of it. Leacock had the boy fixed. Gave him money to swear he hadn't left the house that night. What do you think of that, Mr. Markham? Pretty crude— huh? . . . The kid loosened up when I told him I was thinking of sending him up the river for doing the job himself." Heath laughed unpleasantly. "And he won't spill anything to Leacock, either."

Markham nodded his head slowly.

"What you tell me, Sergeant, bears out certain conclusions I arrived at when I talked to Captain Leacock this morning. Ben put a man on him when he left here, and I'm to get a report to-night. To-morrow may see this thing through. I'll get in touch with you in the morning, and if anything's to be done, you understand, you'll have the handling of it."

When Heath left us, Markham folded his hands behind his head and leaned back contentedly.

"I think I've got the answer," he said. "The girl dined with Benson and returned to his house afterward. The Captain, suspecting the fact, went out, found her there, and shot Benson. That would account not only for her gloves and handbag, but for the hour it took her to go from the Marseilles to her home. It would also account for her attitude here Saturday, and for the Captain's lying about the gun. . . . There, I believe, I have my case. The smashing of the Captain's alibi about clinches it."

"Oh, quite," said Vance airily. "'Hope springs exulting on triumphant wing.'"

Markham regarded him for a moment.

"Have you entirely forsworn human reason as a means of reaching a decision? Here we have an admitted threat, a motive, the time, the place, the opportunity, the conduct, and the criminal agent."

"Those words sound strangely familiar," smiled Vance. "Didn't most of 'em fit the young lady also? . . . And you really haven't got the criminal agent, y'know. But it's no doubt floating about the city somewhere—a mere detail, however."

"I may not have it in my hand," Markham countered. "But with a good man on watch every minute, Leacock won't find much opportunity of disposing of the weapon."

Vance shrugged indifferently.

"In any event go easy," he admonished. "My humble opinion is that you've merely unearthed a conspiracy."

"Conspiracy? . . . Good Lord! What kind?"

"A conspiracy of circumst'nces, don't y'know."

"I'm glad, at any rate, it hasn't to do with international politics," returned Markham good-naturedly.

He glanced at the clock.

"You won't mind if I get to work? I've a dozen things to attend to, and a couple of committees to see. . . . Why don't you go across the hall and have a talk with Ben Hanlon, and then come back at twelve-thirty? We'll have lunch together at the Bankers' Club. Ben's our greatest expert on foreign extradition, and has spent most of his life chasing about the world after fugitives from justice. He'll spin you some good yarns."

"How perfectly fascinatin'!" exclaimed Vance, with a yawn.

But instead of taking the suggestion, he walked to the window and lit a cigarette. He stood for a while puffing at it, rolling it between his fingers, and inspecting it critically.

"Y'know, Markham," he observed, "everything's going to pot these days. It's this silly democracy. Even the nobility is degen'rating. These *Régie* cigarettes, now; they've fallen off frightfully. There was a time when no self-respecting potentate would have smoked such inferior tobacco."

Markham smiled.

"What's the favour you want to ask?"

"Favour? What has that to do with the decay of Europe's aristocracy?"

"I've noticed that whenever you want to ask a favour which you consider questionable etiquette, you begin with a denunciation of royalty."

"Observin' fella," commented Vance drily. Then he, too, smiled. "Do you mind if I invite Colonel Ostrander along to lunch?"

Markham gave him a sharp look.

"Bigsby Ostrander, you mean? . . . Is he the mysterious colonel you've been asking people about for the past two days?"

"That's the lad. Pompous ass and that sort of thing. Might prove a bit edifyin', though. He's the papa of Benson's crowd, so to speak; knows all parties. Regular old scandalmonger."

"Have him along by all means," agreed Markham.

Then he picked up the telephone.

"Now I'm going to tell Ben you're coming over for an hour or so."

CHAPTER XIII

THE GREY "CADILLAC"

(Monday, June 17th; 12.30 p.m.)

WHEN, at half-past twelve, Markham, Vance and I entered the Grill of the Bankers' Club in the Equitable Building, Colonel Ostrander was already at the bar engaged with one of Charlie's prohibition clam-broth-and-Worcestershire-sauce cocktails. Vance had telephoned him immediately upon our leaving the District Attorney's office, requesting him to meet us at the Club; and the Colonel had seemed eager to comply.

"Here is New York's gayest dog," said Vance, introducing him to Markham (I had met him before); "a sybarite and a hedonist. He sleeps till noon, and makes no appointment before tiffin-time. I had to knock him up and threaten him with your official ire to get him down town at this early hour."

"Only too pleased to be of any service," the Colonel assured Markham grandiloquently. "Shocking affair! Gad! I couldn't credit it when I read it in the papers. Fact is, though—I don't mind sayin' it—I've one or two ideas on the subject. Came very near calling you up myself, sir."

When we had taken our seats at the table Vance began interrogating him without preliminaries.

"You know all the people in Benson's set, Colonel. Tell us something about Captain Leacock. What sort of chap is he?"

"Ha! So you have your eye on the gallant Captain?"

Colonel Ostrander pulled importantly at his white moustache. He was a large pink-faced man with bushy eyelashes and small blue eyes; and his manner and bearing were those of a pompous light-opera general.

"Not a bad idea. Might possibly have done it. Hot-headed fellow. He's badly smitten with a Miss St. Clair—fine girl, Muriel. And Benson was smitten, too. If I'd been twenty years younger myself——"

"You're too fascinatin' to the ladies, as it is, Colonel," interrupted Vance. "But tell us about the Captain."

"Ah, yes—the Captain. Comes from Georgia, originally. Served in the war—some kind of decoration. He didn't care for Benson—disliked him, in fact. Quick-tempered, single-track-minded sort of person. Jealous, too. You know the type—a product of that tribal etiquette below the Mason and Dixon line. Puts women on a pedestal—not that they shouldn't be put there, God bless 'em! But he'd go to jail for a lady's honour. A shielder of womanhood. Sentimental cuss, full of chivalry; just the kind to blow out a rival's brains —no question asked—*pop*—and it's all over. Dangerous chap to monkey with. Benson was a confounded idiot to bother with the girl when he knew she was engaged to Leacock. Playin' with fire. I don't mind sayin' I was tempted to warn him. But it was none of my affair—I had no business interferin'. Bad taste."

"Just how well did Captain Leacock know Benson?" asked Vance. "By that I mean: how intimate were they?"

"Not intimate at all," the Colonel replied.

He made a ponderous gesture of negation, and added: "I should say not! Formal, in fact. They met each other here and there a good deal, though. Knowing 'em both pretty well, I've often had 'em to little affairs at my humble diggin's."

"You wouldn't say Captain Leacock was a good gambler— level-headed, and all that?"

"Gambler—huh!" The Colonel's manner was heavily contemptuous. "Poorest I ever saw. Played poker worse than a woman. Too excitable—couldn't keep his feelin's to himself. Altogether too rash."

Then, after a momentary pause:

"By George! I see what you're aimin' at. . . . And you're dead right. It's rash young puppies just like him that go about shootin' people they don't like."

"The Captain, I take it, is quite different in that regard from your friend Leander Pfyfe," remarked Vance.

The Colonel appeared to consider.

"Yes and no," he decided. "Pfyfe's a cool gambler—that I'll grant you. He once ran a private gambling place of his own down on Long Island—roulette, monte, baccarat, that sort of thing. And he popped tigers and wild boar in Africa for a while. But Pfyfe's got his sentimental side, and he'd plunge on a pair of deuces with all the betting odds against him. Not a good scientific gambler. Flighty in his impulses, if you understand me. I don't mind admittin', though, that he could shoot a man and forget all about it in five minutes. But he'd need a lot of provocation. . . . He may have had it—you can't tell."

"Pfyfe and Benson were rather intimate, weren't they?"

"Very—very. Always saw 'em together when Pfyfe was in New York. Known each other years. Boon companions, as they called 'em in the old days. Actually lived together before Pfyfe got married. An exacting woman, Pfyfe's wife; makes him toe the mark. But loads of money."

"Speaking of the ladies," said Vance, "what was the situation between Benson and Miss St. Clair?"

"Who can tell?" asked the Colonel sententiously. "Muriel didn't cotton to Benson—that's sure. And yet . . . women are strange creatures——"

"Oh, no end strange," agreed Vance, a trifle wearily. "But really, y'know, I wasn't prying into the lady's personal relations with Benson. I thought you might know her mental attitude concerning him."

"Ah—I see. Would she, in short, have been likely to take desperate measures against him? . . . Egad! That's an idea!"

The Colonel pondered the point.

"Muriel, now, is a girl of strong character. Works hard at her art. She's a singer, and—I don't mind tellin' you— a mighty fine one. She's deep, too—deuced deep. And capable. Not afraid of taking a chance. Independent. I myself wouldn't want to be in her path if she had it in for me. Might stick at nothing."

He nodded his head sagely.

"Women are funny that way. Always surprisin' you. No sense of values. The most peaceful of 'em will shoot a man in cold blood without warnin'——"

He suddenly sat up, and his little blue eyes glistened like china.

"By Gad!" He fairly blurted the ejaculation. "Muriel had dinner alone with Benson the night he was shot—the very night. Saw 'em together myself at the Marseilles."

"You don't say really!" muttered Vance incuriously. "But I suppose we all must eat. . . . By the bye; how well did you yourself know Benson?"

The Colonel looked startled, but Vance's innocuous expression seemed to reassure him.

"I? My dear fellow! I've known Alvin Benson fifteen years. At least fifteen—maybe longer. Showed him the sights in this old town before the lid was put on. A live town it was then. Wide open. Anything you wanted. Gad! what times we had! Those were the days of the old Haymarket. Never thought of toddlin' home till breakfast——"

Vance again interrupted his irrelevancies.

"How intimate are your relations with Major Benson?"

"The Major? . . . That's another matter. He and I belong to different schools. Dissimilar tastes. We never hit it off. Rarely see each other."

He seemed to think that some explanation was necessary, for before Vance could speak again, he added:

"The Major, you know, was never one of the boys, as we say. Disapproved of gaiety. Didn't mix with our little set. Considered me and Alvin too frivolous. Serious-minded chap."

Vance ate in silence for a while, then asked in an off-hand way:

"Did you do much speculating through Benson and Benson?"

For the first time the Colonel appeared hesitant about answering. He ostentatiously wiped his mouth with his napkin.

"Oh—dabbled a bit," he at length admitted airily. "Not very lucky, though. . . . We all flirted now and then with the Goddess of Chance in Benson's office."

Throughout the lunch Vance kept plying him with questions along these lines; but at the end of an hour he seemed to be no nearer anything definite than when he began. Colonel Ostrander was voluble, but his fluency was vague and disorganised. He talked mainly in parentheses, and insisted on elaborating his answers with rambling opinions, until it was almost impossible to extract what little information his words contained.

Vance, however, did not appear discouraged. He dwelt on Captain Leacock's character, and seemed particularly interested in his personal relationship with Benson. Pfyfe's gambling proclivities also occupied his attention, and he let the Colonel ramble on tiresomely about the man's gambling house on Long Island and his hunting experiences in South Africa. He asked numerous questions about Benson's other friends, but paid scant attention to the answers.

The whole interview impressed me as pointless, and I could not help wondering what Vance hoped to learn. Markham, I was convinced was equally at sea. He pretended polite interest, and nodded appreciatively during the Colonel's incredibly drawn-out periods; but his eyes wandered occasionally and several times I saw him give Vance a look of reproachful inquiry. There was no doubt, however, that Colonel Ostrander knew his people.

When we were back in the District Attorney's office, having taken leave of our garrulous guest at the subway entrance, Vance threw himself into one of the easy chairs with an air of satisfaction.

"Most entertainin', what? As an elim'nator of suspects the Colonel has his good points."

"Eliminator!" retorted Markham. "It's a good thing he's not connected with the police; he'd have half the community jailed for shooting Benson."

"He *is* a bit bloodthirsty," Vance admitted. "He's determined to get somebody jailed for the crime."

"According to that old warrior, Benson's coterie was a camorra of gunmen—not forgetting the women. I couldn't help getting the impression, as he talked, that Benson was miraculously lucky not to have been riddled with bullets long ago."

"It's obvious," commented Vance, "that you overlooked the illuminatin' flashes in the Colonel's thunder."

"Were there any?" Markham asked. "At any rate, I can't say that they exactly blinded me by their brilliance."

"And you received no solace from his words?"

"Only those in which he bade me a fond farewell. The parting didn't exactly break my heart. ... What the old

boy said about Leacock, however, might be called a confirma-
tory opinion. It verified—if verification had been necessary
—the case against the Captain."

Vance smiled cynically.

"Oh, to be sure. And what he said about Miss St. Clair
would have verified the case against her, too—last Saturday.
Also, what he said about Pfyfe would have verified the case
against that Beau Sabreur, if you had happened to suspect
him—eh, what?"

Vance had scarcely finished speaking when Swacker came
in to say that Emery from the Homicide Bureau had been
sent over by Heath, and wished, if possible, to see the District
Attorney.

When the man entered I recognized him at once as the
detective who had found the cigarette butts in Benson's grate.
With a quick glance at Vance and me, he went directly
to Markham.

"We've found the grey Cadillac, sir; and Sergeant Heath
thought you might want to know about it right away. It's
in a small, one-man garage on Seventy-fourth Street near
Amsterdam Avenue, and has been there three days. One
of the men from the Sixth-eighth Street Station located it
and 'phoned in to Headquarters; and I hopped up town at
once. It's the right car—fishing-tackle and all, except for
the rods; so I guess the ones found in Central Park belonged
to the car after all: fell out probably. . . . It seems a fellow
drove the car into the garage about noon last Friday, and
gave the garage-man twenty dollars to keep his mouth shut.
The man's a wop, and says he don't read the papers. Anyway, he came across *pronto* when I put the screws on."

The detective drew out a small notebook.

"I looked up the car's number. . . . It's listed in the name
of Leander Pfyfe, 42 Elm Boulevard, Port Washington, Long
Island."

Markham received this piece of unexpected information
with a perplexed frown. He dismissed Emery almost curtly,
and sat tapping thoughtfully on his desk.

Vance watched him with an amused smile.

"It's really not a madhouse, y'know," he observed com-
fortingly. "I say, don't the Colonel's words bring you any
cheer, now that you know Leander was hovering about the

neighbourhood at the time Benson was translated into the Beyond?"

"Damn your old Colonel!" snapped Markham. "What interests me at present is fitting this new development into the situation."

"It fits beautifully," Vance told him. "It rounds out the mosaic, so to speak. . . . Are you actu'lly disconcerted by learning that Pfyfe was the owner of the mysterious car?"

"Not having your gift of clairvoyance, I am, I confess, disturbed by the fact."

Markham lit a cigar—an indication of worry.

"You, of course," he added, with sarcasm, "knew before Emery came here that it was Pfyfe's car."

"I didn't know," Vance corrected him; "but I had a strong suspicion. Pfyfe overdid his distress when he told us of his breakdown in the Catskills. And Heath's question about his itiner'ry annoyed him frightfully. His hauteur was too melodramatic."

"Your *ex post facto* wisdom is most useful!"

Markham smoked a while in silence.

"I think I'll find out about this matter."

He rang for Swacker.

"Call up the Ansonia," he ordered angrily; "locate Leander Pfyfe, and say I want to see him at the Stuyvesant Club at six o'clock. And tell him he's to be there."

"It occurs to me," said Markham, when Swacker had gone, "that this car episode may prove helpful, after all. Pfyfe was evidently in New York that night, and for some reason he didn't want it known. Why, I wonder? He tipped us off about Leacock's threat against Benson, and hinted strongly that we'd better get on the fellow's track. Of course, he may have been sore at Leacock for winning Miss St. Clair away from his friend, and taken this means of wreaking a little revenge on him. On the other hand, if Pfyfe was at Benson's house the night of the murder, he may have some real information. And now that we've found out about the car, I think he'll tell us what he knows."

"He'll tell you something anyway," said Vance. "He's the type of congenital liar that'll tell anybody anything as long as it doesn't involve himself unpleasantly."

"You and the Cumæan Sibyl, I presume, could inform me in advance what he's going to tell me."

"I couldn't say as to the Cumæan Sibyl, don't y'know," Vance returned lightly; "but speaking for myself, I rather fancy he'll tell you that he saw the impetuous Captain at Benson's house that night."

Markham laughed.

"I hope he does. You'll want to be on hand to hear him, I suppose."

"I couldn't bear to miss it."

Vance was already at the door, preparatory to going, when he turned again to Markham.

"I've another slight favour to ask. Get a *dossier* on Pfyfe —there's a good fellow. Send one of your innumerable Dogberrys to Port Washington and have the gentleman's conduct and social habits looked into. Tell your emiss'ry to concentrate on the woman question. . . . I promise you, you shan't regret it."

Markham, I could see, was decidedly puzzled by this request, and half inclined to refuse it. But after deliberating a few moments, he smiled, and pressed a button on his desk.

"Anything to humour you," he said. "I'll send a man down at once."

CHAPTER XIV

LINKS IN THE CHAIN

(*Monday, June* 17; 6 *p.m.*)

VANCE and I spent an hour or so that afternoon at the Anderson Galleries looking at some tapestries which were to be auctioned the next day, and afterwards had tea at Sherry's. We were at the Stuyvesant Club a little before six. A few minutes later, Markham and Pfyfe arrived, and we went at once into one of the conference rooms.

Pfyfe was as elegant and superior as at the first interview. He wore a rat-catcher suit and Newmarket gaiters of unbleached linen, and was redolent of perfume.

"An unexpected pleasure to see you gentlemen again so soon," he greeted us, like one conferring a blessing.

Markham was far from amiable, and gave him an almost brusque salutation. Vance had merely nodded, and now sat regarding Pfyfe drearily as if seeking to find some excuse for his existence, but utterly unable to do so.

Markham went directly to the point.

"I've found out, Mr. Pfyfe, that you placed your machine in a garage at noon on Friday, and gave the man twenty dollars to say nothing about it."

Pfyfe looked up with a hurt look.

"I've been deeply wronged," he complained sadly. "I gave the man fifty dollars."

"I am glad you admit the fact so readily," returned Markham. "You knew, by the newspapers, of course, that your machine was seen outside Benson's house the night he was shot."

"Why else should I have paid so liberally to have its presence in New York kept secret?" His tone indicated that he was pained at the other's obtuseness.

"In that case, why did you keep it in the city at all?" asked Markham. "You could have driven it back to Long Island."

Pfyfe shook his head sorrowfully, a look of commiseration in his eyes. Then he leaned forward with an air of benign patience: he would be gentle with this dull-witted District Attorney, like a fond teacher with a backward child, and would strive to lead him out of the tangle of his uncertainties.

"I am a married man, Mr. Markham." He pronounced the fact as if some special virtue attached to it. "I started on my trip for the Catskills Thursday after dinner, intending to stop a day in New York to make my adieux to someone residing here. I arrived quite late—after midnight—and decided to call on Alvin. But when I drove up, the house was dark. So, without even ringing the bell, I walked to Pietro's in Forty-third Street to get a night-cap—I keep a bit of my own pinch-bottle Haig and Haig there—but, alas, the place was closed, and I strolled back to my car. . . . To think, that while I was away poor Alvin was shot?"

He stopped and polished his eye-glass.

"The irony of it. . . . I didn't even guess that anything

had happened to the dear fellow—how could I? I drove, all
unsuspecting of the tragedy, to a Turkish bath, and remained
there the night. The next morning I read of the murder;
and in the later editions I saw the mention of my car. It
was then I became—shall I say worried? But no. 'Worried'
is a misleading word. Let me say, rather, that I became
aware of the false position I might be placed in if the car
were traced to me. So I drove it to the garage and paid
the man to say nothing of its whereabouts, lest its discovery
confuse the issue of Alvin's death."

One might have thought, from his tone and the self-
righteous way he looked at Markham, that he had bribed
the garage-man wholly out of consideration for the District
Attorney and the police.

"Why didn't you continue on your trip?" asked Markham.
"That would have made the discovery of the car even less
likely."

Pfyfe adopted an air of compassionate surprise.

"With my dearest friend foully murdered? How could
one have the heart to seek diversion at such a sad moment?
. . . I returned home, and informed Mrs. Pfyfe that my car
had broken down."

"You might have driven home in your car, it seems to
me," observed Markham.

Pfyfe offered a look of infinite forbearance for the other's
inspection, and took a deep sigh, which conveyed the impression, that though he could not sharpen the world's
perceptions, he at least could mourn for its deplorable lack
of understanding.

"If I had been in the Catskills away from any source of
information, where Mrs. Pfyfe believed me to be, how would
I have heard of Alvin's death until, perhaps, days afterward?
You see, unfortunately I had not mentioned it to Mrs. Pfyfe
that I was stopping over in New York. The truth is, Mr.
Markham, I had reason for not wishing my wife to know I
was in the city. Consequently, if I had driven back at once,
she would, I regret to say, have suspected me of breaking
my journey. I therefore pursued the course which seemed
simplest."

Markham was becoming annoyed at the man's fluent
hypocrisy. After a brief silence he asked abruptly:

"Did the presence of your car at Benson's house that night have anything to do with your apparent desire to implicate Captain Leacock in the affair?"

Pfyfe lifted his eyebrows in pained astonishment, and made a gesture of polite protestation.

"My dear sir!" His voice betokened profound resentment of the other's unjust imputation. "If yesterday you detected in my words an undercurrent of suspicion against Captain Leacock, I can account for it only by the fact that I actually saw the Captain in front of Alvin's house when I drove up that night."

Markham shot a curious look at Vance; then said to Pfyfe:

"You are sure you saw Leacock?"

"I saw him quite distinctly, And I would have mentioned the fact yesterday had it not involved the tacit confession of my own presence there."

"What if it had?" demanded Markham. "It was vital information, and I could have used it this morning. You were placing your comfort ahead of the legal demands of justice; and your attitude puts a very questionable aspect on your own alleged conduct that night."

"You are pleased to be severe, sir," said Pfyfe with self-pity. "But, having placed myself in a false position, I must accept your criticism."

"Do you realise," Markham went on, "that many a district attorney, if he knew what I now know about your movements, and had been treated the way you've treated me, would arrest you on suspicion?"

"Then I can only say," was the suave response, "that I am most fortunate in my inquisitor."

Markham rose.

"That will be all for to-day, Mr. Pfyfe. But you are to remain in New York until I give you permission to return home. Otherwise, I will have you held as a material witness."

Pfyfe made a shocked gesture in deprecation of such acerbities, and bade us a ceremonious good afternoon.

When we were alone, Markham looked seriously at Vance.

"Your prophecy was fulfilled, though I didn't dare hope for such luck. Pfyfe's evidence puts the final link in the chain against the Captain."

Vance smoked languidly.

"I'll admit your theory of the crime is most satisfyin'. But alas, the psychological objection remains. Everything fits, with the one exception of the Captain; and he doesn't fit at all. . . . Silly idea, I know. But he has no more business being cast as the murderer of Benson than the bisonic Tetrazzini had being cast as the phthisical *Mimi*."[1]

"In any other circumstances," Markham answered, "I might defer reverently to your charming theories. But with all the circumstantial and presumptive evidence I have against Leacock, it strikes my inferior legal mind as sheer nonsense to say, 'He just couldn't be guilty because his hair is parted in the middle and he tucks his napkin in his collar.' There's too much logic against it."

"I'll grant your logic is irrefutable—as all logic is, no doubt. You've prob'bly convinced many innocent persons by sheer reasoning that they were guilty."

Vance stretched himself wearily.

"What do you say to a light repast on the roof? The unutt'rable Pfyfe has tired me."

In the summer dining-room on the roof of the Stuyvesant Club we found Major Benson sitting alone, and Markham asked him to join us.

"I have good news for you, Major," he said, when we had given our order. "I feel confident I have my man; everything points to him. To-morrow will see the end, I hope."

The Major gave Markham a questioning frown.

"I don't understand exactly. From what you told me the other day, I got the impression there was a woman involved."

Markham smiled awkwardly, and avoided Vance's eyes.

"A lot of water has run under the bridge since then," he said. "The woman I had in mind was eliminated as soon as we began to check up on her. But in the process I was led to the man. There's little doubt of his guilt. I felt pretty sure about it this morning, and just now I learned that he was seen by a credible witness in front of your brother's house within a few minutes of the time the shot was fired."

[1] Obviously a reference to Tetrazzini's performance in *La Bohème* at the Manhattan Opera House in 1908.

"Is there any objection to your telling me who it was?"
The Major was still frowning.

"None whatever. The whole city will probably know it
to-morrow. . . . It was Captain Leacock."

Major Benson stared at him in unbelief.

"Impossible! I simply can't credit it. That boy was
with me three years on the other side, and I got to know
him pretty well. I can't help feeling there's a mistake somewhere. . . . The police," he added quickly, "have got on
the wrong track."

"It's not the police," Markham informed him. "It was
my own investigations that turned up the Captain."

The Major did not answer, but his silence bespoke his
doubt.

"Y'know," put in Vance, "I feel the same way about
the Captain that you do, Major. It rather pleases me to
have my impressions verified by one who has known him so
long."

"What, then, was Leacock doing in front of the house
that night?" urged Markham acidulously.

"He might have been singing carols beneath Benson's
window," suggested Vance.

Before Markham could reply he was handed a card by the
head waiter. When he glanced at it, he gave a grunt of
satisfaction, and directed that the caller be sent up immediately. Then, turning back to us, he said:

"We may learn something more now. I've been expecting
this man Higginbotham. He's the detective that followed
Leacock from my office this morning."

Higginbotham was a wiry, pale-faced youth with fishy
eyes and a shifty manner. He slouched up to the table and
stood hesitantly before the District Attorney.

"Sit down and report, Higginbotham," Markham ordered.
"These gentlemen are working with me on the case."

"I picked up the bird while he was waiting for the elevator,"
the man began, eyeing Markham craftily. "He went to the
subway and rode up town to Seventy-ninth and Broadway.
He walked through Eightieth to Riverside Drive and went
in the apartment house at No. 94. Didn't give his name to
the boy—got right in the elevator. He stayed upstairs a
coupla hours, come down at one-twenty, and hopped a taxi.

I picked up another one, and followed. He went down the
Drive to Seventy-second, through Central Park, and east on
Fifty-ninth. Got out at Avenue A, and walked out on the
Queensborough Bridge. About half way to Blackwell's
Island he stood leaning over the rail for five or six minutes.
Then he took a small package out of his pocket, and dropped
it in the river."

"What size was the package?" There was repressed
eagerness in Markham's question.

Higginbotham indicated the measurements with his hands.

"How thick was it?"

"Inch or so, maybe."

Markham leaned forward.

"Could it have been a gun—a Colt automatic?"

"Sure it could. Just about the right size. And it was
heavy, too—I could tell by the way he handled it, and by
the way it hit the water."

"All right." Markham was pleased. "Anything else?"

"No, sir. After he'd ditched the gun, he went home and
stayed. I left him there."

When Higginbotham had gone, Markham nodded at
Vance with melancholy elation.

"There's your criminal agent. . . . What more would
you like?"

"Oh, lots," drawled Vance.

Major Benson looked up, perplexed.

"I don't quite grasp the situation. Why did Leacock
have to go to Riverside Drive for his gun?"

"I have reason to think," said Markham, "that he took
it to Miss St. Clair the day after the shooting—for safe-keeping
probably. He wouldn't have wanted it found in his place."

"Might he not have taken it to Miss St. Clair's before the
shooting?"

"I know what you mean," Markham answered. (I, too,
recalled the Major's assertion the day before that Miss St.
Clair was more capable of shooting his brother than was the
Captain.) "I had the same idea myself. But certain
evidential facts have eliminated her as a suspect."

"You've doubtlessly satisfied yourself on the point," returned the Major; but his tone was dubious. "However,
I can't see Leacock as Alvin's murderer."

He paused, and laid a hand on the District Attorney's arm.

"I don't want to appear presumptuous, or unappreciative of all you've done; but I really wish you'd wait a bit before clapping that boy into prison. The most careful and conscientious of us are liable to error: even facts sometimes lie damnably; and I can't help believing that the facts in this instance have deceived you."

It was plain that Markham was touched by this request of his old friend; but his instinctive fidelity to duty helped him to resist the other's appeal.

"I must act according to my convictions, Major," he said firmly, but with a great kindness.

CHAPTER XV

"PFYFE—PERSONAL"

(Tuesday, June 18th ; 9 a.m.)

THE next day—the fourth of the investigation—was an important and, in some ways, a momentous one in the solution of the problem posed by Alvin Benson's murder. Nothing of a definite nature came to light, but a new element was injected into the case; and this new element eventually led to the guilty person.

Before we parted from Markham after our dinner with Major Benson, Vance had made the request that he be permitted to call at the District Attorney's office the next morning. Markham, both disconcerted and impressed by his unwonted earnestness, had complied; although, I think, he would rather have made his arrangements for Captain Leacock's arrest without the disturbing influence of the other's protesting presence. It was evident that, after Higginbotham's report, Markham had decided to place the Captain in custody, and to proceed with his preparation of data for the Grand Jury.

Although Vance and I arrived at the office at nine o'clock Markham was already there. As we entered the room. he picked up the telephone receiver, and asked to be put through to Sergeant Heath.

At that moment Vance did an amazing thing. He walked swiftly to the District Attorney's desk, and, snatching the receiver out of Markham's hand, clamped it down on the hook. Then he placed the telephone to one side, and laid both hands on the other's shoulders. Markham was too astonished and bewildered to protest; and before he could recover himself, Vance said in a low, firm voice, which was all the more impelling because of its softness:

"I'm not going to let you jail Leacock—that's what I came here for this morning. You're not going to order his arrest as long as I'm in this office and can prevent it by any means whatever. There's only one way you can accomplish this act of unmitigated folly, and that's by summoning your policemen and having me forcibly ejected. And I advise you to call a goodly number of 'em, because I'll give 'em the battle of their bellicose lives!"

The incredible part of this threat was that Vance meant it literally. And Markham knew he meant it.

"If you do call your henchmen," he went on, "you'll be the laughing stock of the city inside of a week; for, by that time, it'll be known who really did shoot Benson. And I'll be a popular hero and a martyr—God save the mark!—for defying the District Attorney and offering up my sweet freedom on the altar of truth and justice and that sort of thing. . . ."

The telephone rang, and Vance answered it.

"Not wanted," he said, closing off immediately. Then he stepped back and folded his arms.

At the end of a brief silence, Markham spoke, his voice quavering with rage.

"If you don't go at once, Vance, and let me run this office myself, I'll have no choice but to call in those policemen."

Vance smiled. He knew Markham would take no such extreme measures. After all, the issue between these two friends was an intellectual one, and though Vance's actions had placed it for a moment on a physical basis, there was no danger of its so continuing.

Markham's belligerent gaze slowly turned to one of profound perplexity.

"Why are you so damned interested in Leacock?" he

asked gruffly. "Why this irrational insistence that he remain at large?"

"You priceless, inexpressible ass!" Vance strove to keep all hint of affection out of his voice. "Do you think I care particularly what happens to a Southern army captain? There are hundreds of Leacocks, all alike—with their square shoulders and square chins, and their knobby clothes, and their totemistic codes of barbaric chivalry. Only a mother could tell 'em apart. . . . I'm int'rested in *you*, old chap. I don't want to see you make a mistake that's going to injure you more that it will Leacock."

Markham's eyes lost their hardness; he understood Vance's motive, and forgave him. But he was still firm in his belief of the Captain's guilt. He remained thoughtful for some time. Then, having apparently arrived at a decision, he rang for Swacker and asked that Phelps be sent for.

"I've a plan that may nail this affair down tight," he said. "And it'll be evidence that not even you, Vance, can gainsay."

Phelps came in, and Markham gave him instructions.

"Go and see Miss St. Clair at once. Get to her some way, and ask her what was in the package Captain Leacock took away from her apartment yesterday and threw in the East River." He briefly summarised Higginbotham's report of the night before. "Demand that she tell you, and intimate that you know it was the gun with which Benson was shot. She'll probably refuse to answer, and will tell you to get out. Then go downstairs and wait developments. If she 'phones, listen in on the switch-board. If she happens to send a note to anyone, intercept it. And if she goes out—which I hardly think likely—follow her and learn what you can. Let me hear from you the minute you get hold of anything."

"I get you, Chief." Phelps seemed pleased with the assignment, and departed with alacrity.

"Are such burglarious and eavesdropping methods considered ethical by your learned profession?" asked Vance. "I can't harmonise such conduct with your other qualities, y'know."

Markham leaned back and gazed up at the chandelier.

"Personal ethics don't enter into it. Or, if they do, they are crowded out by greater and graver considerations—by

the higher demands of justice. Society must be protected,
and the citizens of this county look to me for their security
against the encroachments of criminals and evil-doers.
Sometimes, in the pursuance of my duty, it is necessary to
adopt courses of conduct that conflict with my personal
instincts. I have no right to jeopardise the whole of society
because of an assumed ethical obligation to an individual.
. . . You understand, of course, that I would not use any
information obtained by these unethical methods unless it
pointed to criminal activities on the part of that individual.
And in such a case I would have every right to use it for the
good of the community."

"I dare say you're right," yawned Vance. "But society
doesn't int'rest me particularly. And I inf'nitely prefer
good manners to righteousness."

As he finished speaking Swacker announced Major Benson,
who wanted to see Markham at once.

The Major was accompanied by a pretty young woman of
about twenty-two with yellow bobbed hair, dressed daintily
and simply in light blue *crêpe de Chine*. But for all her
youthful and somewhat frivolous appearance she possessed
a reserve and competency of manner that immediately evoked
one's confidence.

Major Benson introduced her as his secretary, and Markham placed a chair for her facing his desk.

"Miss Hoffman has just told me something that I think
is vital for you to know," said the Major; "and I brought
her directly to you."

He seemed unusually serious and his eyes held a look of
expectancy coloured with doubt.

"Tell Mr. Markham exactly what you told me, Miss
Hoffman."

The girl raised her head prettily and related her story in
a capable, well-modulated voice.

"About a week ago—I think it was Wednesday—Mr.
Pfyfe called on Mr. Alvin Benson in his private office. I
was in the next room, where my typewriter is located.
There's only a glass partition between the two rooms, and
when anyone talks loudly in Mr. Benson's office I can hear
them. In about five minutes Mr. Pfyfe and Mr. Benson
began to quarrel. I thought it was funny, for they were

such good friends; but I didn't pay much attention to it, and went on with my typing. Their voices got very loud, though, and I caught several words. Major Benson asked me this morning what the words were; so I suppose you want to know, too. Well, they kept referring to a note; and once or twice a cheque was mentioned. Several times I caught the word 'father-in-law,' and once Mr. Benson said 'nothing doing.' . . . Then Mr. Benson called me in and told me to get him an envelope marked 'Pfyfe—Personal' out of his private drawer in the safe. I got it for him, but right after that our book-keeper wanted me for something, so I didn't hear any more. About fifteen minutes later, when Pfyfe had gone, Mr. Benson called me to put the envelope back. And he told me that if Mr. Pfyfe ever called again, I wasn't under any circumstances, to let him into the private office unless he himself was there. He also told me that I wasn't to give the envelope to anybody—not even on a written order. . . . And that is all, Mr. Markham."

During her recital I had been as much interested in Vance's action as in what she had been saying. When first she had entered the room, his casual glance had quickly changed to one of attentive animation, and he had studied her closely. When Markham had placed the chair for her, he had risen and reached for a book lying on the table near her; and, in doing so, he had leaned unnecessarily close to her in order to inspect—or so it appeared to me—the side of her head. And during her story he had continued his observation, at times bending slightly to the right or left to better his view of her. Unaccountable as his actions had seemed, I knew that some serious consideration had prompted the scrutiny.

When she finished speaking Major Benson reached in his pocket, and tossed a long manilla envelope on the desk before Markham.

"Here it is," he said. "I got Miss Hoffman to bring it to me the moment she told me her story."

Markham picked it up hesitantly, as if doubtful of his right to inspect its contents.

"You'd better look at it," the Major advised. "That envelope may very possible have an important bearing on the case."

Markham removed the elastic band, and spread the contents of the envelope before him. They consisted of three items—a cancelled cheque for $10,000 made out to Leander Pfyfe and signed by Alvin Benson; a note of $10,000 to Alvin Benson signed by Pfyfe, and a brief confession, also signed by Pfyfe, saying the cheque was a forgery. The cheque was dated March 20th of the current year. The confession and the note were dated two days later. The note—which was for ninety days—fell due on Friday, June 21st, only three days off.

For fully five minutes Markham studied these documents in silence. Their sudden introduction into the case seemed to mystify him. Nor had any of the perplexity left his face when he finally put them back in the envelope.

He questioned the girl carefully, and had her repeat certain parts of her story. But nothing more could be learned from her; and at length he turned to the Major.

"I'll keep this envelope a while, if you'll let me. I don't see its significance at present, but I'd like to think it over."

When Major Benson and his secretary had gone, Vance rose and extended his legs.

"*A la fin !*" he murmured. "All things journey: sun and moon, morning, noon, and afternoon, night and all her stars. *Videlicet :* we begin to make progress."

"What the devil are you driving at?" The new complication of Pfyfe's peccadilloes had left Markham irritable.

"Int'restin' young woman, this Miss Hoffman—eh, what?" Vance rejoined irrelevantly. "Didn't care especially for the deceased Benson. And she fairly detests the aromatic Leander. He has prob'bly told her he was misunderstood by Mrs. Pfyfe, and invited her to dinner."

"Well, she's pretty enough," commented Markham indifferently. "Benson, too, may have made advances—which is why she disliked him."

"Oh, absolutely," Vance mused a moment. "Pretty—yes; but misleadin'. She's an ambitious gel, and capable too—knows her business. She's no ball of fluff. She has a solid, honest streak in her, a bit of Teutonic blood, I'd say." He paused meditatively. "Y'know, Markham, I have a suspicion you'll hear from little Miss Katinka again."

"Crystal-gazing, eh?" mumbled Markham.

"Oh, dear no!" Vance was looking lazily out of the window.

"But I did enter the silence, so to speak, and indulged in a bit of craniological contemplation."

"I thought I noticed you ogling the girl," said Markham. "But since her hair was bobbed and she had her hat on, how could you analyse the bumps?—if that's the phrase you phrenologists use."

"Forget not Goldsmith's preacher," Vance admonished. "Truth from his lips prevailed, and those who came to scoff remained, et cetera. . . . To begin with, I'm no phrenologist. But I believe in epochal, racial and heredit'ry varieties in skulls. In that respect I'm merely an old-fashioned Darwinian. Every child knows that the skull of the Piltdown man differs from that of the Cromagnard; and even a lawyer could distinguish an Aryan head from a Ural-Altaic head, or a Maylaic from a Negrillo. And, if one is versed at all in the Mendelian theory, herdit'ry cranial similarities can be detected. . . . But all this erudition is beyond you, I fear. Suffice it to say that despite the young woman's hat and hair, I could see the contour of her head, and the bone structure in her face; and I even caught a glimpse of her ear."

"And thereby deduced that we'd hear from her again," added Markham scornfully.

"Indirectly—yes," admitted Vance. Then, after a pause; "I say, in view of Miss Hoffman's revelation, do not Colonel Ostrander's comments of yesterday begin to take on a phosph'rescent aspect?"

"Look here!" said Markham impatiently. "Cut out these circumlocutions, and get to the point."

Vance turned slowly from the window, and regarded him pensively.

"Markham—I put the question academically—doesn't Pfyfe's forged cheque, with its accompanying confession and its shortly-due note, constitute a rather strong motive for doing away with Benson?"

Markham sat up suddenly.

"You think Pfyfe guilty—is that it?"

"Well, here's the touchin' situation: Pfyfe obviously signed Benson's name to a cheque, told him about it, and got the surprise of his life when his dear old pal asked him for a ninety-day note to cover the amount, and also for a written confession to hold over him to insure payment. . . . Now consider the subs'quent facts: First, Pfyfe called on Benson a week ago and had a quarrel in which the cheque was mentioned: Damon was prob'bly pleading with Pythias to extend the note, and was vulgarly informed that there was 'nothing doing.' Secondly, Benson was shot two days later, less than a week before the note fell due. Thirdly, Pfyfe was at Benson's house the hour of the shooting, and not only lied to you about his whereabouts, but bribed a garage owner to keep silent about his car. Fourthly, his explanation, when caught, of his unrewarded search for Haig and Haig was, to say the least, a bit thick. And don't forget that the original tale of his lonely quest for nature's solitudes in the Catskills —with his mysterious stop-over in New York to confer a farewell benediction upon some anonymous person—was not all that one could have hoped for in the line of plausibility. Fifthly, he is an impulsive gambler, given to taking chances; and his experiences in South Africa would certainly have familiarised him with firearms. Sixthly, he was rather eager to involve Leacock, and did a bit of caddish tale-bearing to that end, even informing you that he saw the Captain on the spot at the fatal moment. Seventhly—but why bore you? Have I not supplied you with all the factors you hold so dear—what are they now?—motive, time, place, opportunity, conduct? All that's wanting is the criminal agent. But then, the Captain's gun is at the bottom of the East River; so you're not very much better off in his case, what?"

Markham had listened attentively to Vance's summary. He now sat in rapt silence gazing down at the desk.

"How about a little chat with Pfyfe before you make any final move against the Captain?" suggested Vance.

'I think I'll take your advice," answered Markham slowly, after several minutes' reflection. Then he picked up the telephone. "I wonder if he's at his hotel now."

"Oh, he's there," said Vance. "Watchful, waitin' and all that."

Pfyfe was in; and Markham requested him to come at once to the office.

"There's another thing I wish you'd do for me," said Vance, when the other had finished telephoning. "The fact is, I'm

longing to know what everyone was doing during the hour
of Benson's dissolution—that is, between midnight and one
a.m. on the night of the thirteenth, or to speak pedantically,
the morning of the fourteenth."

Markham looked at him in amazement.

"Seems silly, doesn't it?" Vance went on blithely. "But
you put such faith in alibis—though they do prove disappointin' at times, what? There's Leacock, for instance.
If that hall-boy had told Heath to toddle along and sell his
violets, you couldn't do a blessed thing to the Captain.
Which shows, d'ye see, that you're too trustin'. . . . Why
not find out where everyone was? Pfyfe and the Captain
were at Benson's; and they're about the only ones whose
whereabouts you've looked into. Maybe there were others
hovering around Alvin that night. There may have been
a crush of friends and acquaintances on hand—a regular
soirée, y'know. . . . Then, again, checking up on all these
people will supply the desolate Sergeant with something to
take his mind off his sorrows."

Markham knew, as well as I, that Vance would not have
made a suggestion of this kind unless actuated by some
serious motive; and for several moments he studied the
other's face intently, as if trying to read his reason for this
unexpected request.

"Who, specifically," he asked, "is included in your 'everyone'?" He took up his pencil and held it poised above a
sheet of paper.

"No one is to be left out," replied Vance. "Put down
Miss St. Clair—Captain Leacock—the Major—Pfyfe—Miss
Hoffman——"

"Miss Hoffman!"

"Everyone! . . . Have you Miss Hoffman? Now jot
down Colonel Ostrander——"

"Look here!" cut in Markham.

"——and I may have one or two others for you later.
But that will do nicely for a beginning."

Before Markham could protest further, Swacker came in
to say that Heath was waiting outside.

"What about our friend Leacock, sir?" was the Sergeant's
first question.

"I'm holding that up for a day or so," explained Markham.

"I want to have another talk with Pfyfe before I do anything definite." And he told Heath about the visit of Major Benson and Miss Hoffman.

Heath inspected the envelope and its enclosures, and then handed them back.

"I don't see anything in that," he said. "It looks to me like a private deal between Benson and this fellow Pfyfe. Leacock's our man; and the sooner I get him locked up, the better I'll feel."

"That may be to-morrow," Markham encouraged him. "So don't feel downcast over this little delay. . . . You're keeping the Captain under surveillance, aren't you?"

"I'll say so," grinned Heath.

Vance turned to Markham.

"What about that list of names you made out for the Sergeant?" he asked ingenuously. "I understood you to say something about alibis."

Markham hesitated, frowning. Then he handed Heath the paper containing the names Vance had called off to him.

"As a matter of caution, Sergeant," he said morosely. "I wish you'd get me the alibis of all these people on the night of the murder. It may bring something contributory to light. Verify those you already know, such as Pfyfe's; and let me have the reports as soon as you can."

When Heath had gone Markham turned a look of angry exasperation upon Vance.

"Of all the confounded trouble-makers——" he began.

But Vance interrupted him blandly.

"Such ingratitude! If you only knew it, Markham, I'm your tutelary genius, your *deus ex machina*, your fairy god-mother."

CHAPTER XVI

ADMISSIONS AND SUPPRESSIONS

(Tuesday, June 18th; afternoon.)

An hour later, Phelps, the operative Markham had sent to 94 Riverside Drive, came in radiating satisfaction.

"I think I've got what you want, Chief." His raucous voice was covertly triumphant. "I went up to the St. Clair woman's apartment and rang the bell. She came to the door herself, and I stepped into the hall and put my questions to her. She sure refused to answer. When I let on I knew the package contained the gun Benson was shot with, she just laughed and jerked the door open. 'Leave this apartment, you vile creature,' she says to me."

He grinned.

"I hurried downstairs, and I hadn't any more than got to the switchboard when her signal flashed. I let the boy get the number, and then I stood him to one side, and listened in. . . . She was talking to Leacock, and her first words were: 'They know you took the pistol from here yesterday and threw it in the river.' That must 've knocked him out, for he didn't say anything for a long time. Then he answered, perfectly calm and kinda sweet: 'Don't worry, Muriel; and don't say a word to anybody for the rest of the day. I'll fix everything in the morning." He made her promise to keep quiet until to-morrow, and then he said good-bye."

Markham sat a while digesting the story.

"What impression did you get from the conversation?"

"If you ask me, Chief," said the detective, "I'd lay ten to one that Leacock's guilty and the girl knows it."

Markham thanked him and let him go.

"This sub-Potomac chivalry," commented Vance, "is a frightful nuisance. . . . But aren't we about due to hold police converse with the genteel Leander?"

Almost as he spoke the man was announced. He entered the room with his habitual urbanity of manner, but, for all his suavity, he could not wholly disguise his uneasiness of mind.

"Sit down, Mr. Pfyfe," directed Markham brusquely. "It seems you have a little more explaining to do."

Taking out the manilla envelope, he laid its contents on the desk where the other could see them.

"Will you be so good as to tell me about these?"

"With the greatest pleasure," said Pfyfe; but his voice had lost its assurance. Some of his poise, too, had deserted him, and as he paused to light a cigarette I detected a slight nervousness in the way he manipulated his gold match-box.

"I really should have mentioned these before," he confessed indicating the papers with a delicately inconsequential wave of the hand.

He leaned forward on one elbow, taking a confidential attitude, and as he talked, the cigarette bobbed up and down between his lips.

"It pains me deeply to go into this matter," he began; "but since it is in the interests of truth, I shall not complain. . . . My—ah—domestic arrangements are not all that one could desire. My wife's father has, curiously enough, taken a most unreasonable dislike to me; and it pleases him to deprive me of all but the meagrest financial assistance, although it is really my wife's money that he refuses to give me. A few months ago I made use of certain funds—ten thousand dollars, to be exact—which, I learned later, had not been intended for me. When my father-in-law discovered my error, it was necessary for me to return the full amount to avoid a misunderstanding between Mrs. Pfyfe and myself —a misunderstanding which might have caused my wife's great unhappiness. I regret to say, I used Alvin's name on a cheque. But I explained it to him at once, you understand, offering him the note and this little confession as evidence of my good faith. . . . And that is all, Mr. Markham."

"Was that what your quarrel with him last week was about?"

Pfyfe gave him a look of querulous surprise.

"Ah, you have heard of our little *contretemps?* . . . Yes— we had a slight disagreement as to the—shall I say terms of the transaction?"

"Did Benson insist that the note be paid when due?"

"No—not exactly." Pfyfe's manner became unctuous. "I beg of you, sir, not to press me as to my little chat with Alvin. It was, I assure you, quite irrelevant to the present situation. Indeed, it was of a most personal and private nature." He smiled confidingly. "I will admit, however, that I went to Alvin's house the night he was shot, intending to speak to him about the cheque; but, as you already know, I found the house dark and spent the night in a Turkish bath."

"Pardon me, Mr. Pfyfe,"—it was Vance who spoke— "but did Mr. Benson take your note without security?"

"Of course!" Pfyfe's tone was a rebuke. "Alvin and I, as I have explained, were the closest friends."

"But even a friend, don't y'know," Vance submitted, "might ask for security on such a large amount. How did Benson know that you'd be able to repay him?"

"I can only say that he did know," the other answered, with an air of patient deliberation.

Vance continued to be doubtful.

"Perhaps it was because of the confession you had given him."

Pfyfe rewarded him with a look of beaming approval.

"You grasp the situation perfectly," he said.

Vance withdrew from the conversation, and though Markham questioned Pfyfe for nearly half an hour, nothing further transpired. Pfyfe clung to his story in every detail, and politely refused to go deeper into his quarrel with Benson, insisting that it had no bearing on the case. At last he was permitted to go.

"Not very helpful," Markham observed. "I'm beginning to agree with Heath that we've turned up a mare's nest in Pfyfe's frenzied financial deal."

"You'll never be anything but your own sweet trusting self, will you?" lamented Vance sadly. "Pfyfe has just given you your first intelligent line of investigation—and you say he's not helpful! . . . Listen to me and *nota bene*. Pfyfe's story about the ten thousand dollars is undoubtedly true: he appropriated the money and forged Benson's name to a cheque with which to replace it. But I don't for a second believe there was no security in addition to the confession. Benson wasn't the type of man—friend or no friend—who'd hand over that amount without security. He wanted his money back—not somebody in jail. That's why I put my oar in, and asked about the security. Pfyfe, of course, denied it; but when pressed as to how Benson knew he'd pay the note, he retired into a cloud. I had to suggest the confession as the possible explanation; which showed that something else was in his mind—something he didn't care to mention. And the way he jumped at my suggestion bears out my theory."

"Well, what of it?" Markham asked impatiently.

"Oh, for the gift of tears!" moaned Vance. "Don't you see that there's someone in the background—someone connected with the security? It must be so, y'know; otherwise Pfyfe would have told you the entire tale of the quarrel, if only to clear himself from suspicion. Yet, knowing that his position is an awkward one, he refuses to divulge what passed between him and Benson in the office that day. . . . Pfyfe is shielding someone—and he is not the soul of chivalry, y'know. Therefore I ask: Why?"

He leaned back and gazed at the ceiling.

"I have an idea, amounting to a cerebral cyclone," he added, "that when we put our hands on that security, we'll also put our hands on the murderer."

At this moment the telephone rang, and when Markham answered it a look of startled amusement came into his eyes. He made an appointment with the speaker for half-past five that afternoon. Then, hanging up the receiver, he laughed outright at Vance.

"Your auricular researches have been confirmed," he said. "Miss Hoffman just called me confidentially on an outside 'phone to say she has something to add to her story. She's coming here at five-thirty."

Vance was unimpressed by the announcement.

"I rather imagined she'd telephone during her lunch hour."

Again Markham gave him one of his searching scrutinies.

"There's something damned queer going on around here," he observed.

"Oh, quite," returned Vance carelessly. "Queerer than you could possibly imagine."

For fifteen or twenty minutes Markham endeavoured to draw him out; but Vance seemed suddenly possessed of an ability to say nothing with the blandest fluency. Markham finally became exasperated.

"I'm rapidly coming to the conclusion," he said, "that either you had a hand in Benson's murder, or you're a phenomenally good guesser."

"There is, y'know, an alternative," rejoined Vance. "It might be that my æsthetic hypotheses and metaphysical deductions—as you call 'em—are working out—eh, what?"

A few minutes before we went to lunch Swacker announced that Tracy had just returned from Long Island with his report.

"Is he the lad you sent to look into Pfyfe's *affairs du cour?*" Vance asked Markham. "For, if he is, I am all a-flutter."

"He's the man. . . . Send him in, Swacker."

Tracy entered, smiling silkily, his note-book in one hand, his *pince-nez* in the other.

"I had no trouble learning about Pfyfe," he said. "He's well known in Port Washington—quite a character in fact—and it was easy to pick up gossip about him."

He adjusted his glasses carefully, and referred to his note-book.

"He married a Miss Hawthorn in nineteen-ten. She's wealthy, but Pfyfe doesn't benefit much by it, because her father sits on the money-bags——"

"Mr. Tracy, I say," interrupted Vance; "never mind the *née*-Hawthorn and her doting papa—Mr. Pfyfe himself has confided in us about his sad marriage. Tell us, if you can, about Mr. Pfyfe's extra-nuptial affairs. Are there any other ladies?"

Tracy looked inquiringly at the District Attorney: he was uncertain as to Vance's *locus standi*. Receiving a nod from Markham, he turned a page in his note-book and proceeded.

"I found one other woman in the case. She lives in New York, and often telephones to a drug stores near Pfyfe's house, and leaves messages for him. He uses the same 'phone to call her by. He had made some deal with the proprietor, of course; but I was able to obtain her 'phone number. As soon as I came back to the city I got her name and address from Information, and made a few inquiries. . . . She's a Mrs. Paula Banning, a widow, and a little fast, I should say; and she lives in an apartment at 268 West Seventy-fifth Street."

This exhausted Tracy's information; and when he went out, Markham smiled broadly at Vance.

"He didn't supply you with very much fuel."

"My word! I think he did unbelievably well," said Vance. "He unearthed the very information we wanted."

"*We* wanted?" echoed Markham. "I have more important things to think about than Pfyfe's amours."

"And yet, y'know, this particular amour of Pfyfe's is going to solve the problem of Benson's murder," replied Vance; and would say no more.

Markham, who had an accumulation of other work awaiting him and numerous appointments for the afternoon, de-

cided to have his lunch served in the office; so Vance and
I took leave of him.

We lunched at The Elysée, dropped in at Knoedler's to
see an exhibition of French Pointillism, and then went to
Aeolian Hall, where a string quartette from San Francisco
was giving a programme of Mozart. A little before half-
past five we were again at the District Attorney's office, which
at that hour was deserted except for Markham.

Shortly after our arrival Miss Hoffman came in, and told
the rest of her story in direct, business-like fashion.

"I didn't give you all the particulars this morning," she
said; "and I wouldn't care to do so now unless you are willing
to regard them as confidential, for my telling you might cost
me my position."

"I promise you," Markham assured her, "that I will
entirely respect your confidence."

She hesitated a moment and then continued.

"When I told Major Benson this morning about Mr. Pfyfe
and his brother, he said at once that I should come with him
to your office and tell you also. But on the way over, he
suggested that I might omit a part of the story. He didn't
exactly tell me not to mention it; but he explained that it
had nothing to do with the case and might only confuse you.
I followed his suggestion; but after I got back to the office
I began thinking it over, and knowing how serious a matter
Mr. Benson's death was, I decided to tell you, anyway. In
case it did have some bearing on the situation, I didn't want
to be in the position of having withheld anything from you."

She seemed a little uncertain as to the wisdom of her decision.

"I do hope I haven't been foolish. But the truth is, there
was something else besides that envelope, which Mr. Benson
asked me to bring him from the safe the day he and Mr. Pfyfe
had their quarrel. It was a square, heavy package, and, like
the envelope, was marked 'Pfyfe—Personal.' And it was over
this package that Mr. Benson and Mr. Pfyfe seemed to be
quarrelling."

"Was it in the safe this morning when you went to get
the envelope for the Major?" asked Vance.

"Oh, no. After Mr. Pfyfe left last week, I put the package
back in the safe along with the envelope. But Mr. Benson

took it home with him last Thursday—the day he was killed."

Markham was but mildly interested in the recital, and was about to bring the interview to a close when Vance spoke up.

"It was very good of you, Miss Hoffman, to take this trouble to tell us about the package; and now that you are here, there are one or two questions I'd like to ask. . . . How did Mr. Alvin Benson and the Major get along together?"

She looked at Vance with a curious little smile.

"They didn't get along very well," she said. "They were so different. Mr. Alvin Benson was not a very pleasant person, and not very honourable, I'm afraid. You'd never have thought they were brothers. They were constantly disputing about the business; and they were terribly suspicious of each other."

"That's not unnatural," commented Vance, "seeing how incompatible their temp'raments were. . . . By the bye, how did this suspicion show itself?"

"Well, for one thing, they sometimes spied on each other. You see, their offices were adjoining, and they would listen to each other through the door. I did the secretarial work for both of them, and I often saw them listening. Several times they tried to find out things from me about each other."

Vance smiled at her appreciatively.

"Not a pleasant position for you."

"Oh, I didn't mind it," she smiled back. "It amused me."

"When was the last time you caught either one of them listening?" he asked.

The girl quickly became serious.

"The very last day Mr. Alvin Benson was alive I saw the Major standing by the door. Mr. Benson had a caller —a lady—and the Major seemed very much interested. It was in the afternoon. Mr. Benson went home early that day —only about half an hour after the lady had gone. She called at the office again later, but he wasn't there, of course, and I told her he had already gone home."

"Do you know who the lady was?" Vance asked her.

"No, I don't," she said. "She didn't give her name."

Vance asked a few other questions, after which we rode

up town in the subway with Miss Hoffman, taking leave of her at Twenty-third Street.

Markham was silent and preoccupied during the trip. Nor did Vance make any comments until we were comfortably relaxed in the easy chairs of the Stuyvesant Club's lounge-room. Then, lighting a cigarette lazily, he said:

"You grasp the subtle mental processes leading up to my prophecy about Miss Hoffman's second coming—eh, what, Markham? Y'see, I knew friend Alvin had not paid that forged cheque without security, and I also knew that the tiff must have been about the security, for Pfyfe was not really worrying about being jailed by his *alter ego*. I rather suspect Pfyfe was trying to get the security back before paying off the note, and was told there was 'nothing doing.' . . . Moreover, Little Goldylocks may be a nice girl and all that; but it isn't in the feminine temp'rament to sit next door to an altercation between two such rakes and not listen attentively. I shouldn't care, y'know, to have to decipher the typing she said she did during the episode. I was quite sure she heard more than she told; and I asked myself: Why this curtailment? The only logical answer was: Because the Major had suggested it. And since the *gnädiges Fräulein* was a forthright Germanic soul, with an inbred streak of selfish and cautious honesty, I ventured the prognostication that as soon as she was out from under the benev'lent jurisdiction of her tutor, she would tell us the rest, in order to save her own skin if the matter should come up later. . . . Not so cryptic when explained, what?"

"That's all very well," conceded Markham petulantly. "But where does it get us?"

"I shouldn't say that the forward movement was entirely imperceptible."

Vance smoked a while impassively.

"You realise, I trust," he said, "that the mysterious package contained the security."

"One might form such a conclusion," agreed Markham. "But the fact doesn't dumbfound me—if that's what you're hoping for."

"And, of course," pursued Vance easily, "your legal mind, trained in the technique of ratiocination, has already identified it as the box of jewels that Mrs. Platz espied on Benson's table that fatal afternoon."

Markham sat up suddenly; then sank back with a shrug.

"Even if it was," he said, "I don't see how that helps us. Unless the Major knew the package had nothing to do with the case, he would not have suggested to his secretary that she omit telling us about it."

"Ah! But if the Major knew that the package was an irrelevant item in the case, then he must also know something about the case—eh, what? Otherwise, he couldn't determine what was, and what was not, irrelevant. . . . I have felt all along that he knew more than he admitted. Don't forget that he put us on the track of Pfyfe, and also that he was quite pos'tive Captain Leacock was innocent."

Markham thought for several minutes.

"I'm beginning to see what you're driving at," he remarked slowly. "Those jewels, after all, may have an important bearing on the case. . . . I think I'll have a chat with the Major about things."

Shortly after dinner, at the Club that night, Major Benson came into the lounge-room where we had retired for our smoke; and Markham accosted him at once.

"Major, aren't you willing to help me a little more in getting at the truth about your brother's death?" he asked.

The other gazed at him searchingly: the inflection of Markham's voice belied the apparent casualness of the question.

"God knows it's not my wish to put obstacles in your way," he said, carefully weighing each word. "I'd gladly give you any help I could. But there are one or two things I cannot tell you at this time. . . . If there was only myself to be considered," he added, "it would be different."

"But you do suspect someone?" Vance put the question.

"In a way—yes. I overheard a conversation in Alvin's office one day, that took on added significance after his death."

"You shouldn't let chivalry stand in the way," urged Markham. "If your suspicion is unfounded, the truth will surely come out."

"But when I don't know, I certainly ought not to hazard

a guess," affirmed the Major. "I think it best that you solve this problem without me."

Despite Markham's importunities, he would say no more; and shortly afterwards he excused himself and went out.

Markham, now profoundly worried, sat smoking restlessly, tapping the arm of his chair with his fingers.

"Well, old bean, a bit involved, what?" commented Vance.

"It's not so damned funny," Markham grumbled. "Everyone seems to know more about the case than the police or the District Attorney's office."

"Which wouldn't be so disconcertin' if they all weren't so deucid reticent," supplemented Vance cheerfully. "And the touchin' part of it is that each of 'em appears to be keeping still in order to shield someone else. Mrs. Platz began it: she lied about Benson's having any callers that afternoon, because she didn't want to involve his tea companion. Miss St. Clair declined point-blank to tell you anything, because she obviously didn't desire to cast suspicion on another. The Captain became voiceless the moment you suggested his affianced bride was entangled. Even Leander refused to extricate himself from a delicate situation lest he implicate another. And now the Major! . . . Most annoyin'. On the other hand, don't y'know, it's comfortin'—not to say upliftin' —to be dealing exclusively with such noble, self-sacrificin' souls."

"Hell!" Markham put down his cigar and rose. "The case is getting on my nerves. I'm going to sleep on it, and tackle it in the morning."

"That ancient idea of sleeping on a problem is a fallacy," said Vance—as we walked out into Madison Avenue—"an *apologia*, as it were, for one's not being able to think clearly. Poetic idea, y'know. All poets believe in it—nature's soft nurse, the balm of woe, childhood's mandragore, tired nature's sweet restorer, and that sort of thing. Silly notion. When the brain is keyed up and alive, it works far better than when apathetic from the torpor of sleep. Slumber is an anodyne— not a stimulus."

"Well, you sit up and think," was Markham's surly advice.

"That's what I'm going to do," blithely returned Vance; "but not about the Benson case. I did all the thinking I'm going to do along that line four days ago."

CHAPTER XVII

THE FORGED CHEQUE

(Wednesday, June 19th; forenoon.)

WE rode downtown with Markham the next morning, and though we arrived at his office before nine o'clock, Heath was already there waiting. He appeared worried, and when he spoke his voice held an ill-disguised reproof for the District Attorney.

"What about this Leacock, Mr. Markham?" he asked. "It looks to me like we'd better grab him quick. We've been tailing him right along; and there's something funny going on. Yesterday morning he went to his bank and spent half an hour in the chief cashier's office. After that he visited his lawyer's, and was there over an hour. Then he went back to the bank for another half-hour. He dropped into the Astor Grill for lunch, but didn't eat anything—sat staring at the table. About two o'clock he called on the realty agents who have the handling of the building he lives in; and after he'd left, we found out he'd offered his apartment for sub-lease beginning to-morrow. Then he paid six calls on friends of his, and went home. After dinner my man rang his apartment bell and asked for Mr. Hoozitz: Leacock was packing up! . . . It looks to me like a get-away."

Markham frowned. Heath's report clearly troubled him; but before he could answer, Vance spoke.

"Why this perturbation, Sergeant? You're watching the Captain. I'm sure he can't slip from your vigilant clutches."

Markham looked at Vance a moment; then turned to Heath.

"Let it go at that. But if Leacock attempts to leave the city, nab him."

Heath went out sullenly.

"By the bye, Markham," said Vance, "don't make an appointment for half-past twelve to-day. You already have one, don't y'know. And with a lady."

Markham put down his pen, and stared.

"What new damned nonsense is this?"

"I made an engagement for you. Called the lady by 'phone this morning. I'm sure I woke the dear up."

Markham spluttered, striving to articulate his angry protest. Vance held up his hand soothingly.

"And you simply must keep the engagement. Y'see, I told her it was you speaking; and it would be shocking taste not to appear. . . . I promise, you won't regret meeting her," he added. "Things looked so sadly befuddled last night—I couldn't bear to see you suffering so. Cons'quently, I arranged for you to see Mrs. Paula Banning—Pfyfe's Éloïse, y'know. I'm positive she'll be able to dispel some of this inspissated gloom that's enveloping you."

"See here, Vance!" Markham growled. "I happen to be running this office——" He stopped abruptly, realising the hopelessness of making headway against the other's blandness. Moreover, I think, the prospect of interviewing Mrs. Paula Banning was not wholly alien to his inclinations. His resentment slowly ebbed, and when he again spoke his voice was almost matter-of-fact.

"Since you've committed me, I'll see her. But I'd rather Pfyfe wasn't in such close communication with her. He's apt to drop in—with preconcerted unexpectedness."

"Funny," murmured Vance. "I thought of that myself. . . . That's why I 'phoned him last night that he could return to Long Island."

"You 'phoned him——!"

"Awf'lly sorry and all that," Vance apologised. "But you'd gone to bed. Sleep was knitting up your ravell'd sleave of care; and I couldn't bring myself to disturb you. . . . Pfyfe was so grateful, too. Most touchin'. Said his wife also would be grateful. He was pathetically consid'-rate about Mrs. Pfyfe. But I fear he'll need all his velvety forensic powers to explain his absence."

"In what other quarters have you involved me during my absence?" asked Markham acrimoniously.

"That's all," replied Vance, rising and strolling to the window.

He stood looking out, smoking thoughtfully. When he turned back to the room, his bantering air had gone. He sat down facing Markham.

"The Major has practically admitted to us," he said, "that he knows more about this affair than he has told. You naturally can't push the point, in view of his hon'rable attitude in the matter. And yet, he's willing for you to find out what he knows, as long as he doesn't tell you himself —that was unquestionably the stand he took last night. Now, I believe there's a way you can find out without calling upon him to go against his principles. . . . You recall Miss Hoffman's story of the eavesdropping; and you also recall that he told you he heard a conversation which, in the light of Benson's murder, became significant. It's quite prob'ble, therefore, that the Major's knowledge has to do with something connected with the business of the firm, or at least with one of the firm's clients."

Vance slowly lit another cigarette.

"My suggestion is this: call up the Major, and ask permission to send a man to take a peep at his ledger accounts and his purchase and sales books. Tell him you want to find out about the transactions of one of his clients. Intimate that it's Miss St. Clair—or Pfyfe, if you like. I have a strange mediumistic feeling that, in this way, you'll get on the track of the person he's shielding. And I'm also assailed by the premonition that he'll welcome your interest in his ledger."

The plan did not appeal to Markham as feasible or fraught with possibilities; and it was evident he disliked making such a request of Major Benson. But so determined was Vance, so earnestly did he argue his point, that in the end Markham acquiesced.

"He was quite willing to let me send a man," said Markham, hanging up the receiver. "In fact, he seemed eager to give me every assistance."

"I thought he'd take kindly to the suggestion," said Vance. "Y'see, if you discover for yourself whom he suspects, it relieves him of the onus of having tattled."

Markham rang for Swacker.

"Call up Stitt and tell him I want to see him here before noon—that I have an immediate job for him."

"Stitt," Markham explained to Vance, "is the head of a firm of public accountants over in the New York Life Building. I use him a good deal on work like this."

Shortly before noon Stitt came. He was a prematurely old young man, with a sharp, shrewd face and a perpetual frown. The prospect of working for the District Attorney pleased him.

Markham explained briefly what he wanted, and revealed enough of the case to guide him in his task. The man grasped the situation immediately, and made one or two notes on the back of a dilapidated envelope.

Vance also, during the instructions, had jotted down some notations on a piece of paper.

Markham stood up and took his hat.

"Now, I suppose, I must keep the appointment you made for me," he complained to Vance. Then: "Come, Stitt, I'll take you down with us in the judges' private elevator."

"If you don't mind," interposed Vance, "Mr. Stitt and I will forgo the honour, and mingle with the commoners in the public lift. We'll meet you downstairs."

Taking the accountant by the arm, he led him out through the main waiting-room. It was ten minutes however, before he joined us.

We took the subway to Seventy-second Street and walked up West End Avenue to Mrs. Paula Banning's address. She lived in a small apartment-house just around the corner in Seventy-fifth Street. As we stood before her door, waiting for an answer to our ring, a strong odour of Chinese incense drifted out to us.

"Ah! That facilitates matters," said Vance, sniffing. "Ladies who burn joss-sticks are invariably sentimental."

Mrs. Banning was a tall, slightly adipose woman of indeterminate age, with straw-coloured hair and a pink-and-white complexion. Her face in repose possessed a youthful and vacuous innocence; but the expression was only superficial. Her eyes, a very light blue, were hard; and a slight puffiness about her cheek-bones and beneath her chin attested to years of idle and indulgent living. She was not unattractive, however, in a vivid, flamboyant way; and her manner, when she ushered us into her over-furnished and rococo living-room, was one of easy-going good-fellowship.

When we were seated and Markham had apologised for our intrusion, Vance at once assumed the rôle of interviewer. During his opening explanatory remarks he appraised the woman carefully, as if seeking to determine the best means of approaching her for the information he wanted.

After a few minutes of verbal reconnoitring, he asked permission to smoke, and offered Mrs. Banning one of his cigarettes, which she accepted. Then he smiled at her in a spirit of appreciative geniality, and relaxed comfortably in his chair. He conveyed the impression that he was fully prepared to sympathise with anything she might tell him.

"Mr. Pfyfe strove very hard to keep you entirely out of this affair," said Vance; "and we fully appreciate his delicacy in so doing. But certain circumst'nces connected with Mr. Benson's death have inadvertently involved you in the case; and you can best help us and yourself—and particularly Mr. Pfyfe—by telling us what we want to know, and trusting to our discretion and understanding."

He had emphasised Pfyfe's name, giving it a significant intonation; and the woman had glanced down uneasily. Her apprehension was apparent, and when she looked up into Vance's eyes, she was asking herself: How much does he know? as plainly as if she had spoken the words audibly.

"I can't imagine what you want me to tell you," she said, with an effort at astonishment. "You know that Andy was not in New York that night." (Her designation of the elegant and superior Pfyfe as "Andy" sounded almost like *lèse-majesté*.) "He didn't arrive in the city until nearly nine the next morning."

"Didn't you read in the newspaper about the grey Cadillac that was parked in front of Benson's house?" Vance, in putting the question, imitated her own astonishment.

She smiled confidently.

"That wasn't Andy's car. He took the eight o'clock train to New York the next morning. He said it was lucky that he did, seeing that a machine just like his had been at Mr. Benson's the night before."

She had spoken with the sincerity of complete assurance. It was evident that Pfyfe had lied to her on this point.

Vance did not disabuse her; in fact, he gave her to understand that he accepted her explanation, and consequently dismissed the idea of Pfyfe's presence in New York on the night of the murder.

"I had in mind a connection of a somewhat diff'rent nature

when I mentioned you and Mr. Pfyfe as having been drawn into the case. I referred to a personal relationship between you and Mr. Benson."

She assumed an attitude of smiling indifference.

"I'm afraid you've made another mistake." She spoke lightly. "Mr. Benson and I were not even friends. Indeed, I scarcely knew him."

There was an overtone of emphasis in her denial—a slight eagerness which, in indicating a conscious desire to be believed, robbed her remark of the complete casualness she had intended.

"Even a business relationship may have its personal side," Vance reminded her; "especially when the intermediary is an intimate friend of both parties to the transaction."

She looked at him quickly; then turned her eyes away.

"I really don't know what you're talking about," she affirmed: and her face for a moment lost its contours of innocence and became calculating. "You're surely not implying that I had any business dealings with Mr. Benson?"

"Not directly," replied Vance. "But certainly Mr. Pfyfe had business dealings with him; and one of them, I rather imagined, involved you consid'rably."

"Involved me?" She laughed scornfully, but it was a strained laugh.

"It was a somewhat unfortunate transaction, I fear," Vance went on, "unfortunate in that Mr. Pfyfe was necessitated to deal with Mr. Benson; and doubly unfortunate, y'know, in that he should have had to drag you into it."

His manner was easy and assured, and the woman sensed that no display of scorn or contempt, however well simulated, would make an impression on him. Therefore, she adopted an attitude of tolerantly incredulous amusement.

"And where did you learn about all this?" she asked playfully.

"Alas! I didn't learn about it," answered Vance, falling in with her manner. "That's the reason, d'ye see, that I indulged in this charming little visit. I was foolish enough to hope that you'd take pity on my ignorance and tell me all about it."

"But I wouldn't think of doing such a thing," she said, "even if this mysterious transaction had really taken place."

"My word!" sighed Vance. "That *is* disappointin'. . . . Ah, well. I see that I must tell you what little I know about it, and trust to your sympathy to enlighten me further."

Despite the ominous undercurrent of his words, his levity acted like a sedative to her anxiety. She felt that he was friendly, however much he might know about her.

"Am I bringing you news when I tell you that Mr. Pfyfe forged Mr. Benson's name to a cheque for ten thousand dollars?" he asked.

She hesitated, gauging the possible consequences of her answer.

"No, that isn't news. Andy tells me everything."

"And did you also know that Mr. Benson, when informed of it, was rather put out?—that, in fact, he demanded a note and a signed confession before he would pay the cheque?"

The woman's eyes flashed angrily.

"Yes, I knew that too. And after all Andy had done for him! If ever a man deserved shooting, it was Alvin Benson. He was a dog. And he pretended to be Andy's best friend. Just think of it—refusing to lend Andy the money without a confession! . . . You'd hardly call that a business deal, would you? I'd call it a dirty, contemptible, underhand trick."

She was enraged. Her mask of breeding and good-fellowship had fallen from her; and she poured out vituperation on Benson with no thought of the words she was using. Her speech was devoid of all the ordinary reticencies of intercourse between strangers.

Vance nodded consolingly during her tirade.

"Y'know, I sympathise fully with you." The tone in which he made the remark seemed to establish a closer *rapprochement*.

After a moment he gave her a friendly smile.

"But, after all, one could almost forgive Benson for holding the confession, if he hadn't also demanded security."

"What security?"

Vance was quick to sense the change in her tone. Taking advantage of her rage, he had mentioned the security while the barriers of her pose were down. Her frightened, almost involuntary query told him that the right moment had arrived. Before she could gain her equilibrium or dispel the momentary fear which had assailed her, he said, with suave deliberation:

"The day Mr. Benson was shot he took home with him from the office a small blue box of jewels."

She caught her breath, but otherwise gave no outward sign of emotion.

"Do you think he had stolen them?"

The moment she had uttered the question she realised it was a mistake in technique. An ordinary man might have been temporarily diverted from the truth by it. But by Vance's smile she recognised that he had accepted it as an admission.

"It was rather fine of you, y'know, to lend Mr. Pfyfe your jewels to cover the note with."

At this she threw her head up. The blood had left her face, and the rouge on her cheeks took on a mottled and unnatural hue.

"You say I lent my jewels to Andy! I swear to you——"

Vance halted her denial with a slight movement of the hand and a *coup d'œil*. She saw that his intention was to save her from the humiliation she might feel later at having made too emphatic and unqualified a statement; and the graciousness of his action, although he was an antagonist, gave her more confidence in him.

She sank back into her chair, and her hands relaxed.

"What makes you think I lent Andy my jewels?"

Her voice was colourless, but Vance understood the question. It was the end of her deceptions. The pause which followed was an amnesty—recognised as such by both. The next spoken words would be the truth."

"Andy had to have them," she said, "or Benson would have put him in jail." One read in her words a strange, self-sacrificing affection for the worthless Pfyfe. "And if Benson hadn't done it, and had merely refused to honour the cheque, his father-in-law would have done it. . . . Andy is so careless, so unthinking. He does things without weighing the consequences: I am all the time having to hold him down. . . . But this thing has taught him a lesson—I'm sure of it."

I felt that if anything in the world could teach Pfyfe a lesson, it was the blind loyalty of this woman.

"Do you know what he quarrelled about with Mr. Benson in his office last Wednesday?" asked Vance.

"That was all my fault," she explained, with a sigh. "It was getting very near to the time when the note was due, and I knew Andy didn't have all the money. So I asked him to go to Benson and offer him what he had, and see if he couldn't get my jewels back. . . . But he was refused—I thought he would be."

Vance looked at her for a while sympathetically.

"I don't want to worry you any more than I can help," he said; "but won't you tell me the real cause of your anger against Benson a moment ago?"

She gave him an admiring nod.

"You're right—I had good reason to hate him." Her eyes narrowed unpleasantly. "The day after he had refused to give Andy the jewels, he called me up—it was in the afternoon—and asked me to have breakfast with him at his house the next morning. He said he was home and had the jewels with him; and he told me—hinted, you understand— that maybe—*maybe* I could have them. That's the kind of beast he was! . . . I telephoned to Port Washington to Andy and told him about it, and he said he'd be in New York the next morning. He got here about nine o'clock, and we read in the paper that Benson had been shot that night."

Vance was silent for a long time. Then he stood up and thanked her.

"You have helped us a great deal. Mr. Markham is a friend of Major Benson, and, since we have the cheque and the confession in our possession, I shall ask him to use his influence with the Major to permit us to destroy them— very soon."

CHAPTER XVIII

A CONFESSION

(*Wednesday, June 19th; 1 p.m.*)

WHEN we were again outside, Markham asked:

"How in heaven's name did you know she had put up her jewels to help Pfyfe?"

"My charmin' metaphysical deductions, don't y'know," answered Vance. "As I told you, Benson was not the open-handed, big-hearted altruist who would have lent money without security; and certainly the impecunious Pfyfe had no collateral worth ten thousand dollars, or he wouldn't have forged the cheque. *Ergo:* someone lent him the security. Now, who would be so trustin' as to lend Pfyfe that amount of security except a sentimental woman who was blind to his amazin' defects? Y'know, I was just evil-minded enough to suspect there was a Calypso in the life of this Ulysses when he told us of stopping over in New York to murmur *au revoir* to someone. When a man like Pfyfe fails to specify the sex of a person, it is safe to assume the female gender. So I suggested that you send a Paul Pry to Port Washington to peer into his trans-matrimonial activities: I felt certain a *bonne amie* would be found. Then, when the mysterious package, which obviously was the security, seemed to identify itself as the box of jewels seen by the inquisitive housekeeper, I said to myself: 'Ah! Leander's misguided Dulcinea has lent him her gewgaws to save him from the yawning dungeon.' Nor did I overlook the fact that he had been shielding someone in his explanation about the cheque. Therefore, as soon as the lady's name and address were learned by Tracy, I made the appointment for you. . . ."

We were passing the Gothic-Renaissance Schwab residence which extends from West End Avenue to Riverside Drive at Seventy-third Street, and Vance stopped for a moment to contemplate it.

Markham waited patiently. At length Vance walked on.

". . . . Y'know, the moment I saw Mrs. Banning I knew my conclusions were correct. She was a sentimental soul, and just the sort of professional good sport who would have handed over her jewels to her *amoroso*. Also, she was bereft of gems when we called—and a woman of her stamp always wears her jewels when she desires to make an impression on strangers. Moreover, she's the kind that would have jewellery even if the larder was empty. It was therefore merely a question of getting her to talk."

"On the whole, you did very well," observed Markham.

Vance gave him a condescending bow.

"Sir Hubert is too generous. But tell me, didn't my little chat with the lady cast a gleam into your darkened mind?"

"Naturally," said Markham. "I'm not utterly obtuse. She played unconsciously into our hands. She believed Pfyfe did not arrive in New York until the morning after the murder, and therefore told us quite frankly that she had 'phoned him that Benson had the jewels at home. The situation now is: Pfyfe knew they were in Benson's house, and was there himself at about the time the shot was fired. Furthermore, the jewels are gone; and Pfyfe tried to cover up his tracks that night."

Vance sighed hopelessly.

Markham, there are altogther too many trees for you in this case. You simply can't see the forest, y'know, because of 'em."

"There is the remote possibility that you are so busily engaged in looking at one particular tree that you are unaware of the others."

A shadow passed over Vance's face.

"I wish you were right," he said.

It was nearly half-past one, and we dropped into the Fountain Room of the Ansonia Hotel for lunch. Markham was preoccupied throughout the meal, and when we entered the subway later, he looked uneasily at his watch.

"I think I'll go on down to Wall Street and call on the Major a moment before returning to the office. I can't understand his asking Miss Hoffman not to mention the package to me. . . . It might not have contained the jewels, after all."

"Do you imagine for one moment," rejoined Vance, "that Alvin told the Major the truth about the package? It was not a very cred'table transaction, y'know; and the Major most likely would have given him what-for."

Major Benson's explanation bore out Vance's surmise. Markham, in telling him of the interview with Paula Banning, emphasised the jewel episode in the hope that the Major would voluntarily mention the package; for his promise to Miss Hoffman prevented him from admitting that he was aware of the other's knowledge concerning it.

The Major listened with considerable astonishment, his eyes gradually growing angry.

"I'm afraid Alvin deceived me," he said. He looked straight ahead for a moment, his face softening. "And I don't like to think it, now that he's gone. But the truth is, when Miss Hoffman told me this morning about the envelope, she also mentioned a small parcel that had been in Alvin's private safe-drawer; and I asked her to omit any reference to it from her story to you. I knew the parcel contained Mrs. Banning's jewels, but I thought the fact would only confuse matters, if brought to your attention. You see, Alvin told me that a judgment had been taken against Mrs. Banning, and that, just before the Supplementary Proceedings, Pfyfe had brought her jewels here and asked him to sequester them temporarily in his safe."

On our way back to the Criminal Courts Building Markham took Vance's arm and smiled.

"Your guessing luck is holding out, I see."

"Rather!" agreed Vance. "It would appear that the late Alvin, like Warren Hastings, resolved to die in the last dyke of prevarication. . . . *Splendide mendax*, what?"

"In any event," replied Markham, "the Major has unconsciously added another link in the chain against Pfyfe."

"You seem to be making a collection of chains," commented Vance drily. "What have you done with the ones you forged about Miss St. Clair and Leacock?"

"I haven't entirely discarded them—if that's what you think," asserted Markham gravely.

When we reached the office Sergeant Heath was awaiting us with a beatific grin.

"It's all over, Mr. Markham," he announced. "This noon, after you'd gone, Leacock came here looking for you. When he found you were out, he 'phoned Headquarters, and they connected him with me. He wanted to see me— very important, he said; so I hurried over. He was sitting in the waiting-room when I came in, and he called me over and said: 'I came to give myself up. I killed Benson.' I got him to dictate a confession to Swacker, and then he signed it. . . . Here it is." He handed Markham a type-written sheet of paper.

Markham sank wearily into a chair. The strain of the past few days had begun to tell on him. He sighed heavily.

"Thank God! Now our troubles are ended."

Vance looked at him lugubriously, and shook his head.

"I rather fancy y'know, that your troubles are only beginning," he drawled.

When Markham had glanced through the confession he handed it to Vance, who read it carefully with an expression of growing amusement.

"Y'know," he said, "this document isn't at all legal. Any judge worthy the name would throw it precip'tately out of court. It's far too simple and precise. It doesn't begin with 'greetings'; it doesn't contain a single 'where-fore-be-it' or 'be-it-known' or 'do-hereby'; it says nothing about 'free will' or 'sound mind' or 'disposin' mem'ry'; and the Captain doesn't once refer to himself as 'the party of the first part.' . . . Utterly worthless, Sergeant. If I were you, I'd chuck it."

Heath was feeling too complacently triumphant to be annoyed. He smiled with magnanimous tolerance.

"It strikes you as funny, doesn't it, Mr. Vance?"

"Sergeant, if you knew how inord'nately funny this con-fession is, you'd positively have hysterics."

Vance then turned to Markham.

"Really, y'know, I shouldn't put too much stock in this. It may, however, prove a valuable lever with which to prise open the truth. In fact, I'm jolly glad the Captain has gone in for imag'native lit'rature. With this entrancin' fable in our possession, I think we can overcome the Major's scruples, and get him to tell us what he knows. Maybe I'm wrong, but it's worth trying."

He stepped to the District Attorney's desk, and leaned over it cajolingly.

"I haven't led you astray yet, old dear; and I'm going to make another suggestion. Call up the Major and ask him to come here at once. Tell him you've secured a con-fession—but don't you dare say whose. Imply it's Miss St. Clair's, or Pfyfe's—or Pontius Pilate's. But urge his im-mediate presence. Tell him you want to discuss it with him before proceeding with the indictment."

"I can't see the necessity of doing that," objected Markham. "I'm pretty sure to see him at the Club to-night and I can tell him then."

"That wouldn't do at all," insisted Vance. "If the Major can enlighten us on any point, I think Sergeant Heath should be present to hear him."

"I don't need any enlightenment," cut in Heath.

Vance regarded him with admiring surprise.

"What a wonderful man! Even Goethe cried for *mehr Licht;* and here you are in a state of luminous saturation! . . . Astonishin'!"

"See here, Vance," said Markham, "why try to complicate the matter? It strikes me as a waste of time, besides being an imposition, to ask the Major here to discuss Leacock's confession. We don't need his evidence now, anyway."

Despite his gruffness there was a hint of reconsideration in his voice; for, though his instinct had been to dismiss the request out of hand, the experiences of the past few days had taught him that Vance's suggestions were not made without an object.

Vance, sensing the other's hesitancy, said:

"My request is based on something more than an idle desire to gaze upon the Major's rubicund features at this moment. I'm telling you, with all the meagre earnestness I possess, that his presence here now would be most helpful."

Markham deliberated, and argued the point at some length. But Vance was so persistent that in the end he was convinced of the advisability of complying.

Heath was patently disgusted, but he sat down quietly and sought solace in a cigar.

Major Benson arrived with astonishing promptness, and when Markham handed him the confession, he made little attempt to conceal his eagerness. But as he read it his face clouded, and a look of puzzlement came into his eyes.

At length he looked up, frowning.

"I don't quite understand this; and I'll admit I'm greatly surprised. It doesn't seem credible that Leacock shot Alvin. . . . And yet, I may be mistaken, of course."

He laid the confession on Markham's desk with an air of disappointment, and sank into a chair.

"Do *you* feel satisfied?" he asked.

"I don't see any way around it," said Markham. "If he isn't guilty, why should he come forward and confess? God knows, there's plenty of evidence against him. I was ready to arrest him two days ago."

"He's guilty all right," put in Heath. "I've had my eye on him from the first."

Major Benson did not reply at once; he seemed to be framing his next words.

"It might be—that is, there's the bare possibility—that Leacock had an ulterior motive in confessing."

We all, I think, recognised the thought which his words strove to conceal.

"I'll admit," acceded Markham, "that at first I believed Miss St. Clair guilty, and I intimated as much to Leacock. But later I was persuaded that she was not directly involved."

"Does Leacock know this?" the Major asked quickly.

Markham thought a moment.

"No, I can't say that he does. In fact, it's more than likely he still thinks I suspect her."

"Ah!"

The Major's exclamation was almost involuntary.

"But what's that got to do with it?" asked Heath irritably. "Do you think he's going to the chair to save her reputation? —Bunk! That sort of thing's all right in the movies, but no man's that crazy in real life."

"I'm not so sure, Sergeant," ventured Vance lazily. "Women are too sane and practical to make such foolish gestures; but men, y'know, have an illim'table capacity for idiocy."

He turned an inquiring gaze on Major Benson.

"Won't you tell us why you think Leacock is playing Sir Galahad?"

But the Major took refuge in generalities, and was disinclined even to follow up his original intimation as to the cause of the Captain's action. Vance questioned him for some time, but was unable to penetrate his reticence.

Heath, becoming restless, finally spoke up.

"You can't argue Leacock's guilt away, Mr. Vance. Look at the facts. He threatened Benson that he'd kill him if he caught him with the girl again. The next time Benson goes out with her, he's found shot. Then Leacock hides his gun

at her house, and when things begin to get hot, he takes it
away and ditches it in the river. He bribes the hall-boy to
alibi him, and he's seen at Benson's house at twelve-thirty
that night. When he's questioned he can't explain anything.
. . . If that ain't an open-and-shut case, I'm a mock-turtle."

"The circumstances are convincing," admitted Major
Benson. "But couldn't they be accounted for on other
grounds?"

Heath did not deign to answer the question.

"The way I see it," he continued, "is like this: Leacock
gets suspicious along about midnight, takes his gun and goes
out. He catches Benson with the girl, goes in, and shoots
him like he threatened. They're both mixed up in it, if you
ask me; but Leacock did the shooting. And now we got his
confession. . . . There isn't a jury in the country that
wouldn't convict him."

"*Probi et legales homines*—oh, quite!" murmured Vance.

Swacker appeared at the door.

"The reporters are clamouring for attention," he announced
with a wry face.

"Do they know about the confession?" Markham asked
Heath.

"Not yet. I haven't told 'em anything so far—that's
why they're clamouring, I guess. But I'll give 'em an earful
now, if you say the word."

Markham nodded, and Heath started for the door. But
Vance quickly planted himself in the way.

"Could you keep this thing quiet till to-morrow, Markham?" he asked.

Markham was annoyed.

"I could if I wanted to—yes. But why should I?"

"For your own sake, if for no other reason. You've
got your prize safely locked up. Control your vanity for
twenty-four hours. The Major and I both know that Leacock's innocent, and by this time to-morrow the whole
country'll know it."

Again an argument ensued; but the outcome, like that
of the former argument, was a foregone conclusion. Markham
had realized for some time that Vance had reason to be convinced of something which as yet he was unwilling to divulge.
His opposition to Vance's requests were, I had suspected,

largely the result of an effort to ascertain this information; and I was positive of it now as he leaned forward and gravely debated the advisability of making public the Captain's confession.

Vance, as heretofore, was careful to reveal nothing; but in the end his sheer determination carried his point; and Markham requested Heath to keep his own counsel until the next day. The Major, by a slight nod, indicated his approbation of the decision.

"You might tell the newspaper lads, though," suggested Vance, "that you'll have a rippin' sensation for 'em to-morrow."

Heath went out, crestfallen and glowering.

"A rash fella, the Sergeant—so impetuous!"

Vance again picked up the confession, and perused it.

"Now, Markham, I want you to bring your prisoner forth—*habeas corpus* and that sort of thing. Put him in that chair facing the window, give him one of the good cigars you keep for influential politicians, and then listen attentively while I politely chat with him. . . . The Major, I trust, will remain for the interlocut'ry proceedings."

"That request, at least, I'll grant without objections," smiled Markham. "I had already decided to have a talk with Leacock."

He pressed a buzzer, and a brisk, ruddy-faced clerk entered.

"A requisition for Captain Philip Leacock," he ordered.

When it was brought to him he initialled it.

"Take it to Ben, and tell him to hurry."

The clerk disappeared through the door leading to the outer corridor.

Ten minutes later a deputy sheriff from the Tombs entered with the prisoner.

CHAPTER XIX

VANCE CROSS-EXAMINES

(*Wednesday, June 19th ; 3.30 p.m.*)

CAPTAIN LEACOCK walked into the room with a hopeless indifference of bearing. His shoulders drooped; his arms hung listlessly. His eyes were haggard like those of a man who had not slept for days. On seeing Major Benson, he straightened a little and, stepping towards him, extended his hand. It was plain that, however much he may have disliked Alvin Benson, he regarded the Major as a friend. But suddenly realising the situation, he turned away, embarrassed.

The Major went quickly to him and touched him on the arm.

"It's all right, Leacock," he said softly. "I can't think that you really shot Alvin."

The Captain turned apprehensive eyes upon him.

"Of course, I shot him." His voice was flat. "I told him I was going to."

Vance came forward, and indicated a chair.

"Sit down, Captain. The District Attorney wants to hear your story of the shooting. The law, you understand, does not accept murder confessions without corroborat'ry evidence. And since, in the present case, there are suspicions against others than yourself, we want you to answer some questions in order to substantiate your guilt. Otherwise, it will be necess'ry for us to follow up our suspicions."

Taking a seat facing Leacock, he picked up the confession.

"You say here you were satisfied that Mr. Benson had wronged you, and you went to his house at about half-past twelve on the night of the thirteenth. . . . When you speak of his wronging you, do you refer to his attentions to Miss St. Clair?"

Leacock's face betrayed a sulky belligerence.

"It doesn't matter why I shot him. Can't you leave Miss St. Clair out of it?"

"Certainly," agreed Vance. "I promise you she shall not be brought into it. But we must understand your motive thoroughly."

After a brief silence Leacock said:

"Very well, then. That was what I referred to."

"How did you know Miss St. Clair went to dinner with Mr. Benson that night?"

"I followed them to the Marseilles."

"And then you went home?"

"Yes."

"What made you go to Mr. Benson's house later?"

"I got to thinking about it more and more, until I couldn't stand it any longer. I began to see red, and at last I took my Colt and went out, determined to kill him."

A note of passion had crept into his voice. It seemed unbelievable that he could be lying.

Vance again referred to the confession.

"You dictated: 'I went to 87 West Forty-eighth Street, and entered the house by the front door.' . . . Did you ring the bell? Or was the front door unlatched?"

Leacock was about to answer, but hesitated. Evidently he recalled the newspaper accounts of the housekeeper's testimony in which she asserted positively that the bell had not rung that night.

"What difference does it make?" He was sparring for time.

"We'd like to know—that's all," Vance told him. "But no hurry."

"Well, if it's so important to you: I didn't ring the bell; and the door wasn't unlocked." His hesitancy was gone. "Just as I reached the house, Benson drove up in a taxicab ——"

"Just a moment. Did you happen to notice another car standing in front of the house? A grey Cadillac?"

"Why—yes."

"Did you recognise its occupant?"

There was another short silence.

"I'm not sure. I think it was a man named Pfyfe."

"He and Mr. Benson were outside at the same time, then?"

Leacock frowned.

"No—not at the same time. There was nobody there when I arrived. . . . I didn't see Pfyfe until I came out a few minutes later."

"He arrived in his car when you were inside—is that it?"

"He must have."

"I see. . . . And now to go back a little: Benson drove up in a taxicab. Then what?"

"I went up to him and said I wanted to speak to him He told me to come inside, and we went in together. He used his latch-key."

"And now, Captain, tell us just what happened after you and Mr. Benson entered the house."

"He laid his hat and stick on the hat rack, and we walked into the living-room. He sat down by the table, and I stood up and said—what I had to say. Then I drew my gun and shot him."

Vance was closely watching the man, and Markham was leaning forward tensely.

"How did it happen that he was reading at the time?"

"I believe he did pick up a book while I was talking. . . . Trying to appear indifferent, I reckon."

"Think now: you and Mr. Benson went into the living-room directly from the hall, as soon as you entered the house?"

"Yes."

"Then how do you account for the fact, Captain, that when Mr. Benson was shot he had on his smoking-jacket and slippers?"

Leacock glanced nervously about the room. Before he answered he wet his lips with his tongue.

"Now that I think of it, Benson did go upstairs for a few minutes first. . . . I guess I was too excited," he added desperately, "to recollect everything."

"That's natural," Vance said sympathetically. "But when he came downstairs did you happen to notice anything peculiar about his hair?"

Leacock looked up vaguely.

"His hair? I—don't understand."

"The colour of it, I mean. When Mr. Benson sat before you under the table lamp, didn't you remark some—difference let us say—in the way his hair looked?"

The man closed his eyes, as if striving to visualise the scene.

"No—I don't remember."

"A minor point," said Vance indifferently. "Did Benson's speech strike you as peculiar when he came downstairs—that is, was there a thickness, or slight impediment of any kind, in his voice?"

Leacock was manifestly puzzled.

"I don't know what you mean," he said. "He seemed to talk the way he always talked."

"And did you happen to see a blue jewel-case on the table?"

"I didn't notice."

Vance smoked a moment thoughtfully.

"When you left the room after shooting Mr. Benson, you turned out the lights, of course?"

When no immediate answer came, Vance volunteered the suggestion:

"You must have done so, for Mr. Pfyfe says the house was dark when he drove up."

Leacock then nodded an affirmative.

"That's right. I couldn't recollect for the moment."

"Now that you remember the fact, just how did you turn them off?"

"I——" he began, and stopped. Then, finally: "At the switch."

"And where is that switch located, Captain?"

"I can't just recall."

"Think a moment. Surely you can remember."

"By the door leading into the hall, I think."

"Which side of the door?"

"How can I tell?" the man asked piteously. "I was too —nervous. . . . But I think it was on the right-hand side of the door."

"The right-hand side when entering or leaving the room?"

"As you go out."

"That would be where the bookcase stands?"

"Yes."

Vance appeared satisfied.

"Now, there's the question about the gun," he said. "Why did you take it to Miss St. Clair?"

"I was a coward," the man replied. "I was afraid they might find it at my apartment. And I never imagined she would be suspected."

"And when she was suspected, you at once took the gun away and threw it into the East River?"

"Yes."

"I suppose there was one cartridge missing from the magazine, too—which in itself would have been a suspicious circumstance."

"I thought of that. That's why I threw the gun away."

Vance frowned.

"That's strange. There must have been two guns. We dredged the river, y'know, and found a Colt automatic, but the magazine was full. . . . Are you sure, Captain, that it was *your* gun you took from Miss St. Clair's and threw over the bridge?"

I knew no gun had been retrieved from the river, and I wondered what he was driving at. Was he, after all, trying to involve the girl? Markham, too, I could see, was in doubt.

Leacock made no answer for several moments. When he spoke, it was with dogged sullenness.

"There weren't two guns. The one you found was mine. . . . I refilled the magazine myself."

"Ah, that accounts for it." Vance's tone was pleasant and reassuring. "Just one more question, Captain. Why did you come here to-day and confess?"

Leacock thrust his chin out, and for the first time during the cross-examination his eyes became animated.

"Why? It was the only honourable thing to do. You had unjustly suspected an innocent person; and I didn't want anybody else to suffer."

This ended the interview. Markham had no questions to ask; and the deputy-sheriff led the Captain out.

When the door had closed on him a curious silence fell over the room. Markham sat smoking furiously, his hands folded behind his head, his eyes fixed on the ceiling. The Major had settled back in his chair, and was gazing at Vance with admiring satisfaction. Vance was watching Markham out of the corner of his eye, a drowsy smile on his lips. The expressions and attitudes of the three men conveyed perfectly their varying individual reactions to the interview—Markham troubled, the Major pleased, Vance cynical. It was Vance who broke the silence. He spoke easily, almost lazily.

"You see how silly the confession is, what? Our pure and lofty Captain is an incredibly poor Munchausen. No one could lie as badly as he did who hadn't been born into the world that way. It's simply impossible to imitate such stupidity. And he did so want us to think him guilty. Very affectin'. He prob'bly imagined you'd merely stick the confession in his shirt-front and send him to the hangman. You noticed, he hadn't even decided how he got into

Benson's house that night. Pfyfe's admitted presence outside almost spoiled his impromptu explanation of having
entered *bras dessus bras dessous* with his intended victim.
And he didn't recall Benson's semi-négligé attire. When I
reminded him of it, he had to contradict himself, and send
Benson trotting upstairs to make a rapid change. Luckily
the toupee wasn't mentioned by the newspapers. The
Captain couldn't imagine what I meant when I intimated
that Benson had dyed his hair when changing his coat and
shoes. . . . By the bye, Major, did your brother speak
thickly when his false teeth were out?"

"Noticeably so," answered the Major. "If Alvin's plate
had been removed that night—as I gathered it had been
from your question—Leacock would surely have noticed it."

"There were other things he didn't notice," said Vance:
"the jewel-case, for instance, and the location of the electric-
light switch."

"He went badly astray on that point," added the Major.
"Alvin's house is old-fashioned, and the only switch in the
room is a pendant one attached to the chandelier."

"Exactly," said Vance. "However, his worst break was
in connection with the gun. He gave his hand away completely there. He said he threw the pistol into the river
largely because of the missing cartridge, and when I told him
the magazine was full, he explained that he had refilled it, so
I wouldn't think it was anyone else's gun that was found.
. . . It's plain to see what's the matter. He thinks Miss
St. Clair is guilty, and is determined to take the blame."

"That's my impression," said Major Benson.

"And yet," mused Vance, "the Captain's attitude bothers
me a little. There's no doubt he had something to do with
the crime, else why should he have concealed his pistol the
next day in Miss St. Clair's apartment? He's just the kind
of silly beggar, d'ye see, who would threaten any man he
thought had designs on his fiancée, and then carry out the
threat if anything happened. And he has a guilty conscience
—that's obvious. But for what? Certainly not the shooting.
The crime was planned; and the Captain never plans. He's
the kind that gets an *idée fixe*, girds up his loins, and does the
deed in knightly fashion, prepared to take the cons'quences.
That sort of chivalry, y'know, is sheer *beau geste*: its acolytes

want everyone to know of their valour. And when they go forth to rid the world of a Don Juan, they're always clear-minded. The Captain, for instance, wouldn't have overlooked his Lady Fair's gloves and handbag—he would have taken 'em away. In fact, it's just as certain he would have shot Benson as it is he didn't shoot him. That's the beetle in the amber. It's psychologically possible he would have done it, and psychologically impossible he would have done it the way it was done."

He lit a cigarette and watched the drifting spirals of smoke.

"If it wasn't so fantastic, I'd say he started out to do it, and found it already done. And yet, that's about the size of it. It would account for Pfyfe's seeing him there, and for his secreting the gun at Miss St. Clair's the next day."

The telephone rang: Colonel Ostrander wanted to speak to the District Attorney. Markham, after a short conversation, turned a disgruntled look upon Vance.

"Your bloodthirsty friend wanted to know if I'd arrested anyone yet. He offered to confer more of his invaluable suggestions upon me in case I was still undecided as to who was guilty."

"I heard you thanking him fulsomely for something or other. . . . What did you give him to understand about your mental state?"

"That I was still in the dark."

Markham's answer was accompanied by a sombre, tired smile. It was his way of telling Vance that he had entirely rejected the idea of Captain Leacock's guilt.

The Major went to him and held out his hand.

"I know how you feel," he said. "This sort of thing is discouraging; but it's better that the guilty person should escape altogether than that an innocent man should be made to suffer. . . . Don't work too hard, and don't let these disappointments get to you. You'll soon hit on the right solution, and when you do——" His jaw snapped shut, and he uttered the rest of the sentence between clenched teeth "——you'll meet with no opposition from me. I'll help you put the thing over."

He gave Markham a grim smile, and took up his hat.

"I'm going back to the office now. If you want me at any time, let me know. I may be able to help you—later on."

With a friendly, appreciative bow to Vance, he went out. Markham sat in silence for several minutes.

"Damn it, Vance!" he said irritably. "This case gets more difficult by the hour. I feel worn out."

"You really shouldn't take it so seriously, old dear," Vance advised lightly. "It doesn't pay, y'know, to worry over the *trivia* of existence.

> 'Nothing's new,
> And nothing's true,
> And nothing really matters.'

Several million johnnies were killed in the War, and you don't let the fact bedevil your phagocytes or inflame your brain cells. But when one rotter is mercifully shot in your district, you lie awake nights perspiring over it, what? My word! You're deucedly inconsistent."

"Consistency——" began Markham; but Vance interrupted him.

"Now don't quote Emerson. I inf'nitely prefer Erasmus. Y'know, you ought to read his *Praise of Folly;* it would cheer you no end. That goaty old Dutch professor would never have grieved inconsolably over the destruction of Alvin *Le Chauve.*"

"I'm not a *fruges consumere natus* like you," snapped Markham. "I was elected to this office——"

"Oh, quite—'loved I not honour more' and all that," Vance chimed in. "But don't be so sens'tive. Even if the Captain has succeeded in bungling his way out of jail, you have at least five possibilities left. There's Mrs. Platz . . . and Pfyfe . . . and Colonel Ostrander . . . and Miss Hoffman . . . and Mrs. Banning. I say! Why don't you arrest 'em all, one at a time, and get 'em to confess? Heath would go crazy with joy."

Markham was in too crestfallen a mood to resent this chaffing. Indeed, Vance's light-heartedness seemed to buoy him up.

"If you want the truth," he said, "that's exactly what I feel like doing. I am restrained merely by my indecision as to which one to arrest first."

"Stout fella!" Then Vance asked: "What are you going to do with the Captain now? It'll break his heart if you release him."

"His heart'll have to break, I'm afraid."   Markham reached for the telephone.   "I'd better see to the formalities now."

"Just a moment!" Vance put forth a restraining hand. "Don't end his rapturous martyrdom just yet.   Let him be happy for another day at least.   I've a notion he may be most useful to us, pining away in his lonely cell like the prisoner of Chillon."

Markham put down the telephone without a word.   More and more, I had noticed, he was becoming inclined to accept Vance's leadership.   This attitude was not merely the result of the hopeless confusion in his mind, though his uncertainty probably influenced him to some extent; but it was due in large measure to the impression Vance had given him of knowing more than he cared to reveal.

"Have you tried to figure out just how Pfyfe and his Turtledove fit into the case?" Vance asked.

"Along with a few thousand other enigmas—yes," was the petulant reply.   "But the more I try to reason it out, the more of a mystery the whole thing becomes."

"Loosely put, my dear Markham," criticised Vance. "There are no mysteries originating in human beings, y'know; there are only problems.   And any problem originating in one human being can be solved by another human being. It merely requires a knowledge of the human mind, and the application of that knowledge to human acts.   Simple, what?"

He glanced at the clock.

"I wonder how your Mr. Stitt is getting along with the Benson and Benson books.   I await his report with antici-pat'ry excitement."

This was too much for Markham.   The wearing-down pro-cess of Vance's intimations and veiled innuendoes had at last dissipated his self-control.   He bent forward and struck the desk angrily with his hand.

"I'm damned tired of this superior attitude of yours," he complained hotly.   "Either you know something or you don't.   If you don't know anything, do me the favour of dropping these insinuations of knowledge.   If you do know anything, it's up to you to tell me.   You've been hinting around in one way or another ever since Benson was shot. If you've got any idea who killed him, I want to know it."

He leaned back and took out a cigar.   Not once did he

look up as he carefully clipped the end and lit it. I think he
was a little ashamed at having given way to his anger.

Vance had sat apparently unconcerned during the outburst. At length he stretched his legs, and gave Markham
a long contemplative look.

"Y'know, Markham, old bean, I don't blame you a bit
for your unseemly ebullition. The situation has been most
provokin'. But now, I fancy, the time has come to put an
end to the comedietta. I really haven't been spoofing,
y'know. The fact is, I've some most int'restin' ideas on the
subject."

He stood up and yawned.

"It's a beastly hot day, but it must be done—eh, what?

> 'So nigh is grandeur to our dust,
>   So near is God to man.
> When duty whispers low, *Thou must,*
>   The youth replies, *I can.*'

I'm the noble youth, don't y'know. And you're the voice
of duty—though you didn't exactly whisper, did you? . . .
Was aber ist deine Pflicht? And Goethe answered: *Die
Forderung des Tages.* But—deuce take it—I wish the demand
had come on a cooler day!"

He handed Markham his hat.

"Come, *Postume.* To everything there is a season, and
a time to every purpose under the heaven.[1] You are through
with the office for to-day—inform Swacker of the fact, will
you?—there's a dear! We attend upon a lady—Miss St.
Clair, no less."

Markham realised that Vance's jesting manner was only
the masquerade of a very serious purpose. Also, he knew
that Vance would tell him what he knew or suspected only
in his own way, and that, no matter how circuitous and unreasonable that way might appear, Vance had excellent

---

[1] This quotation from Ecclesiastes reminds me that Vance
regularly read the Old Testament. "When I weary of the professional liter'ry man," he once said, "I find stimulation in the
majestic prose of the Bible. If the moderns feel that they simply
must write, they should be made to spend at least two hours a
day with the Biblical historians."

reasons for following it. Furthermore, since the unmasking
of Captain Leacock's purely fictitious confession, he was in
a state of mind to follow any suggestion that held the faintest
hope of getting at the truth. He therefore rang at once
for Swacker, and informed him he was quitting the office for
the day.

In ten minutes we were in the subway on our way to
94 Riverside Drive.

CHAPTER XX

A LADY EXPLAINS

(*Wednesday, June 19th; 4.30 p.m.*)

"THE quest for enlightenment upon which we are now em-
barked," said Vance, as we rode up town, "may prove a bit
tedious. But you must exert your will-power, and bear
with me. You can't imagine what a ticklish task I have on
my hands. And it's not a pleasant one either. I'm a bit
too young to be sentimental, and yet, d'ye know, I'm half
inclined to let your culprit go."

"Would you mind telling me why we are calling on Miss
St. Clair?" asked Markham resignedly.

Vance amiably complied.

"Not at all. Indeed, I deem it best for you to know.
There are several points connected with the lady that need
eluc'dation. First, there are the gloves and the handbag.
Nor poppy nor mandragora shall ever medicine thee to that
sweet sleep which thou ow'dst yesterday until you have
learned about those articles—eh, what? Then, you recall,
Miss Hoffman told us that the Major was lending an ear
when a certain lady called upon Benson the day he was
shot. I suspect that the visitor was Miss St. Clair; and I
am rather curious to know what took place in the office
that day, and why she came back later. Also, why did she
go to Benson's for tea that afternoon? And what part did
the jewels play in the chit-chat? But there are other items.
For example: Why did the Captain take his gun to her?

What makes him think she shot Benson?—he really believes it, y'know. And why did she think that he was guilty from the first?".

Markham looked sceptical.

"You expect her to tell us all this?"

"My hopes run high," returned Vance. "With her *verray parfit gentil knight* jailed as a self-confessed murderer, she will have nothing to lose by unburdening her soul. . . . But we must have no blustering. Your police brand of aggressive cross-examination will, I assure you, have no effect upon the lady."

"Just how do you propose to elicit your information?"

"With *morbidezza*, as the painters say. Much more refined and gentlemanly, y'know."

Markham considered a moment.

"I think I'll keep out of it, and leave the Socratic *elenchus* entirely to you."

"An extr'ordin'rily brilliant suggestion," said Vance.

When we arrived Markham announced over the house-telephone that he had come on a vitally important mission; and we were received by Miss St. Clair without a moment's delay. She was apprehensive, I imagine, concerning the whereabouts of Captain Leacock.

As she sat before us in her little drawing-room overlooking the Hudson, her face was quite pale, and her hands, though tightly clasped, trembled a little. She had lost much of her cold reserve, and there were unmistakable signs of sleepless worry about her eyes.

Vance went directly to the point. His tone was almost flippant in its lightness: it at once relieved the tension of the atmosphere, and gave an air bordering on inconsequentiality to our visit.

"Captain Leacock has, I regret to inform you, very foolishly confessed to the murder of Mr. Benson. But we are not entirely satisfied with his *bona fides*. We are, alas! awash between Scylla and Charybdis. We cannot decide whether the Captain is a deep-dyed villain or a *chevalier sans peur et sans reproche*. His story of how he accomplished the dark deed is a bit sketchy: he is vague on certain essential details; and—what's most confusin'—he turned the lights off in Benson's hideous living-room by a switch which pos'tively doesn't exist. Cons'quently, the suspicion has crept into my mind that he has concocted this tale of derring-do in order to shield someone whom he really believes guilty."

He indicated Markham with a slight movement of the head. "The District Attorney here does not wholly agree with me. But then, d'ye see, the legal mind is incredibly rigid and unreceptive once it has been invaded by a notion. You will remember that, because you were with Mr. Alvin Benson on his last evening on earth, and for other reasons equally irrelevant and trivial, Mr. Markham actu'lly concluded that you had had something to do with the gentleman's death."

He gave Markham a smile of waggish reproach, and went on:

"Since you, Miss St. Clair, are the only person whom Captain Leacock would shield so heroically, and since I, at least, am convinced of your own innocence, will you not clear up for us a few of those points where your orbit crossed that of Mr. Benson? . . . Such information cannot do the Captain or yourself any harm, and it very possibly will help to banish from Mr. Markham's mind his lingering doubts as to the Captain's innocence."

Vance's manner had an assuaging effect upon the woman; but I could see that Markham was boiling inwardly at Vance's animadversions on him, though he refrained from any interruption.

Miss St. Clair stared steadily at Vance for several minutes.

"I don't know why I should trust you, or even believe you," she said evenly; "but now that Captain Leacock has confessed—I was afraid he was going to, when he last spoke to me—I see no reason why I should not answer your questions. . . . Do you truly think he is innocent?"

The question was like an involuntary cry: her pent-up emotion had broken through her carapace of calm.

"I truly do," Vance avowed soberly. "Mr. Markham will tell you that before we left his office I pleaded with him to release Captain Leacock. It was with the hope that your explanations would convince him of the wisdom of such a course, that I urged him to come here."

Something in his tone and manner seemed to inspire her confidence.

"What do you wish to ask me?" she asked.

Vance cast another reproachful glance at Markham, who was restraining his outraged feelings only with difficulty; and then turned back to the woman.

"First of all, will you explain how your gloves and hand-bag found their way into Mr. Benson's house? Their presence there has been preying most distressin'ly on the District Attorney's mind."

She turned a direct, frank gaze upon Markham.

"I dined with Mr. Benson at his invitation. Things between us were not pleasant, and when we started for home, my resentment of his attitude increased. At Times Square I ordered the chauffeur to stop—I preferred returning home alone. In my anger and my haste to get away, I must have dropped my gloves and bag. It was not until Mr. Benson had driven off that I realised my loss, and having no money, I walked home. Since my things were found in Mr. Benson's house, he must have taken them there himself."

"Such was my own belief," said Vance. "And—my word!—it's a deucedly long walk out here, what?"

He turned to Markham with a tantalising smile.

"Really, y'know, Miss St. Clair couldn't have been expected to reach here before one."

Markham, grim and resolute, made no reply.

"And now," pursued Vance, "I should love to know under what circumstances the invitation to dinner was extended."

A shadow darkened her face, but her voice remained even.

"I had been losing a lot of money through Mr. Benson's firm, and suddenly my intuition told me that he was purposely seeing to it that I did lose, and that he could, if he desired, help me to recoup." She dropped her eyes. "He had been annoying me with his attentions for some time; and I didn't put any despicable scheme past him. I went to his office, and told him quite plainly what I suspected. He replied that if I'd dine with him that night we could talk it over. I knew what his object was, but I was so desperate I decided to go any way, hoping I might plead with him."

"And how did you happen to mention to Mr. Benson the exact time your little dinner would terminate?"

She looked at Vance in astonishment, but answered un-hesitatingly.

"He said something about—making a gay night of it;

and then I told him—very emphatically—that if I went I would leave him sharply at midnight, as was my invariable rule on all parties. . . . You see," she added, "I study very hard at my singing, and going home at midnight, no matter what the occasion, is one of the sacrifices—or rather, restrictions—I impose on myself."

"Most commendable and most wise!" commented Vance. "Was this fact generally known among your acquaintances?"

"Oh, yes. It even resulted in my being nicknamed Cinderella."

"Specifically, did Colonel Ostrander and Mr. Pfyfe know it?"

"Yes."

Vance thought a moment.

"How did you happen to go to tea at Mr. Benson's home the day of the murder, if you were to dine with him that night?"

A flush stained her cheeks.

"There was nothing wrong in that," she declared. "Somehow, after I had left Mr. Benson's office, I revolted against my decision to dine with him, and I went to his house—I had gone back to the office first, but he had left—to make a final appeal, and to beg him to release me from my promise. But he laughed the matter off, and after insisting that I have tea, sent me home in a taxicab to dress for dinner. He called for me about half-past seven."

"And when you pleaded with him to release you from your promise you sought to frighten him by recalling Captain Leacock's threat; and he said it was only bluff."

Again the woman's astonishment was manifest.

"Yes," she murmured.

Vance gave her a soothing smile.

"Colonel Ostrander told me he saw you and Mr. Benson at the Marseilles."

"Yes; and I was terribly ashamed. He knew what Mr. Benson was, and had warned me against him only a few days before."

"I was under the impression that the Colonel and Mr. Benson were good friends."

"They were—up to a week ago. But the Colonel lost more money than I did in a stock pool which Mr. Benson

engineered recently, and he intimated to me very strongly
that Mr. Benson had deliberately misadvised us to his own
benefit. He didn't even speak to Mr. Benson that night
at the Marseilles."

"What about these rich and precious stones that accompanied your tea with Mr. Benson?"

"Bribes," she answered; and her contemptuous smile
was a more eloquent condemnation of Benson than if she
had resorted to the bitterest castigation. "The gentleman
sought to turn my head with them. I was offered a string
of pearls to wear to dinner; but I declined them. And
I was told that, if I saw things in the right light—or some
such charming phrase—I could have jewels like them for
my very, very own—perhaps even those identical ones, on
the twenty-first."

"Of course—the twenty-first," grinned Vance. "Markham, are you listening? On the twenty-first Leander's note
falls due, and if it's not paid the jewels are forfeited."

He addressed himself again to Miss St. Clair.

"Did Mr. Benson have the jewels with him at dinner?"

"Oh, no! I think my refusal of the pearls rather discouraged him."

Vance paused, looking at her with ingratiating cordiality.

"Tell us now, please, of the gun episode—in your own
words, as the lawyers say, hoping to entangle you
later."

But she evidently feared no entanglement.

"The morning after the murder Captain Leacock came
here and said he had gone to Mr. Benson's house about
half-past twelve with the intention of shooting him. But
he had seen Mr. Pfyfe outside and, assuming he was calling
had given up the idea and gone home. I feared that Mr.
Pfyfe had seen him, and I told him it would be safer to
bring his pistol to me and to say, if questioned, that he'd
lost it in France. . . . You see, I really thought he had
shot Mr. Benson and was—well, lying like a gentleman, to
spare my feelings. Then, when he took the pistol from me
with the purpose of throwing it away altogether, I was even
more certain of it."

She smiled faintly at Markham.

"That was why I refused to answer your questions. I

wanted you to think that maybe I had done it, so you'd not suspect Captain Leacock."

"But he wasn't lying at all," said Vance.

"I know now that he wasn't. And I should have known it before. He'd never have brought the pistol to me if he'd been guilty."

A film came over her eyes.

"And—poor boy!—he confessed because he thought that I was guilty."

"That's precisely the harrowin' situation," nodded Vance. "But where did he think you had obtained a weapon?"

"I know many army men—friends of his and of Major Benson's. And last summer at the mountains I did considerable pistol practice for the fun of it. Oh, the idea was reasonable enough."

Vance rose and made a courtly bow.

"You've been most gracious—and most helpful," he said. "Y'see, Mr. Markham had various theories about the murder. The first, I believe, was that you alone were the Madame Borgia. The second was that you and the Captain did the deed together—*à quatre mains*, as it were. The third was that the Captain pulled the trigger *a cappella*. And the legal mind is so exquisitely developed that it can believe in several conflicting theories at the same time. The sad thing about the present case is that Mr. Markham still leans towards the belief that both of you are guilty, individually and collectively. I tried to reason with him before coming here; but I failed. Therefore, I insisted upon his hearing from your own charming lips your story of the affair."

He went up to Markham, who sat glaring at him with lips compressed.

"Well, old chap," he remarked pleasantly, "surely you are not going to persist in your obsession that either Miss St. Clair or Captain Leacock is guilty, what? . . . And won't you relent and unshackle the Captain as I begged you to?"

He extended his arms in a theatrical gesture of supplication.

Markham's wrath was at the breaking point, but he got up deliberately and, going to the woman, held out his hand.

"Miss St. Clair," he said kindly—and again I was impressed by the bigness of the man—"I wish to assure you that I have dismissed the idea of your guilt, and also Captain Leacock's, from what Mr. Vance terms my incredibly rigid and unreceptive mind. . . . I forgive him, however, because he has saved me from doing you a very grave injustice. And I will see that you have your Captain back as soon as the paper can be signed for his release."

As we walked out on to Riverside Drive, Markham turned savagely on Vance.

"So! *I* was keeping her precious Captain locked up, and *you* were pleading with me to let him go! You know damned well I didn't think either one of them was guilty—you—you lounge lizard!"

Vance sighed.

"Dear me! Don't you want to be of any help at all in this case?" he asked sadly.

"What good did it do you to make an ass of me in front of that woman?" spluttered Markham. "I can't see that you got anywhere, with all your tomfoolery."

"What!" Vance registered utter amazement. "The testimony you've heard to-day is going to help immeasurably in convicting the culprit. Furthermore, we know about the gloves and handbag, and who the lady was that called at Benson's office, and what Miss St. Clair did between twelve and one, and why she dined alone with Alvin, and why she first had tea with him, and how the jewels came to be there, and why the Captain took her his gun and then threw it away, and why he confessed. . . . My word! Doesn't all this knowledge soothe you? It rids the situation of so much debris."

He stopped and lit a cigarette.

"The really important thing the lady told us was that her friends knew she invariably departed at midnight when she went out of an evening. Don't overlook or belittle that point, old dear; it's most pert'nent. I told you long ago that the person who shot Benson knew she was dining with him that night."

"You'll be telling me next you know who killed him," Markham scoffed.

Vance sent a ring of smoke circling upward.

"I've known all along who shot the blighter."

Markham snorted derisively.

"Indeed!   And when did this revelation burst upon you?"

"Oh, not more than five minutes after I entered Benson's house that first morning," replied Vance.

"Well, well!   Why didn't you confide in me, and avoid all these trying activities?"

"Quite impossible," Vance explained jocularly. "You were not ready to receive my apocryphal knowledge. It was first necess'ry to lead you patiently by the hand out of the various dark forests and morasses into which you insisted upon straying. You're so dev'lishly unimag'native, don't y'know."

A taxicab was passing, and he hailed it.

"Eighty-seven West Forty-eighth Street," he directed.

Then he took Markham's arm confidingly.

"Now for a brief chat with Mrs. Platz. And then—then I shall pour into your ear all my maidenly secrets."

CHAPTER XXI

SARTORIAL REVELATIONS

(Wednesday, June 19th; 5.30 p.m.)

THE housekeeper regarded our visit that afternoon with marked uneasiness. Though she was a large powerful woman, her body seemed to have lost some of its strength, and her face showed signs of prolonged anxiety. Snitkin informed us, when we entered, that she had carefully read every newspaper account of the progress of the case, and had questioned him interminably on the subject.

She entered the living-room with scarcely an acknowledgment of our presence, and took the chair Vance placed for her like a woman resigning herself to a dreaded but inevitable ordeal. When Vance looked at her keenly, she gave him a frightened glance and turned her face away, as if, in the second their eyes met, she had read his knowledge of some secret she had been jealously guarding.

Vance began his questioning without prelude or protasis.

"Mrs. Platz, was Mr. Benson very particular about his toupee—that is, did he often receive his friends without having it on?"

The woman appeared relieved.

"Oh, no, sir—never."

"Think back, Mrs. Platz. Has Mr. Benson never, to your knowledge, been in anyone's company without his toupee?"

She was silent for some time, her brows contracted.

"Once I saw him take off his wig and show it to Colonel Ostrander, an elderly gentleman who used to call here very often. But Colonel Ostrander was an old friend of his. He told me they lived together once."

"No one else?"

Again she frowned thoughtfully.

"No," she said, after several minutes.

"What about the tradespeople?"

"He was very particular about them. . . . And strangers, too," she added. "When he used to sit in here in hot weather without his wig, he always pulled the shade on that window." She pointed to the one nearest the hallway. "You can look in it from the steps."

"I'm glad you brought up that point," said Vance. "And anyone standing on the steps could tap on the window or the iron bars, and attract the attention of anyone in this room?"

"Oh, yes, sir—easily. I did it myself once, when I went on an errand and forgot my key."

"It's quite likely, don't you think, that the person who shot Mr. Benson obtained admittance that way?"

"Yes, sir." She grasped eagerly at the suggestion.

"The person would have had to know Mr. Benson pretty well to tap on the window instead of ringing the bell. Don't you agree with me, Mrs. Platz?"

"Yes—sir." Her tone was doubtful: evidently the point was a little beyond her.

"If a stranger had tapped on the window, would Mr. Benson have admitted him without his toupee?"

"Oh, no—he wouldn't have let a stranger in."

"You are sure the bell didn't ring that night?"

"Positive, sir." The answer was very emphatic.

"Is there a light on the front steps?"

"No, sir."

"If Mr. Benson had looked out of the window to see who was tapping, could he have recognised the person at night?"

The woman hesitated.

"I didn't know—I don't think so."

"Is there any way you can see through the front door, who is outside, without opening it?"

"No, sir. Sometimes I wished there was."

"Then, if the person knocked on the window, Mr. Benson must have recognised the voice?"

"It looks that way, sir."

"And you're certain no one could have got in without a key?"

"How could they? The door locks by itself."

"It's the regulation spring-lock, isn't it?"

"Yes, sir."

"Then it must have a catch you can turn off so that the door will open from either side even though it's latched."

"It did have a catch like that," she exclaimed, "but Mr. Benson had it fixed so's it wouldn't work. He said it was too dangerous—I might go out and leave the house unlocked."

Vance stepped into the hallway, and I heard him opening and shutting the front door.

"You're right, Mrs. Platz," he observed, when he came back. "Now tell me: are you quite sure no one had a key?"

"Yes, sir. No one but me and Mr. Benson had a key."

Vance nodded his acceptance of her statement.

"You said you left your bedroom door open on the night Mr. Benson was shot. . . . Do you generally leave it open?"

"No, I 'most always shut it. But it was terrible close that night."

"Then it was merely an accident you left it open?"

"As you might say."

"If your door had been closed as usual, could you have heard the shot, do you think?"

"If I'd been awake, maybe. Not if I was sleeping, though. They got heavy doors in these old houses, sir."

"And they're beautiful, too," commented Vance.

He looked admiringly at the massive mahogany double door that opened into the hall.

"Y'know, Markham, our so-called civ'lisation is nothing

more than the persistent destruction of everything that's beautiful and enduring, and the designing of cheap make-shifts. You should read Oswald Spengler's *Untergang des Abendlands*—a most penetratin' document. I wonder some enterprisin' publisher hasn't embalmed it in our native argot.[1] The whole history of this degen'rate era we call modern civ'lisa-tion can be seen in our woodwork. Look at that fine old door, for instance, with its bevelled panels and ornamented bolec-tion, and its Ionic pilasters and carved lintel. And then compare it with the flat, flimsy, machine-made, shellacked boards which are turned out by the thousand to-day. *Sic transit. . . .*"

He studied the door for some time: then turned abruptly back to Mrs. Platz, who was eyeing him curiously and with mounting apprehension.

"What did Mr. Benson do with the box of jewels when he went out to dinner?" he asked.

"Nothing, sir," she answered nervously. "He left them on the table there."

"Did you see them after he had gone?"

"Yes; and I was going to put them away. But I decided I'd better not touch them."

"And nobody came to the door, or entered the house, after Mr. Benson left?"

"No, sir."

"You're quite sure?"

"I'm positive, sir."

Vance rose, and began to pace the floor. Suddenly, just as he was passing the woman, he stopped and faced her.

"Was your maiden name Hoffman, Mrs. Platz?"

The thing she had been dreading had come. Her face paled, her eyes opened wide, and her lower lip drooped a little.

Vance stood looking at her, not unkindly. Before she could regain control of herself, he said:

"I had the pleasure of meeting your charmin' daughter recently."

"My daughter . . .?" the woman managed to stammer.

---

[1] The book—or a part of it—has, I believe, been recently translated into English.

"Miss Hoffman, y'know—the attractive young lady with the blond hair—Mr. Benson's secret'ry."

The woman sat erect, and spoke through clamped teeth. "She's not my daughter."

"Now, now, Mrs. Platz!" Vance chid her, as if speaking to a child. "Why this foolish attempt at deception? You remember how worried you were when I accused you of having a personal interest in the lady who was here to tea with Mr. Benson? You were afraid I thought it was Miss Hoffman. . . . But why should you be anxious about her, Mrs. Platz? I'm sure she's a very nice girl. And you really can't blame her for preferring the name of Hoffman to that of Platz. *Platz* means generally a place, though it also means a crash or an explosion; and sometimes a *Platz* is a bun or a yeast-cake. But a *Hoffman* is a courtier—much nicer than being a yeast-cake, what?"

He smiled engagingly, and his manner had a quieting effect upon her.

"It isn't that, sir," she said, looking at him appealingly. "I made her take the name. In this country any girl who's smart can get to be a lady, if she's given a chance. And——"

"I understand perfectly," Vance interposed pleasantly. "Miss Hoffman is clever, and you feared that the fact of your being a housekeeper, if it became known, would stand in the way of her success. So you elim'nated yourself, as it were, for her welfare. I think it was very generous of you. . . . Your daughter lives alone?"

"Yes, sir—in Morningside Heights. But I see her every week." Her voice was barely audible.

"Of course—as often as you can, I'm sure. . . . Did you take the position as Mr. Benson's housekeeper because she was his secret'ry?"

She looked up, a bitter expression in her eyes.

"Yes, sir—I did. She told me the kind of man he was; and he often made her come to the house here in the evenings to do extra work."

"And you wanted to be here to protect her?"

"Yes, sir—that was it."

"Why were you so worried the morning after the murder, when Mr. Markham here asked you if Mr. Benson kept any firearms around the house?"

The woman shifted her gaze.

"I—wasn't worried."

"Yes, you were, Mrs. Platz. And I'll tell you why. You were afraid we might think Miss Hoffman shot him."

"Oh, no, sir, I wasn't!" she cried. "My girl wasn't even here that night—I swear it!—she wasn't here. . . ."

She was badly shaken: the nervous tension of a week had snapped, and she looked helplessly about her.

"Come, come, Mrs. Platz," pleaded Vance consolingly. "No one believes for a moment that Miss Hoffman had a hand in Mr. Benson's death."

The woman peered searchingly into his face. At first she was loath to believe him—it was evident that fear had long been prying on her mind—and it took him fully a quarter of an hour to convince her that what he had said was true. When, finally, we left the house, she was in a comparatively peaceful state of mind.

On our way to the Stuyvesant Club Markham was silent, completely engrossed with his thoughts. It was evident that the new facts educed by the interview with Mrs. Platz troubled him considerably.

Vance sat smoking dreamily, turning his head now and then to inspect the buildings we passed. We drove east through Forty-eighth Street, and when we came abreast of the New York Bible Society House he ordered the chauffeur to stop, and insisted that we admire it.

"Christianity," he remarked, "has almost vindicated itself by its architecture alone. With few exceptions, the only buildings in this city that are not eyesores are the churches and their allied structures. The American æsthetic credo is: Whatever's big is beautiful. These depressin' gargantuan boxes with rectangular holes in 'em, which are called skyscrapers, are worshipped by Americans simply because they're huge. A box with forty rows of holes is twice as beautiful as a box with twenty rows. Simple formula, what? . . . Look at this little five-storey affair across the street. It's inf'nitely lovelier—and more impressive, too—than any skyscraper in the city. . . ."

Vance referred but once to the crime during our ride to the Club, and then only indirectly.

"Kind hearts, y'know, Markham, are more than coronets,

I've done a good deed to-day, and I feel pos'tively virtuous. Frau Platz will *schlafen* much better to-night. She has been frightfully upset about little Gretchen. She's a doughty old soul; motherly and all that. And she couldn't bear to think of the future Lady Vere de Vere being suspected. . . . Wonder why she worried so?" And he gave Markham a sly look.

Nothing further was said until after dinner, which we ate in the Roof Garden. We had pushed back our chairs, and sat looking out over the tree-tops of Madison Square.

"Now, Markham," said Vance, "give over all prejudices and consider the situation judiciously—as you lawyers euphemistically put it. . . . To begin with, we now know why Mrs. Platz was so worried at your question regarding firearms, and why she was upset by my ref'rence to her personal int'rest in Benson's tea-companion. So, those two mysteries are elim'nated. . . ."

"How did you find out about her relation to the girl?" interjected Markham.

"'Twas my ogling did it." Vance gave him a reproving look. "You recall that I 'ogled' the young lady at our first meeting—but I forgive you. . . . And you remember our little discussion about cranial idiosyncrasies? Miss Hoffman, I noticed at once, possessed all the physical formations of Benson's housekeeper. She was brachy-cephalic; she had over-articulated cheek-bones, an ortho-gnathous jaw, a low flat parietal structure, and a meso-rhinian nose. . . . Then I looked for her ear, for I had noted that Mrs. Platz had the pointed, lobeless, 'satyr' ear—sometimes called the Darwin ear. These ears run in families; and when I saw that Miss Hoffman's were of the same type, even though modified, I was fairly certain of the relationship. But there were other similarities—in pigment, for instance; and in height—both are tall, y'know. And the central masses of each were very large in comparison with the peripheral masses: the shoulders were narrow and the wrists and ankles small, while the hips were bulky. . . . That Hoffman was Platz's maiden name was only a guess. But it didn't matter."

Vance adjusted himself more comfortably in his chair.

"Now for your judicial considerations. . . . First, let

us assume that at a little before half-past twelve on the night of the thirteenth the villain came to Benson's house, saw the light in the living-room, tapped on the window, and was instantly admitted. . . . What, would you say, do these assumptions indicate regarding the visitor?"

"Merely that Benson was acquainted with him," returned Markham. "But that doesn't help us any. We can't extend the *sus. per coll.* to everybody the man knew."

"The indications go much further than that, old chap," Vance retorted. "They show unmistakably that Benson's murderer was a most intimate crony, or, at least, a person before whom he didn't care how he looked. The absence of the toupee, as I once suggested to you, was a prime essential of the situation. A toupee, don't y'know, is the sartorial *sine qua non* of every middle-aged Beau Brummel afflicted with baldness. You heard Mrs. Platz on the subject. Do you think for a second that Benson, who hid his hirsute deficiency even from the grocer's boy, would visit with a mere acquaintance thus bereft of his crowning glory? And besides being thus denuded, he was without his full complement of teeth. Moreover, he was without collar or tie, and attired in an old smoking-jacket and bedroom slippers! Picture the spectacle, my dear fellow. . . . A man does not look fascinatin' without his collar and with his shirtband and gold stud exposed. Thus attired he is the equiv'lent of a lady in curl-papers. . . . How many men do you think Benson knew with whom he would have sat down to a *tête-à-tête* in this undress condition?"

"Three or four, perhaps," answered Markham. "But I can't arrest them all."

"I'm sure you would if you could. But it won't be necess'ry."

Vance selected another cigarette from his case, and went on:

"There are other helpful indications, y'know. For instance, the murderer was fairly well acquainted with Benson's domestic arrangements. He must have known that the housekeeper slept a good distance from the living-room and would not be startled by the shot if her door was closed as usual. Also, he must have known there was no one else in the house at that hour. And another thing; don't forget his voice was perfectly familiar to Benson. If there had been the slightest doubt about it Benson would not have let him in, in view of his natural fear of housebreakers, and with the Captain's threat hanging over him."

"That's a tenable hypothesis. . . . What else?"

"The jewels, Markham—those orators of love. Have you thought of them? They were on the centre-table when Benson came home that night; and they were gone in the morning. Wherefore, it seems inev'table that the murderer took 'em—eh, what? . . . And may they not have been one reason for the murderer's coming there that night? If so, who of Benson's most intimate *personæ gratæ* knew of their presence in the house? And who wanted 'em particularly?"

"Exactly, Vance." Markham nodded his head slowly. "You've hit it. I've had an uneasy feeling about Pfyfe right along. I was on the point of ordering his arrest to-day when Heath brought word of Leacock's confession; and then, when that blew up, my suspicions reverted to him. I said nothing this afternoon because I wanted to see where your ideas had led you. What you've been saying checks up perfectly with my own notions. Pfyfe's our man——"

He brought the front legs of his chair down suddenly.

"And now, damn it, you've let him get away from us!"

"Don't fret, old dear," said Vance. "He's safe with Mrs. Pfyfe, I fancy. And anyhow, your friend, Mr. Ben Hanlon, is well versed in retrieving fugitives. . . . Let the harassed Leander alone for the moment. You don't need him to-night —and to-morrow you won't want him."

Markham wheeled about.

"What's that?—I don't want him? . . . And why, pray?"

"Well," Vance explained indolently. "He hasn't a congenial and lovable nature, has he? And he's not exactly an object of blindin' beauty. I shouldn't want him around me more than was necess'ry, don't y'know. . . . Incidentally he's not guilty."

Markham was too nonplussed to be exasperated. He regarded Vance searchingly for a full minute.

"I don't follow you," he said. "If you think Pfyfe's innocent, who in God's name, do you think is guilty?"

Vance glanced at his watch.

"Come to my house to-morrow for breakfast, and bring those alibis you asked Heath for; and I'll tell you who shot Benson."

Something in his tone impressed Markham. He realised that Vance would not have made so specific a promise unless he was confident of his ability to keep it. He knew Vance too well to ignore, or even minimise his statement.

"Why not tell me now?" he asked.

"Awf'lly sorry, y'know," apologised Vance; "but I'm going to the Philharmonic's 'special' to-night. They're playing César Franck's D-minor, and Stransky's temp'rament is em'nently suited to its diatonic sentimentalities. . . . You'd better come along, old man. Soothin' to the nerves and all that."

"Not me!" grumbled Markham. "What I need is a brandy-and-soda."

He walked down with us to the taxicab.

"Come at nine to-morrow," said Vance, as we took our seats. "Let the office wait a bit. And don't forget to 'phone Heath for those alibis."

Then, just as we started off, he leaned out of the car.

"And I say, Markham: how tall would you say Mrs. Platz was?"

CHAPTER XXII

VANCE OUTLINES A THEORY

(Thursday, June 20th; 9 a.m.)

MARKHAM came to Vance's apartment at promptly nine o'clock the next morning. He was in bad humour.

"Now, see here, Vance," he said, as soon as he was seated at the table; "I want to know what was the meaning of your parting words last night."

"Eat your melon, old dear," said Vance. "It comes from Northern Brazil, and is very delicious. But don't devitalise its flavour with pepper or salt. An amazin' practice, that—

though not as amazin' as stuffing a melon with ice-cream. The American does the most dumbfoundin' things with ice-cream. He puts it on pie; he puts it in soda water; he encases it in hard chocolate like a *bon-bon*; he puts it between sweet biscuits and calls the result an ice-cream sandwich; he even uses it instead of whipped cream in a Charlotte-Russe. . . ."

"What I want to know——" began Markham; but Vance did not permit him to finish.

"It's surprisin', y'know, the erroneous ideas people have about melons. There are only two species—the muskmelon and the watermelon. All breakfast melons—like cantaloups, citrons, nut-megs, Cassabas, and Honeydews—are varieties of the muskmelon. But people have the notion, d'ye see, that cantaloup is a generic term. Philadelphians call all melons cantaloups; whereas this type of muskmelon was first cultivated in Cantalupo, Italy. . . ."

"Very interesting," said Markham, with only partly disguised impatience. "Did you intend by your remark last night——"

"And after the melon, Currie has prepared a special dish for you. It's my own gustat'ry *chef-d'œuvre*—with Currie's collaboration, of course. I've spent months on its conception —composing and organising it, so to speak. I haven't named it yet—perhaps you can suggest a fitting appellation. . . . To achieve this dish, one first chops a hard-boiled egg and mixes it with grated *Por du Salut* cheese, adding a *soupçon* of tarragon. This paste is then enclosed in a *filet* of white perch—like a French pancake. It is tied with silk, rolled in a specially prepared almond batter, and cooked in sweet butter. That, of course, is the barest outline of its manufacture, with all the truly exquisite details omitted."

"It sounds appetising." Markham's tone was devoid of enthusiasm. "But I didn't come here for a cooking lesson."

"Y'know, you underestimate the importance of your ventral pleasures," pursued Vance. "Eating is the one infallible guide to a people's intellectual advancement, as well as the inev'table gauge of the individual's temp'rament. The savage cooked and ate like a savage. In the early days of the human race, mankind was cursed with one vast epidemic of indigestion. There's where his devils and demons and ideas of hell came from; they were the nightmares of his dyspepsia.

Then, as man began to master the technique of cooking, he became civilised; and when he achieved the highest pinnacles of the culin'ry art, he also achieved the highest pinnacles of cultural and intellectual glory. When the art of the *gourmet* retrogressed, so did man. The tasteless, standardised cookery of America is typical of our decadence. A perfectly blended soup, Markham, is more ennoblin' than Beethoven's C-minor Symphony. . . ."

Markham listened stolidly to Vance's chatter during breakfast. He made several attempts to bring up the subject of the crime, but Vance glibly ignored each essay. It was not until Currie had cleared away the dishes that he referred to the object of Markham's visit.

"Did you bring the alibi reports?" was his first question.

Markham nodded.

"And it took me five hours to find Heath after you'd gone last night."

"Sad," breathed Vance.

He went to the desk, and took a closely-written double sheet of foolscap from one of the compartments.

"I wish you'd glance this over and give me your learned opinion." he said, handing the paper to Markham. "I prepared it last night after the concert."

I later took possession of the document, and filed it with my other notes and papers pertaining to the Benson case. The following is a verbatim copy:

HYPOTHESIS

Mrs. Anna Platz shot and killed Alvin Benson on the night of June 13th.

PLACE

She lived in the house, and admitted being there at the time the shot was fired.

OPPORTUNITY

She was alone in the house with Benson.

All the windows were either barred or locked on the inside. The front door was locked. There was no other means of ingress.

Her presence in the living-room was natural; she might have entered ostensibly to ask Benson a domestic question.

Her standing directly in front of him would not necessarily have caused him to look up. Hence, his reading attitude.

Who else could have come so close to him for the purpose of shooting him, without attracting his attention?

He would not have cared how he appeared before his housekeeper. He had become accustomed to being seen by her without his teeth and toupee and in *négligé* condition.

Living in the house, she was able to choose a propitious moment for the crime.

TIME

She waited up for him. Despite her denial, he might have told her when he would return.

When he came in alone and changed to his smoking-jacket, she knew he was not expecting any late visitors.

She chose a time shortly after his return because it would appear that he had brought someone home with him, and that this other person had killed him.

MEANS

She used Benson's own gun. Benson undoubtedly had more than one; for he would have been more likely to keep a gun in his bedroom than in his living-room; and since a Smith and Wesson was found in the living-room, there probably was another in the bedroom.

Being his housekeeper, she knew of the gun upstairs. After he had gone down to the living-room to read, she secured it, and took it with her, concealed under her apron.

She threw the gun away or hid it after the shooting. She had all night in which to dispose of it.

She was frightened when asked what firearms Benson kept about the house, for she was not sure whether or not we knew of the gun in the bedroom.

MOTIVE

She took up the position of housekeeper because she feared Benson's conduct towards her daughter. She always listened when her daughter came to his house at night to work.

Recently she discovered that Benson had dishonourable intentions and believed her daughter to be in imminent danger.

A mother who would sacrifice herself for her daughter's future, as she has done, would not hesitate at killing to save her.

And: there are the jewels. She has them hidden and is keeping them for her daughter. Would Benson have gone out and left them on the table? And if he had put them away, who but she, familiar with the house and having plenty of time, could have found them?

CONDUCT

She lied about St. Clair's coming to tea, explaining later that she knew St. Clair could not have had anything to do with the crime. Was this feminine intuition? No. She could know St. Clair was innocent only because she herself was guilty. She was too motherly to want an innocent person suspected.

She was markedly frightened yesterday when her daughter's name was mentioned because she feared the discovery of the relationship might reveal her motive for shooting Benson.

She admitted hearing the shot, because, if she had denied it, a test might have proved that a shot in the living-room would have sounded loudly in her room; and this would have aroused suspicion against her. Does a person, when awakened, turn on the lights and determine the exact hour? And if she had heard a report which sounded like a shot being fired in the house, would she not have investigated, or given an alarm?

When first interviewed, she showed plainly she disliked Benson.

Her apprehension has been pronounced each time she has been questioned.

She is the hard-headed, shrewd, determined German type, who could both plan and perform such a crime.

HEIGHT

She is about five feet ten inches tall—the demonstrated height of the murderer.

Markham read the *précis* through several times—he was fully fifteen minutes at the task—and when he had finished he sat silent for ten minutes more.

Then he rose and walked up and down the room.

"Not a fancy legal document, that," remarked Vance. "But I think even a Grand Juror could understand it. You, of course, can rearrange and elab'rate it, and bedeck it with innum'rable meaningless phrases and recondite legal idioms."

Markham did not answer at once. He paused by the French windows and looked down into the street. Then he said:

"Yes, I think you've made out a case. . . . Extraordinary! I've wondered from the first what you were getting at; and your questioning of Platz yesterday impressed me as pointless. I'll admit it never occurred to me to suspect her. Benson must have given her good cause."

He turned and came slowly towards us, his head down, his hands behind him.

"I don't like the idea of arresting her. . . . Funny I never thought of her in connection with it."

He stopped in front of Vance.

"And you yourself didn't think of her at first, despite your boast that you knew who did it after you'd been in Benson's house five minutes."

Vance smiled mirthfully, and sprawled in his chair.

Markham became indignant.

"Damn it! You told me the next day that no woman could have done it, no matter what evidence was adduced, and harangued me about art and psychology and God knows what."

"Quite right," murmured Vance, still smiling. "No woman did it."

"No woman did it!" Markham's gorge was rising rapidly.

"Oh, dear, no!"

He pointed to the sheet of paper in Markham's hand.

"That's just a bit of spoofing, don't y'know. . . . Poor old Mrs. Platz—she's as innocent as a lamb!"

Markham threw the paper on the table and sat down. I had never seen him so furious; but he controlled himself admirably.

"Y'see, my dear old bean," explained Vance, in his unemotional drawl, "I had an irresistible longing to demonstrate to you how utterly silly your circumst'ntial and material evidence is. I'm rather proud, y'know, of my case against Mrs. Platz. I'm sure you could convict her on the strength of it. But, like the whole theory of your exalted law, it's wholly specious and erroneous. . . . Circumst'ntial evidence, Markham, is the utt'rest tommy-rot imag'nable. Its theory is not unlike that of our present-day democracy. The democratic theory is that if you accumulate enough ignorance at the polls you produce intelligence; and the theory of circumst'ntial evidence is that if you accumulate a sufficient number of weak links you produce a strong chain."

"Did you get me here this morning," demanded Markham coldly, "to give me a dissertation on legal theory?"

"Oh, no," Vance blithely assured him. "But I simply must prepare you for the acceptance of my revelation; for I haven't a scrap of material or circumst'ntial evidence against the guilty man. And yet, Markham, I know he's guilty as well as I know you're sitting in that chair planning how you can torture and kill me without being punished."

"If you have no evidence, how did you arrive at your conclusion?" Markham's tone was vindictive.

"Solely by psychological analysis—by what might be called the science of personal possibilities. A man's psychological nature is as clear a brand to one who can read it as was Hester Prynne's scarlet letter. . . . I never read Hawthorne, by the bye. I can't abide the New England temp'rament."

Markham set his jaw, and gave Vance a look of arctic ferocity.

"You expect me to go into court, I suppose, leading your victim by the arm, and say to the Judge: ' Here's the man that shot Alvin Benson. I have no evidence against him, but I want you to sentence him to death, because my brilliant and sagacious friend, Mr. Philo Vance, the inventor of stuffed perch, says this man has a wicked nature."

Vance gave an almost imperceptible shrug.

"I shan't wither away with grief if you don't even arrest the guilty man. But I thought it no more than humane to tell you who he was, if only to stop you from chivvying all these innocent people."

"All right—tell me; and let me get on about my business."

I don't believe there was any longer a question in Markham's mind that Vance actually knew who had killed Benson. But it was not until considerably later in the morning that he fully understood why Vance had kept him for days upon tenter-hooks. When, at last, he did understand it, he forgave Vance; but at the moment he was angered to the limit of his control.

"There are one or two things that must be done before I can reveal the gentleman's name." Vance told him. "First, let me have a peep at those alibis."

Markham took from his pocket a sheaf of typewritten pages and passed them over.

Vance adjusted his monocle, and read through them carefully. Then he stepped out of the room; and I heard him telephoning. When he returned he re-read the reports. One in particular he lingered over, as if weighing its possibilities.

"There's a chance, y'know," he murmured at length, gazing indecisively into the fireplace.

He glanced at the report again.

"I see here," he said, "that Colonel Ostrander, accompanied by a Bronx alderman named Moriarty, attended the Midnight Follies at the Piccadilly Theatre in Forty-seventh Street on the night of the thirteenth, arriving there a little before twelve and remaining through the performance, which was over about half-past two a.m. . . . Are you acquainted with this particular alderman?"

Markham's eyes lifted sharply to the other's face.

"I've met Mr. Moriarty. What about him?" I thought I detected a note of suppressed excitement in his voice.

"Where do Bronx aldermen loll about in the forenoons?" asked Vance.

"At home, I should say. Or possibly at the Samoset

Club. . . . Sometimes they have business at City Hall."

"My word—such unseemly activity for a politician! . . . Would you mind ascertaining if Moriarty is at home or at his club? If it's not too much bother, I'd like to have a brief word with him."

Markham gave Vance a penetrating gaze. Then, without a word, he went to the telephone in the den.

"Mr. Moriarty was at home, about to leave for City Hall," he announced, on returning. "I asked him to drop by here on his way down town."

"I do hope he doesn't disappoint us," sighed Vance. "But it's worth trying."

"Are you composing a charade?" asked Markham; but there was neither humour nor good-nature in the question.

"'Pon my word, old man, I'm not trying to confuse the main issue," said Vance. "Exert a little of that simple faith with which you are so gen'rously supplied—it's more desirable than Norman blood, y'know. I'll give you the guilty man before the morning's over. But, d'ye see, I must make sure that you'll accept him. These alibis are, I trust, going to prove most prof'table to paving the way for my *coup de boutoir*. . . . An alibi—as I recently confided to you—is a tricky and dang'rous thing, and open to grave suspicion. And the absence of an alibi means nothing at all. For instance, I see by these reports that Miss Hoffman has no alibi for the night of the thirteenth. She says she went to a motion-picture theatre and then home. But no one saw her at any time. She was prob'bly at Benson's, visiting mamma, until late. Looks suspicious—eh, what? And yet, even if she was there, her only crime that night was filial affection. . . . On the other hand, there are several alibis here which are, as one says, cast-iron—silly metaphor; cast-iron's easily broken —and I happen to know one of 'em is spurious. So be a good fellow and have patience; for it's most necess'ry that these alibis be minutely inspected."

Fifteen minutes later Mr. Moriarty arrived. He was a serious, good-looking, well-dressed youth in his late twenties —not at all my idea of an alderman—and he spoke clear and precise English with almost no trace of the Bronx accent.

Markham introduced him, and briefly explained why he had been requested to call.

"One of the men from the Homicide Bureau." answered Moriarty, "was asking me about the matter only yesterday."

"We have the report," said Vance, "but it's a bit too general. Will you tell us exactly what you did that night after you met Colonel Ostrander?"

"The Colonel had invited me to dinner and the Follies. I met him at the Marseilles at ten. We had dinner there, and went to the Piccadilly a little before twelve, where we remained until about two-thirty. I walked to the Colonel's apartment with him had a drink and a chat, and then took the subway home about three-thirty."

"You told the detective yesterday you sat in a box at the theatre?"

"That's correct."

"Did you and the Colonel remain in the box throughout the performance?"

"No. After the first act a friend of mine came to the box, and the Colonel excused himself and went to the wash-room. After the second act, the Colonel and I stepped outside into the alley-way and had a smoke."

"What time, would you say, was the first act over?"

"Twelve-thirty or thereabouts."

"And where is this alley-way situated?" asked Vance. "As I recall, it runs along the side of the theatre to the street."

"You're right."

"And isn't there an 'exit' door very near the boxes, which leads into the alley-way?"

"There is. We used it that night."

"How long was the Colonel gone after the first act?"

"A few minutes—I couldn't say exactly."

"Had he returned when the curtain went up on the second act?"

Moriarty reflected.

"I don't believe he had. I think he came back a few minutes after the act began."

"Ten minutes?"

"I couldn't say. Certainly no more."

"Then allowing for a ten-minute intermission, the Colonel might have been away twenty minutes?"

"Yes—it's possible."

This ended the interview; and when Moriarty had gone, Vance lay back in his chair and smoked thoughtfully.

"Surprisin' luck!" he commented. "The Piccadilly Theatre, y'know, is practically round the corner from Benson's house. You grasp the possibilities of the situation, what? . . . The Colonel invites an alderman to the Midnight Follies, and gets box seats near an exit giving on an alley. At a little before half-past twelve he leaves the box, sneaks out *via* the alley, goes to Benson's taps, and is admitted, shoots his man, and hurries back to the theatre. Twenty minutes would have been ample."

Markham straightened up, but made no comment.

"And now," continued Vance, "let's look at the indicat'ry circumst'nces and the confirmat'ry facts. . . . Miss St. Clair told us the Colonel had lost heavily in a pool of Benson's manipulation, and had accused him of crookedness. He hadn't spoken to Benson for a week; so it's plain there was bad blood between 'em. He saw Miss St. Clair at the Marseilles with Benson; and, knowing she always went home at midnight, he chose half-past twelve as a propitious hour; although originally he may have intended to wait until much later; say, one-thirty or two—before sneaking out of the theatre. Being an army officer he would have had a Colt forty-five; and he was probably a good shot. He was most anxious to have you arrest someone—he didn't seem to care who; and he even 'phoned you to inquire about it. He was one of the very few persons in the world whom Benson would have admitted, attired as he was. He'd known Benson int'mately for fifteen years, and Mrs. Platz once saw Benson take off his toupee and show it to him. Moreover, he would have known all about the domestic arrangements of the house; he no doubt had slept there many a time, when showing his old pal the wonders of New York's night life. . . . How does all that appeal to you?"

Markham had risen and was pacing the floor, his eyes almost closed.

"So that was why you were so interested in the Colonel—asking people if they knew him, and inviting him to lunch? . . . What gave you the idea, in the first place, that he was guilty?"

"Guilty!" exclaimed Vance. "That priceless old dunder-head guilty! Really, Markham, the notion's prepost'rous. I'm sure he went to the wash-room that night to comb his eyebrows and arrange his tie. Sitting, as he was, in a box, the gels on the stage could see him, y'know."

Markham halted abruptly. An ugly colour crept into his cheeks, and his eyes blazed. But before he could speak Vance went on, with serene indifference to his anger.

"And I played in the most astonishin' luck. Still, he's just the kind of ancient popinjay who'd go to the wash-room and dandify himself—I rather counted on that, don't y'know. . . . My word! We've made amazin' progress this morning, despite your injured feelings. You now have five different people, anyone of whom you can, with a little legal ingenuity, convict of the crime—in any event, you can get indictments against 'em."

He leaned his head back meditatively.

"First there's Miss St. Clair. You were quite pos'tive she did the deed, and you told the Major you were all ready to arrest her. My demonstration of the murderer's height could be thrown out on the grounds that it was intelligent and con-clusive, and therefore had no place in a court of law. I'm sure the judge would concur. Secondly, I give you Captain Leacock. I actu'lly had to use physical force to keep you from jailing the chap. You had a beautiful case against him —to say nothing of his delightful confession. And if you met with any diff'culties, he'd help you out: he'd adore having you convict him. Thirdly, I submit Leander the Lovely. You had a better case against him than against almost any one of the others—a perfect wealth of circumst'ntial evidence— an *embarras de richesse*, in fact. And any jury would delight in convicting him—I would, myself, if only for the way he dresses. Fourthly, I point with pride to Mrs. Platz. Another perfect circumst'ntial case, fairly bulging with clues and inf'rences and legal whatnots. Fifthly, I present the Colonel. I have just rehearsed your case against him; and I could elab'rate it touchin'ly, given a little more time."

He paused, and gave Markham a smile of cynical affability.

"Observe, please, that each member of this quintette meets all the demands of presumptive guilt: each one fulfils the legal requirements as to time, place, opportunity, means,

motive, and conduct. The only drawback, d'ye see, is that
all five are quite innocent. A most discomposin' fact—but
there you are. . . . Now, if all the people against whom
there's the slightest suspicion, are innocent, what's to be
done? . . . Annoyin', ain't it?"

He picked up the alibi reports.

"There's pos'tively nothing to be done but to go on
checking up these alibis."

I could not imagine what goal he was trying to reach by
these apparently irrelevant digressions; and Markham, too,
was mystified. But neither of us doubted for a moment
that there was method in his madness.

"Let's see," he mused. "The Major's is the next in
order. What do you say to tackling it? It shouldn't
take long; he lives near here; and the entire alibi hinges
on the evidence of the night-boy at his apartment house.
Come!" He got up.

"How do you know the boy is there now?" objected
Markham.

"I 'phoned a while ago and found out."

"But this is damned nonsense!"

Vance now had Markham by the arm, playfully urging
him toward the door.

"Oh, undoubtedly," he agreed. "But I've often told
you, old dear, you take life much too seriously."

Markham, protesting vigorously, held back, and endeavoured to disengage his arm from the other's grip.
But Vance was determined; and after a somewhat heated
dispute, Markham gave in.

"I'm about through with this hocus-pocus," he growled,
as we got into a taxicab.

"I'm through already," said Vance.

CHAPTER XXIII

CHECKING AN ALIBI

(*Thursday, June 20th ; 10.30 a.m.*)

THE Chatham Arms, where Major Benson lived, was a small,
exclusive, bachelor apartment-house in Forty-sixth Street,

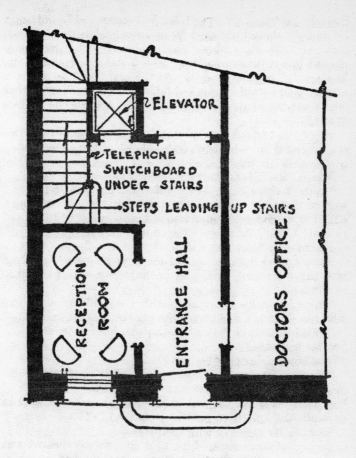

WEST 46TH. STREET

First floor of Chatham Arms Apartment in
West Forty-sixth Street.

Labels within the plan:
- ELEVATOR
- TELEPHONE SWITCHBOARD UNDER STAIRS
- STEPS LEADING UP STAIRS
- RECEPTION ROOM
- ENTRANCE HALL
- DOCTORS OFFICE

midway between Fifth and Sixth Avenues. The entrance, set in a simple and dignified façade, was flush with the street, and only two steps above the pavement. The front door opened into a narrow hall-way with a small reception room, like a *cul-de-sac*, on the left. At the rear could be seen the elevator; and beside it, tucked under a narrow flight of steps which led round the elevator shaft, was a telephone switch-board.

When we arrived two youths in uniform were on duty, one lounging in the door of the elevator, the other seated at the switchboard.

Vance halted Markham near the entrance.

"One of these boys, I was informed over the telephone, was on duty the night of the thirteenth. Find out which one it was, and scare him into submission by your exalted title of District Attorney. Then turn him over to me."

Reluctantly Markham walked down the hall-way.

After a brief interrogation of the boys he led one of them into the reception room, and peremptorily explained what he wanted.[1]

Vance began his questioning with the confident air of one who has no doubt whatever as to another's exact knowledge.

"What time did Major Benson get home the night his brother was shot?"

The boy's eyes opened wide.

"He came in about 'leven—right after show time," he answered, with only a momentary hesitation.

(I have set down the rest of the questions and answers in dramatic-dialogue form, for the purposes of space economy.)

VANCE: He spoke to you, I suppose?

BOY: Yes, sir. He told me he'd been to the theatre, and said what a rotten show it was—and that he had an awful headache.

VANCE: How do you happen to remember so well what he said a week ago?

BOY: Why, his brother was murdered that night!

VANCE: And the murder caused so much excitement that you naturally recalled everything that happened at the time in connection with Major Benson?

---

[1] The boy was Jack Prisco, of 621 Kelly Street.

BOY: Sure—he was the murdered guy's brother.

VANCE: When he came in that night did he say anything about the day of the month?

BOY: Nothin' except that he guessed his bad luck in pickin' a bum show was on account of it bein' the thirteenth.

VANCE: Did he say anything else?

BOY (*grinning*): He said he'd make the thirteenth my lucky day, and he gave me all the silver he had in his pocket—nickels and dimes and quarters and one fifty-cent piece.

VANCE: How much altogether?

BOY: Three dollars and forty-five cents.

VANCE: And then he went to his room?

BOY: Yes, sir—I took him up. He lives on the third floor.

VANCE: Did he go out again later?

BOY: No, sir.

VANCE: How do you know?

BOY: I'd 've seen him. I was either answerin' the switchboard or runnin' the elevator all night. He couldn't 've got out without my seein' him.

VANCE: Were you alone on duty?

BOY: After ten o'clock there's never but one boy on.

VANCE: And there's no other way a person could leave the house except by the front door?

BOY: No, sir.

VANCE: When did you next see Major Benson?

BOY (*after thinking a moment*): He rang for some cracked ice, and I took it up.

VANCE: What time?

BOY: Why—I don't know exactly. . . . Yes, I do! It was half-past twelve.

VANCE (*smiling faintly*): He asked you the time perhaps?

BOY: Yes, sir, he did. He asked me to look at his clock in his parlour.

VANCE: How did he happen to do that?

BOY: Well, I took up the ice, and he was in bed; and he asked me to put it in his pitcher in the parlour. When I was doin' it he called to me to look at the clock on the mantel and tell him what time it was. He said his watch had stopped and he wanted to set it.

VANCE: What did he say then?

BOY: Nothin' much. He told me not to ring his bell, no

matter who called up. He said he wanted to sleep, and didn't want to be woke up.

VANCE: Was he emphatic about it?

BOY: Well—he meant it, all right.

VANCE: Did he say anything else?

BOY: No. He just said good night and turned out the light, and I came on downstairs.

VANCE: What light did he turn out?

BOY: The one in his bedroom.

VANCE: Could you see into his bedroom from the parlour?

BOY: No. The bedroom's off the hall.

VANCE: How could you tell the light was turned off then?

BOY: The bedroom door was open, and the light was shinin' into the hall.

VANCE: Did you pass the bedroom door when you went out?

BOY: Sure—you have to.

VANCE: And was the door still open?

BOY: Yes.

VANCE: Is that the only door to the bedroom?

BOY: Yes.

VANCE: Where was Major Benson when you entered the apartment?

BOY: In bed.

VANCE: How do you know?

BOY (*mildly indignant*): I saw him.

VANCE (*after a pause*): You're quite sure he didn't come downstairs again?

BOY: I told you I'd 've seen him if he had.

VANCE: Couldn't he have walked down at some time when you had the elevator upstairs, without your seeing him?

BOY: Sure, he could. But I didn't take the elevator up after I'd took the Major his cracked ice until round two-thirty, when Mr. Montagu came in.

VANCE: You took no one up in the elevator, then, between the time you brought Major Benson the ice and when Mr. Montagu came in at two-thirty?

BOY: Nobody.

VANCE: And you didn't leave the hall here between those hours?

BOY: No. I was sittin' here all the time.

VANCE: Then the last time you saw him was in bed at twelve-thirty?

BOY: Yes—until early in the morning when some dame[1] 'phoned him and said his brother had been murdered. He came down and went out about ten minutes after.

VANCE (*giving the boy a dollar*): That's all. But don't you open your mouth to anyone about our being here, or you may find yourself in the lock-up—understand? . . . Now, get back to your job."

When the boy had left us, Vance turned a pleading gaze upon Markham.

"Now, old man, for the protection of society, and the higher demands of justice, and the greatest good for the greatest number, and *pro bono publico*, and that sort of thing, you must once more adopt a course of conduct contr'ry to your innate promptings—or whatever the phrase you used. Vulgarly put, I want to snoop through the Major's apartment at once."

"What for?" Markham's tone was one of exclamatory protest. "Have you completely lost your senses? There's no getting round the boy's testimony. I may be weak-minded, but I know when a witness like that is telling the truth."

"Certainly, he's telling the truth," agreed Vance serenely. "That's just why I want to go up. Come, my Markham. There's no danger of the Major returning *en surprise* at this hour. . . . And"—he smiled cajolingly—"you promised me every assistance, don't y'know."

Markham was vehement in his remonstrances, but Vance was equally vehement in his insistence; and a few minutes later we were trespassing, by means of a pass-key, in Major Benson's apartment.

The only entrance was a door leading from the public hall into a narrow passageway which extended straight ahead into the living-room at the rear. On the right of this passageway, near the entrance, was a door opening into the bedroom.

Vance walked directly back into the living-room. On the right-hand wall was a fireplace and a mantel on which sat

[1] Obviously Mrs. Platz.

an old-fashioned mahogany clock. Near the mantel, in the far corner, stood a small table containing a silver ice-water service consisting of a pitcher and six goblets.

"There is our very convenient clock," said Vance. "And there is the pitcher in which the boy put the ice—imitation Sheffield plate."

Going to the window he glanced down into the paved rear court twenty-five or thirty feet below.

"The Major certainly couldn't have escaped through the window," he remarked.

He turned and stood a moment looking into the passage-way.

"The boy could easily have seen the light go out in the bedroom, if the door was open. The reflection on the glazed white wall of the passage would have been quite brilliant."

Then, retracing his steps, he entered the bedroom. It contained a small canopied bed facing the door, and beside it stood a night-table on which was an electric lamp. Sitting down on the edge of the bed, he looked about him, and turned the lamp on and off by the socket-chain. Presently he fixed his eyes on Markham.

"You see how the Major got out without the boy's knowing it—eh, what?"

"By levitation, I suppose," submitted Markham.

"It amounted to that, at any rate," replied Vance. "Deuced ingenious, too. . . . Listen, Markham. At half-past twelve the Major rang for cracked ice. The boy brought it, and when he entered he looked in through the door, which was open, and saw the Major in bed. The Major told him to put the ice in the pitcher in the living-room. The boy walked on down the passage and across the living-room to the table in the corner. The Major then called to him to learn the time by the clock on the mantel. The boy looked: it was half-past twelve. The Major replied that he was not to be disturbed again, said good night, turned off this light on this night-table, jumped out of bed—he was dressed, of course—and stepped quickly out into the public hall before the boy had time to empty the ice and return to the passage. The Major ran down the stairs and was in the street before the elevator descended. The boy, when he passed the bedroom door

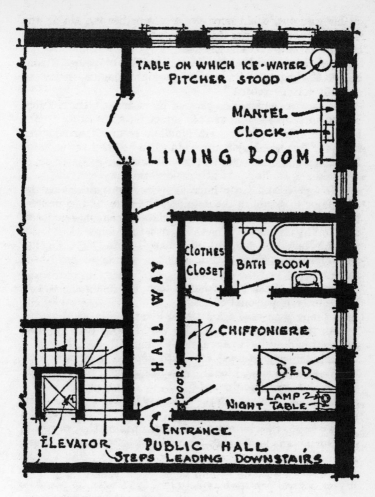

Third floor of Chatham Arms Apartment in
West Forty-sixth Street.

on his way out, could not have seen whether the Major was still in bed or not, even if he had looked in, for the room was then in darkness. Clever, what?"

"The thing would have been possible, of course," conceded Markham. "But your specious imaginings fail to account for his return."

"That was the simplest part of the scheme. He prob'bly waited in a doorway across the street for some other tenant to go in. The boy said a Mr. Montagu returned about two-thirty. Then the Major slipped in when he knew the elevator had ascended, and walked up the stairs."

Markham, smiling patiently, said nothing.

"You perceived," continued Vance, "the pains taken by the Major to establish the date and the hour, and to impress them on the boy's mind. Poor show—headache—unlucky day. Why unlucky? The thirteenth, to be sure. But lucky for the boy. A handful of money—all silver. Singular way of tipping, what? But a dollar bill might have been forgotten."

A shadow clouded Markham's face, but his voice was as indulgently impersonal as ever.

"I prefer your case against Mrs. Platz."

"Ah, but I've not finished." Vance stood up. "I have hopes of finding the weapon, don't y'know."

Markham now studied him with amused incredulity.

"That, of course, would be a contributory factor. . . . You really expect to find it?"

"Without the slightest diff'culty," Vance pleasantly assured him.

He went to the chiffonier and began opening the drawers.

"Our absent host didn't leave the pistol at Alvin's house; and he was far too canny to throw it away. Being a major in the late war, he'd be expected to have such a weapon: in fact, several persons may actu'lly have known he possessed one. And if he is innocent—as he fully expects us to assume —why shouldn't it be in its usual place? Its absence, d'ye see, would be more incriminatin' than its presence. Also, there's a most int'restin' psychological factor involved. An innocent person who was afraid of being thought guilty, would have hidden it, or thrown it away—like Captain Leacock, for example. But a guilty man, wishing to create an appearance of innocence, would have put it back exactly where it was before the shooting."

He was still searching through the chiffonier.

"Our only problem, then, is to discover the custom'ry abiding place of the Major's gun. . . . It's not here in the chiffonier," he added, closing the last drawer.

He opened a kitbag standing at the foot of the bed, and rifled its contents.

"Not here," he murmured indifferently. "The clothes-closet is the only other likely place."

Going across the room, he opened the closet door. Un-hurriedly he switched on the light. There, on the upper shelf, in plain view, lay an army belt with a bulging holster.

Vance lifted it with extreme delicacy and placed it on the bed near the window.

"There you are, old chap," he cheerfully announced, bending over it closely. "Please take particular note that the entire belt and holster—with only the exception of the holster's flap—is thickly coated with dust. The flap is comparatively clean, showing it has been opened recently. . . . Not conclusive, of course; but you're so partial to clues, Markham."

He carefully removed the pistol from the holster.

"Note, also, that the gun itself is innocent of dust. It has been recently cleaned, I surmise."

His next act was to insert a corner of his handkerchief into the barrel. Then, withdrawing it, he held it up.

"You see—eh, what? Even the inside of the barrel is immaculate. . . . And I'll wager all my Cézannes against an LL.B. degree that there isn't a cartridge missing."

He extracted the magazines, and poured the cartridges on to the night-table, where they lay in a neat row before us. There were seven—the full number for that style of gun.

"Again, Markham, I present you with one of your revered clues. Cartridges that remain in a magazine for a long time become slightly tarnished, for the catch-plate is not air-tight. But a fresh box of cartridges is well sealed, and its contents retain their lustre much longer."

He pointed to the first cartridge that had rolled out of the magazine.

"Observe that this one cartridge—the last to be inserted

into the magazine—is a bit brighter than its fellows. The inf'rence is—you're an adept at inf'rences, y'know—that it is a newer cartridge, and was placed in the magazine rather recently."

He looked straight into Markham's eyes.

"It was placed there to take the place of the one which Captain Hagedorn is keeping."

Markham lifted his head jerkily, as if shaking himself out of an encroaching spell of hypnosis. He smiled, but with an effort.

"I still think your case against Mrs. Platz is your master-piece."

"My picture of the Major is merely blocked in," answered Vance. "The revealin' touches are to come. But first, a brief catechism. . . . How did the Major know that brother Alvin would be home at twelve-thirty on the night of the thirteenth? He heard Alvin invite Miss St. Clair to dinner —remember Miss Hoffman's story of his eavesdropping?— and he also heard her say she'd unfailingly leave at mid-night. When I said yesterday, after we had left Miss St. Clair, that something she told us would help convict the guilty person, I referred to her statement that midnight was her invariable hour of departure. The Major therefore knew Alvin would be home about half-past twelve, and he was pretty sure that no one else would be there. In any event, he could have waited for him, what? . . .   Could he have secured an immediate audience with his brother *en déshabillé?* Yes. He tapped on the window; his voice was recognised beyond any shadow of doubt; and he was ad-mitted instanter. Alvin had no sartorial modesties in front of his brother, and would have thought nothing of receiving him without his teeth and toupee. . . . Is the Major the right height?—He is. I purposely stood beside him in your office the other day; and he is almost exactly five feet ten and a half."

Markham sat staring silently at the disembowelled pistol. Vance had been speaking in a voice quite different from that he had used when constructing his hypothetical cases against the others; and Markham had sensed the change.

"We now come to the jewels," Vance was saying. "I once expressed the belief, you remember, that when we

found the security for Pfyfe's note, we would put our hands
on the murderer. I thought then the Major had the jewels;
and after Miss Hoffman told us of his requesting her not
to mention the package, I was sure of it. Alvin took them
home on the afternoon of the thirteenth, and the Major undoubtedly knew it. This fact, I imagine, influenced his
decisions to end Alvin's life that night. He wanted those
baubles, Markham."

He rose jauntily and stepped to the door.

"And now, it remains only to find 'em. . . . The murderer
took 'em away with him; they couldn't have left the house
any other way. Therefore, they're in this apartment. If
the Major had taken them to the office, someone might have
seen them; and if he had placed them in a safe deposit-box,
the clerk at the bank might have remembered the episode.
Moreover, the same psychology that applies to the gun,
applies to the jewels. The Major has acted throughout on
the assumption of his innocence; and, as a matter of fact, the
trinkets were safer here than elsewhere. There'd be time
enough to dispose of them when the affair blew over. . . .
Come with me a moment, Markham. It's painful, I know;
and your heart's too weak for an anæsthetic."

Markham followed him down a passageway in a kind of
daze. I felt a great sympathy for the man, for now there
was no question that he knew Vance was serious in his demonstration of the Major's guilt. Indeed, I have always felt that
Markham suspected the true purpose of Vance's request to
investigate the Major's alibi, and that his opposition was due
as much to his fear of the results as to his impatience with
the other's irritating methods. Not that he would have
balked ultimately at the truth, despite his long friendship
for Major Benson; but he was struggling—as I see it now—
with the inevitability of circumstances, hoping against hope
that he had read Vance incorrectly, and that, by vigorously
contesting each step of the way, he might alter the very shape
of destiny itself.

Vance led the way to the living-room, and stood for five
minutes inspecting the various pieces of furniture, while
Markham remained in the doorway watching him through
narrowed lids, his hands crowded deep into his pockets.

"We could, of course, have an expert searcher rake the

apartment over inch by inch," observed Vance. "But I don't think it necess'ry. The Major's a bold, cunning soul: witness his wide square forehead, the dominating stare of his globular eyes, the perpendicular spine, and the indrawn abdomen. He's forthright in all his mental operations. Like Poe's Minister D——, he would recognise the futility of painstakingly secreting the jewels in some obscure corner. And anyhow, he had no object in secreting them. He merely wished to hide 'em where there'd be no chance of their being seen. This naturally suggests a lock and key, what? There was no such *cache* in the bedroom—which is why I came here."

He walked to a squat rosewood desk in the corner, and tried all its drawers; but they were unlocked. He next tested the table drawer; but that, too, was unlocked. A small Spanish cabinet by the window proved equally disappointing.

"Markham, I simply must find a locked drawer," he said.

He inspected the room again and was about to return to the bedroom when his eyes fell on a Circassian-walnut humidor half hidden by a pile of magazines on the undershelf of the centre-table. He stopped abruptly, and going quickly to the box, endeavoured to lift the top. It was locked.

"Let's see," he mused. "What does the Major smoke? *Romeo y Julieta Perfeccionados*, I believe—but they're not sufficiently valuable to keep under lock and key."

He picked up a strong bronze paper-knife lying on the table, and forced its point into the crevice of the humidor just above the lock.

"You can't do that!" cried Markham; and there was as much pain as reprimand in his voice.

Before he could reach Vance, however, there was a sharp click, and the lid flew open. Inside was a blue-velvet jewel-case.

"Ah! 'Dumb jewels more quick than words,'" said Vance, stepping back.

Markham stood staring into the humidor with an expression of tragic distress. Then slowly he turned and sank heavily into a chair.

"Good God!" he murmured. "I don't know what to believe."

"In that respect," returned Vance, "you're in the same

disheartenin' predicament as all the philosophers. But you were ready enough, don't y'know, to believe in the guilt of half a dozen innocent people. Why should you gag at the Major, who aotu'lly is guilty?"

His tone was contemptuous, but a curious inscrutable look in his eyes belied his voice; and I remembered that, although these two men were welded in an indissoluble friendship, I had never heard a word of sentiment, or even sympathy, pass between them.

Markham had leaned forward in an attitude of hopelessness, elbows on knees, his head in his hands.

"But the motive!" he urged. "A man doesn't shoot his brother for a handful of jewels."

"Certainly not," agreed Vance. "The jewels were a mere addendum. There was a vital motive—rest assured. And, I fancy, when you get your report from the expert accountant, all—or at least a goodly part—will be revealed."

"So that was why you wanted his books examined?" Markham stood up resolutely.

"Come: I'm going to see this thing through."

Vance did not move at once. He was intently studying small antique candlestick of oriental design on the mantel. "I say!" he muttered. "That's dev'lish fine copy!"

CHAPTER XXIV

THE ARREST

(Thursday, June 20th ; noon.)

On leaving the apartment, Markham took with him the pistol and the case of jewels. In the drug store at the corner of Sixth Avenue he telephoned Heath to meet him immediately at the office, and to bring Captain Hagedorn. He also telephoned Stitt, the public accountant, to report as soon as possible.

"You observe, I trust," said Vance, when we were in the taxicab headed for the Criminal Courts Building, "the great

advantage of my methods over yours. When one knows
at the outset who committed a crime, one isn't misled by
appearances. Without that foreknowledge, one is apt to be
deceived by a clever alibi, for example . . . I asked you to
secure the alibis because, knowing the Major was guilty, I
thought he'd have prepared a good one."

"But why ask for all of them? And why waste time trying
to disprove Colonel Ostrander's?"

"What chance would I have had of securing the Major's
alibi, if I had not injected his name surreptitiously, as it were,
into a list of other names? . . . And had I asked you to
check the Major's alibi first, you'd have refused. I chose
the Colonel's alibi to start with because it seemed to offer a
loophole—and I was lucky in the choice. I knew that if I
could puncture one of the other alibis, you would be more
inclined to help me test the Major's."

"But if, as you say, you knew from the first that the
Major was guilty, why, in God's name, didn't you tell me,
and save me this week of anxiety?"

"Don't be ingenuous, old man," returned Vance. "If
I had accused the Major at the beginning, you'd have had
me arrested for *scandalum magnatum* and criminal libel.
It was only by deceivin' you every minute about the Major's
guilt, and drawing a whole school of red herrings across the
trail, that I was able to get you to accept the fact even to-day.
And yet, not once did I actu'lly lie to you. I was constantly
throwing out suggestions, and pointing to significant facts, in
the hope that you'd see the light for yourself; but you ignored
all my intimations, or else misinterpreted them, with the most
irritatin' perversity."

Markham was silent a moment.

"I see what you mean. But why did you keep setting up
these straw men and then knocking them over?"

"You were bound, body and soul, to circumst'ntial evidence,"
Vance pointed out. "It was only by letting you see that it
led you nowhere that I was able to foist the Major on you.
There was no evidence against him—he naturally saw to that.
No one even regarded him as a possibility; fratricide has been
held as inconceivable—a *lusus naturæ*—since the days of
Cain. Even with all my finessing you fought every inch of
the way, objectin' to this and that, and doing everything

imag'nable to thwart my humble efforts. . . . Admit, like a good fellow, that, had it not been for my assiduousness, the Major would never have been suspected."

"And yet, there are some things I don't understand even now. Why, for instance, should he have objected so strenuously to my arresting the Captain?"

Vance wagged his head.

"How deuced obvious you are! Never attempt a crime, my Markham—you'd be instantly apprehended. I say, can't you see how much more impregnable the Major's position would be if he showed no int'rest in your arrests—if, indeed, he appeared actu'lly to protest against your incarc'ration of a victim. Could he, by any other means, have elim'nated so completely all possible suspicion against himself? Moreover, he knew very well that nothing he could say would swerve you from your course. You're so noble, don't y'know."

"But he did give me the impression once or twice that he thought Miss St. Clair was guilty."

"Ah! There you have a shrewd intelligence taking advantage of an opportunity. The Major unquestionably planned the crime so as to cast suspicion on the Captain. Leacock had publicly threatened his brother in connection with Miss St. Clair; and the lady was about to dine alone with Alvin. When, in the morning, Alvin was found shot with an army Colt, who but the Captain would be suspected? The Major knew the Captain lived alone, and that he would have diff'culty in establishing an alibi. Do you now see how cunning he was in recommending Pfyfe as a source of information? He knew that if you interviewed Pfyfe, you'd hear of the threat. And don't ignore the fact that his suggestion of Pfyfe was an apparent afterthought: he wanted to make it appear casual, don't y'know. Astute devil, what?"

Markham, sunk in gloom, was listening closely.

"Now for the opportunity of which he took advantage," continued Vance. "When you upset his calculations by telling him you knew whom Alvin dined with, and that you had almost enough evidence to ask for an indictment, the idea appealed to him. He knew no charmin' lady could ever be convicted of murder in this most chivalrous city, no matter what the evidence; and he had enough of the sporting instinct in him to prefer that no one should actu'lly be punished for the crime. Cons'quently, he was willing to switch you back to the lady. And he played his hand cleverly, making it appear that he was most reluctant to involve her."

"Was that why, when you wanted me to examine his books and to ask him to the office to discuss the confession, you told me to intimate that I had Miss St. Clair in mind?"

"Exactly!"

"And the person the Major was shielding——"

"Was himself. But he wanted you to think it was Miss St. Clair."

"If you were certain he was guilty, why did you bring Colonel Ostrander into the case?"

"In the hope that he could supply us with faggots for the Major's funeral pyre. I knew he was acquainted intimately with Alvin Benson and his entire *camarilla;* and I knew, too, that he was an egregious quidnunc who might have got wind of some enmity between the Benson boys, and have suspected the truth. And I also wanted to get a line on Pfyfe, by way of elim'nating every remote counter possibility."

"But we already had a line on Pfyfe."

"Oh, I don't mean material clues. I wanted to learn about Pfyfe's nature—his psychology, y'know—particularly his personality as a gambler. Y'see, it was the crime of a calculating, cold-blooded gambler; and no one but a man of that particular type could possibly have committed it."

Markham apparently was not interested just now in Vance's theories.

"Did you believe the Major," he asked, "when he said his brother had lied to him about the presence of the jewels in the safe?"

"The wily Alvin prob'bly never mentioned 'em to Anthony," rejoined Vance. "An ear at the door during one of Pfyfe's visits was, I fancy, his source of information. . . . And speaking of the Major's eavesdropping, it was that which suggested to me a possible motive for the crime. Your man, Stitt, I hope, will clarify that point."

"According to your theory, the crime was rather hastily conceived." Markham's statement was in reality a question.

"The details of its execution were hastily conceived," corrected Vance. "The Major undoubtedly had been contemplating for some time elim'nating his brother. Just how or when he was to do it, he hadn't decided. He may have thought out and rejected a dozen plans. Then, on the thirteenth, came the opportunity: all the conditions adjusted themselves to his purpose. He heard St. Clair's promise to go to dinner; and he therefore knew that Alvin would prob'bly be home alone at twelve-thirty, and that, if he were done away with at that hour, suspicion would fall on Captain Leacock. He saw Alvin take home the jewels—another prov'dential circumst'nce. The propitious moment for which he had been waiting, d'ye see, was at hand. All that remained was to establish an alibi and work out a *modus operandi*. How he did this, I've already eluc'dated."

Markham sat thinking for several minutes. At last he lifted his head.

"You've about convinced me of his guilt," he admitted, "But, damn it man! I've got to prove it; and there's not much actual legal evidence."

Vance gave a slight shrug.

"I'm not int'rested in your stupid courts and your silly rules of evidence. But, since I've convinced you, you can't charge me with not having met your challenge, don't y'know."

"I suppose not," Markham assented gloomily.

Slowly the muscles about his mouth tightened.

"You've done your share, Vance. I'll carry on."

Heath and Captain Hagedorn were waiting when we arrived at the office, and Markham greeted them in his customary reserved, matter-of-fact way. By now he had himself well in hand, and he went about the task before him with the sombre forcefulness that characterised him in the discharge of his duties.

"I think we at last have the right man, Sergeant," he said. "Sit down, and I'll go over the matter with you in a moment. There are one or two things I want to attend to first."

He handed Major Benson's pistol to the firearms expert.

"Look that gun over, Captain, and tell me if there's any way of identifying it as the weapon that killed Benson."

Hagedorn moved ponderously to the window. Laying

the pistol on the sill, he took several tools from the pockets of his voluminous coat, and placed them beside the weapon. Then, adjusting a jeweller's magnifying glass to his eye, he began what seemed an interminable series of tinkerings. He opened the plates of the stock, and drawing back the sear, took out the firing-pin. He removed the slide, unscrewed the link, and extracted the recoil spring. ` I thought he was going to take the weapon entirely apart, but apparently he merely wanted to let light into the barrel; for presently he held the gun to the window and placed his eye at the muzzle. He peered into the barrel for nearly five minutes, moving it slightly back and forth to catch the reflection of the sun on different points of the interior.

At last, without a word, he slowly and painstakingly went through the operation of redintegrating the weapon. Then he lumbered back to his chair, and sat blinking heavily for several moments.

"I'll tell you," he said, thrusting his head forward and gazing at Markham over the tops of his steel-rimmed spectacles. "This, now, may be the right gun. I wouldn't say for sure. But when I saw the bullet the other morning I noticed some peculiar rifling marks on it; and the rifling in this gun here looks to me as though it would match up with the marks on the bullet. I'm not certain. I'd like to look at this barrel through my helixometer."[1]

"But you believe it's the gun?" insisted Markham.

"I couldn't say, but I think so. I might be wrong."

"Very good, Captain. Take it along, and call me the minute you've inspected it thoroughly."

"It's the gun, all right," asserted Heath, when Hagedorn had gone. "I know that bird. He wouldn't 've said as much as he did if he hadn't been sure. . . . Whose gun is it, sir?"

"I'll answer you presently." Markham was still battling against the truth—withholding, even from himself, his pronouncement of the Major's guilt until every loophole of doubt should be closed. "I want to hear from Stitt before I say any-

---

[1] A helixometer, I learned later, is an instrument that makes it possible to examine every portion of the inside of a gun's barrel through a microscope.

thing. I sent him to look over Benson and Benson's books. He'll be here any moment."

After a wait of a quarter of an hour, during which time Markham attempted to busy himself with other matters, Stitt came in. He said a sombre good morning to the District Attorney and Heath; then, catching sight of Vance, smiled appreciatively.

"That was a good tip you gave me. You had the dope. If you'd kept Major Benson away longer, I could have done more. While he was there he was watching me every minute."

"I did the best I could," sighed Vance. He turned to Markham: "Y'know, I was wondering all through lunch yesterday how I could remove the Major from his office during Mr. Stitt's investigation; and when we learned of Leacock's confession, it gave me just the excuse I needed. I really didn't want the Major here—I simply wished to give Mr. Stitt a free hand."

"What did you find out?" Markham asked the accountant.

"Plenty!" was the laconic reply.

He took a sheet of paper from his pocket, and placed it on the desk.

"There's a brief report. . . . I followed Mr. Vance's suggestion, and took a look at the stock record and the cashier's collateral blotter, and traced the transfer receipts. I ignored the journal entries against the ledger, and concentrated on the activities of the firm heads. Major Benson, I found, has been consistently hypothecating securities transferred to him as collateral for marginal trading, and has been speculating heavily in mercantile curb stocks. He has lost heavily—how much, I can't say."

"And Alvin Benson?" asked Vance.

"He was up to the same tricks. But he played in luck. He made a wad on a Columbus Motors pool a few weeks back; and he has been salting the money away in his safe—or, at least, that's what the secretary told me."

"And if Major Benson has possession of the key to that safe," suggested Vance, "then it's lucky for him his brother was shot."

"Lucky?" retorted Stitt. "It'll save him from State prison."

When the accountant had gone, Markham sat like a man of stone, his eyes fixed on the wall opposite. Another straw at which he had grasped in his instinctive denial of the Major's guilt, had been snatched from him.

The telephone rang. Slowly he took up the receiver, and as he listened I saw a look of complete resignation come in his eyes. He leaned back in his chair, like a man exhausted.

"It was Hagedorn," he said. "That was the right gun."

Then he drew himself up and turned to Heath.

"The owner of that gun, Sergeant, was Major Benson."

The detective whistled softly and his eyes opened slightly with astonishment. But gradually his face assumed its habitual stolidity of expression.

"Well, it don't surprise me any," he said.

Markham rang for Swacker.

"Get Major Benson on the wire, and tell him—tell him I'm about to make an arrest, and would appreciate his coming here immediately." His deputizing of the telephone call to Swacker was understood by all of us, I think.

Markham then summarized, for Heath's benefit, the case against the Major. When he had finished, he rose and re-arranged the chairs at the table in front of his desk.

"When Major Benson comes, Sergeant," he said, "I am going to seat him here." He indicated a chair directly facing his own. "I want you to sit at his right; and you'd better get Phelps—or one of the other men, if he isn't in—to sit at his left. But you're not to make any move until I give the signal. Then you can arrest him."

When Heath had returned with Phelps and they had taken their seats at the table, Vance said:

"I'd advise you, Sergeant, to be on your guard. The minute the Major knows he's in for it, he'll go bald-headed for you."

Heath smiled with heavy contempt.

"This isn't the first man I've arrested, Mr. Vance—with many thanks for your advice. And what's more, the Major isn't that kind; he's too nervy."

"Have it your own way," replied Vance indifferently. "But I've warned you. The Major is cool-headed; he'd take big chances, and he could lose his last dollar without

turning a hair. But when he is finally cornered, and sees
ultimate defeat, all his repressions of a lifetime, having had
no safety-valve, will explode physically. When a man lives
without passions or emotions or enthusiasms, there's bound
to be an outlet some time. Some men explode, and some
commit suicide—the principle is the same; it's a matter of
psychological reaction. The Major isn't the self-destructive
type—that's why I say he'll blow up."

Heath snorted.

"We may be short on psychology down here," he rejoined,
"but we know human nature pretty well."

Vance stifled a yawn, and carelessly lit a cigarette. I
noticed, however, that he pushed his chair back a little from
the end of the table where he and I were sitting.

"Well, Chief," rasped Phelps, "I guess your troubles are
about over—though I sure did think that fellow Leacock
was your man. . . . Who got the dope on this Major
Benson?"

"Sergeant Heath and the Homicide Bureau will receive
entire credit for the work," said Markham; and added:
"I'm sorry, Phelps, but the District Attorney's office, and
everyone connected with it, will be kept out of it altogether."

"Oh, well, it's all in a lifetime," observed Phelps philo-
sophically.

We sat in strained silence until the Major arrived.
Markham smoked abstractedly. He glanced several times
over the sheet of notations left by Stitt, and once he went
to the water-cooler for a drink. Vance opened at random
a law book before him, and perused with an amused smile
a bribery case decision by a Western judge. Heath and
Phelps, habituated to waiting, scarcely moved.

When Major Benson entered, Markham greeted him with
exaggerated casualness, and busied himself with some papers
in a drawer to avoid shaking hands. Heath, however, was
almost jovial. He drew out the Major's chair for him, and
uttered a ponderous banality about the weather. Vance
closed the law book and sat erect with his feet drawn
back.

Major Benson was cordially dignified. He gave Markham
a swift glance; but if he suspected anything, he showed no
outward sign of it.

"Major, I want you to answer a few questions—if you care to." Markham's voice, though low, had in it a resonant quality.

"Anything at all," returned the other easily.

"You own an army pistol, do you not?"

"Yes—a Colt automatic," he replied, with a questioning lift of the eyebrows.

"When did you last clean and refill it?"

Not a muscle of the Major's face moved.

"I don't exactly remember," he said. "I've cleaned it several times. But it hasn't been refilled since I returned from overseas."

"Have you lent it to anyone recently?"

"Not that I recall."

Markham took up Stitt's report, and looked at it a moment.

"How did you hope to satisfy your clients if suddenly called upon for their marginal securities?"

The Major's upper lip lifted contemptuously, exposing his teeth.

"So! That was why—under the guise of friendship— you sent a man to look over my books!"

I saw a red blotch of colour appear on the back of his neck, and swell upward to his ears.

"It happens that *I* didn't send him there for that purpose." The accusation had cut Markham. "But I did enter your apartment this morning."

"You're a house-breaker, too, are you?" The man's face was now crimson; the veins stood out on his forehead.

"And I found Mrs. Banning's jewels. . . . How did they get there, Major?"

"It's none of your damned business how they got there," he said, his voice as cold and even as ever.

"Why did you tell Miss Hoffman not to mention them to me?"

"That's none of your damned business either."

"Is it any of my business," asked Markham quietly, "that the bullet which killed your brother was fired from your gun?"

The Major looked at him steadily, his mouth a sneer.

"That's the kind of double-crossing you do—invite me here to arrest me, and then ask me questions to incriminate myself when I'm unaware of your suspicions.   A fine dirty sport *you* are!"

Vance leaned forward.

"You fool!"   His voice was very low, but it cut like a whip. "Can't you see he's your friend, and is asking you these questions in a last desp'rate hope that you're not guilty?"

The Major swung round on him hotly.

"Keep out of this—you damned sissy!"

"Oh, quite," murmured Vance.

"And as for *you*"—he pointed a quivering finger at Markham—"I'll make you sweat for this! . . ."

Vituperation and profanity poured from the man.   His nostrils were expanded, his eyes blazing.   His wrath seemed to surpass all human bounds; he was like a person in an apoplectic fit—contorted, repulsive, insensate.

Markham sat through it patiently, his head resting on his hands, his eyes closed.   When, at length, the Major's rage became inarticulate, he looked up and nodded to Heath.   It was the signal the detective had been watching for.

But before Heath could make a move, the Major sprang to his feet.   With the motion of rising he swung his body swiftly about, and brought his fist against Heath's face with terrific impact.   The Sergeant went backward in his chair, and lay on the floor dazed.   Phelps leaped forward, crouching; but the Major's knee shot upward and caught him in the lower abdomen.   He sank to the floor, where he rolled back and forth groaning.

The Major then turned on Markham.   His eyes were glaring like a maniac's, and his lips were drawn back.   His nostrils dilated with each stertorous breath.   His shoulders were hunched, and his arms hung away from his body, his fingers rigidly flexed.   His attitude was the embodiment of a terrific, uncontrolled malignity.

"You're next!"   The words, guttural and venomous, were like a snarl.

As he spoke he sprang forward.

Vance, who had sat quietly during the mêlée, looking on with half-closed eyes and smoking indolently, now stepped sharply round the end of the table.   His arms shot forward. With one hand he caught the Major's right wrist; with the other he grasped the elbow.   Then he seemed to fall back with a swift pivotal motion. The Major's pinioned arm was twisted upward behind his shoulder-blades. There was a cry of pain, and the man suddenly relaxed in Vance's grip.

By this time Heath had recovered. He scrambled quickly to his feet and stepped up. There was the click of handcuffs and the Major dropped heavily into a chair, where he sat moving his shoulder back and forth painfully.

"It's nothing serious," Vance told him. "The capsular ligament is torn a little. It'll be all right in a few days."

Heath came forward and, without a word, held out his hand to Vance. The action was at once an apology and a tribute. I liked Heath for it.

When he and his prisoner had gone, and Phelps had been assisted into an easy chair, Markham put his hand on Vance's arm.

"Let's get away," he said. "I'm done up."

CHAPTER XXV

VANCE EXPLAINS HIS METHODS

(Thursday, June 20th ; 9 p.m.)

THAT same evening, after a Turkish bath and dinner, Markham, grim and weary, and Vance, bland and debonair, and myself were sitting together in the alcove of the Stuyvesant Club's lounge-room.

We had smoked in silence for half an hour or more, when Vance, as if giving articulation to his thoughts, remarked:

"And it's stubborn, unimag'native chaps like Heath who constitute the human barrage between the criminal and society! . . . Sad, sad."

"We have no Napoleons to-day," Markham observed. "And if we had, they'd probably not be detectives."

"But even should they have yearnings towards that profession," said Vance, "they would be rejected on their physical measurements. As I understand it, your policemen are chosen by their height and weight; they must meet certain requirements as to heft—as though the only crimes they had to cope with were riots and gang feuds. Bulk—the great American ideal, whether in art, architecture, table d'hôte meals, or detectives. An entrancin' notion."

"At any rate, Heath has a generous nature," said Markham palliatingly. "He has completely forgiven you for everything."

Vance smiled.

"The amount of credit and emulsification he received in the afternoon papers would have mellowed anyone. He should even forgive the Major for hitting him. A clever blow, that; based on rotary leverage. Heath's constitution must be tough, or he wouldn't have recovered so quickly. . . . And poor Phelps! He'll have a horror of knees the rest of his life."

"You certainly guessed the Major's reaction," said Markham. "I'm almost ready to grant there's something in your psychological flummery, after all. Your æsthetic deductions seemed to put you on the right track."

After a pause he turned and looked inquisitively at Vance.

"Tell me exactly why, at the outset, you were convinced of the Major's guilt?"

Vance settled back in his chair.

"Consider, for a moment, the characteristics—the outstanding features—of the crime. Just before the shot was fired Benson and the murderer undoubtedly had been talking or arguing—the one seated, the other standing. Then Benson had pretended to read: he had said all he had to say. His reading was his gesture of finality; for one doesn't read when conversing with another unless for a purpose. The murderer, seeing the hopelessness of the situation, and having come prepared to meet it heroically, took out a gun, aimed it at Benson's temple, and pulled the trigger. After that, he turned out the lights and went away. . . . Such are the facts, indicated and actual."

He took several puffs on his cigarette.

"Now, let's analyse 'em. . . . As I pointed out to you, the murderer didn't fire at the body, where, though the chances of hitting would have been much greater, the chances of death would have been less. He chose the more diff'cult and hazardous—and, at the same time, the more certain and efficient—course. His technique, so to speak, was bold, direct, and fearless. Only a man with iron nerves and a highly developed gambler's instinct would have done it in just this forthright and audacious fashion. Therefore, all nervous, hot-headed, impulsive, or timid persons were automatically elim'nated as suspects. The neat, business-like aspect of the crime, together with the absence of any material clues that could possibly have incrim'nated the culprit, indicated unmistakably that it had been premeditated and planned with coolness and precision by a person of tre-mendous self-assurance, and one used to taking risks. There was nothing subtle or in the least imag'native about the crime. Every feature of it pointed to an aggressive, blunt mind—a mind at once static, determined and intrepid and accustomed to dealing with facts and situations in a direct, concrete and unequivocal manner. . . . I say, Markham, surely you're a good enough judge of human nature to read the indications, what?"

"I think I get the drift of your reasoning," the other ad-mitted a little doubtfully.

"Very well, then," Vance continued. "Having deter-mined the exact psychological nature of the deed, it only remained to find some int'rested person whose mind and temp'rament were such that, if he undertook a task of this kind in the given circumstances, he would inev'tably do it in precisely the manner in which it was done. As it happened, I had known the Major for a long time; and so it was obvious to me, the moment I had looked over the situation that first morning, that he had done it. The crime, in every respect and feature, was a perfect psychological expression of his character and mentality. But even had I not known him personally, I would have been able—since I possessed so clear and accurate a knowledge of the murderer's personality —to pick him out from any number of suspects."

"But suppose another person of the Major's type had done it?" asked Markham.

"We all differ in our natures—however similar two persons may appear at times," Vance explained. "And while, in the present case, it is barely conceivable that another man of the Major's type and temp'rament might have done it, the

law of probability must be taken into account. Even suppos-
ing there were two men, almost identical in personality and
instincts in New York, what would be the chance of their
both having had a reason to kill Benson? However, despite
the remoteness of the possibility, when Pfyfe came into the
case, and I learned he was a gambler and a hunter, I took
occasion to look into his qualifications. Not knowing him
personally, I appealed to Colonel Ostrander for my information; and what he told me put Pfyfe at once *hors de combat.*"

"But he had nerve: he was a rash plunger; and he certainly
had enough at stake," objected Markham.

"Ah! But between a rash plunger and a bold, level-
headed gambler like the Major, there is a great difference—
a psychological abyss. In fact, their animating impulses
are opposites. The plunger is actuated by fear and hope
and desire; the cool-headed gambler is actuated by expediency
and belief and judgment. The one is emotional, the other
mental. The Major, unlike Pfyfe, is a born gambler, and
inf'nitely self-confident. This kind of self-confidence, however, is not the same as recklessness, though superficially the
two bear a close resemblance. It is based on an instinctive
belief in one's own infallibility and safety. It's the reverse
of what the Freudians call the inferiority complex—a form
of egomania, a variety of *folie de grandeur.* The Major
possessed it, but it was absent from Pfyfe's composition;
and as the crime indicated its possession by the perpetrator,
I knew Pfyfe was innocent."

"I begin to grasp the thing in a nebulous sort of way,"
said Markham after a pause.

"But there were other indications, psychological and otherwise," went on Vance: "the undress attire of the body,
the toupee and teeth upstairs, the inferred familiarity of the
murderer with the domestic arrangements, the fact that he
had been admitted by Benson himself, and his knowledge
that Benson would be at home alone at that time—all pointing
to the Major as the guilty person. Another thing: the height
of the murderer corresponded to the Major's height. This
indication, though, was of minor importance; for had my
measurements not tallied with the Major, I would have
known that the bullet had been deflected, despite the opinions
of all the Captain Hagedorns in the universe."

"Why were you so positive a woman couldn't have done it?"

"To begin with: it wasn't a woman's crime—that is, no woman would have done it in the way it was done. The most mentalised women are emotional when it comes to a fundamental issue like taking a life. That a woman could have coldly planned such a murder and then executed it with such business-like efficiency—aiming a single shot at her victim's temple at a distance of five or six feet—would be contr'ry, d'ye see, to everything we know of human nature. Again: women don't stand up to argue a point before a seated antagonist. Somehow they seem to feel more secure sitting down. They talk better sitting; whereas men talk better standing. And even had a woman stood before Benson, she could not have taken out a gun and aimed it without his looking up. A man's reaching in his pocket is a natural action; but a woman has no pockets and no place to hide a gun except her handbag. And a man is always on guard when an angry woman opens a handbag in front of him—the very uncertainty of women's natures has made men suspicious of their actions when aroused. . . . But—above all—it was Benson's bald pate and bedroom slippers that made the woman hypothesis untenable."

"You remarked a moment ago," said Markham, "that the murderer went there that night prepared to take heroic measures if necessary. And yet you say he planned the murder."

"True. The two statements don't conflict, y'know. The murder was planned—without doubt. But the Major was willing to give his victim a last chance to save his life. My theory is this: The Major, being in a tight financial hole, with State prison looming before him, and knowing that his brother had sufficient funds in the safe to save him plotted the crime, and went to the house that night prepared to commit it. First, however, he told his brother of his predic'ment and asked for the money; and Alvin prob'ly told him to go to the devil. The Major may even have pleaded a bit in order to avoid killing him; but when the liter'ry Alvin turned to reading, he saw the futility of appealing further, and proceeded with the dire business."

Markham smoked a while.

"Granting all you've said," he remarked at length, "I still don't see how you could know, as you asserted this morning, that the Major had planned the murder so as to throw suspicion deliberately on Captain Leacock."

"Just as a sculptor, who thoroughly understands the principles of form and composition, can accurately supply any missing integral part of a statue," Vance explained, "so can the psychologist, who understands the human mind, supply any missing factor in a given human action. I might add, parenthically, that all this blather about the missing arms of the Aphrodite of Melos—the Milo Venus, y'know—is the utt'rest fiddle-faddle. Any competent artist who knew the laws of æsthetic organisation could restore the arms exactly as they were originally. Such restorations are merely a matter of context—the missing factor, d'ye see, simply has to conform and harmonise with what is already known."

He made one of his rare gestures of delicate emphasis.

"Now, the problem of circumventing suspicion is an important detail in every deliberated crime. And since the general conception of this particular crime was pos'tive, conclusive and concrete, it followed that each one of its component parts would be pos'tive, conclusive and concrete. Therefore, for the Major merely to have arranged things so that he himself should *not* be suspected, would have been too negative a conception to fit consistently with the other psychological aspects of the deed. It would have been too vague, too indirect, too indef'nite. The type of literal mind which conceived this crime would logically have provided a specific and tangible object of suspicion. Cons'quently, when the material evidence began to pile up against the Captain, and the Major waxed vehement in defending him, I knew he had been chosen as the dupe. At first, I admit, I suspected the Major of having selected Miss St. Clair as the victim; but when I learned that the presence of her gloves and handbag at Benson's was only an accident, and remembered that the Major had given us Pfyfe as a source of information about the Captain's threat, I realised that her projection into the rôle of murder was unpremeditated."

A little later Markham rose and stretched himself.

"Well, Vance," he said, "your task is finished. Mine has just begun. And I need sleep."

Before a week had passed, Major Anthony Benson was indicted for the murder of his brother. His trial before Judge Rudolph Hansacker, as you remember, created a nation-wide sensation. The Associated Press sent columns daily to its members; and for weeks the front pages of the country's newspapers were emblazoned with spectacular reports of the proceedings. How the District Attorney's office won the case after a bitter struggle; how, because of the indirect character of the evidence, the verdict was for murder in the second degree; and how, after a retrial in the Courts of Appeals, Anthony Benson finally received a sentence of from twenty years to life—all these facts are a matter of official and public record.

Markham personally did not appear as Public Prosecutor. Having been a life-long friend of the defendant, his position was an unenviable and difficult one, and no word of criticism was directed agaist his assignment of the case to Chief Assistant District Attorney Sullivan. Major Benson surrounded himself with an array of counsel such as is rarely seen in our criminal courts. Both Blashfield and Bauer were among the attorneys for the defence—Blashfield fulfilling the duties of the English solicitor, and Bauer acting as advocate. They fought with every legal device at their disposal, but the accumulation of evidence against their client overwhelmed them.

After Markham had been convinced of the Major's guilt, he had made a thorough examination of the business affairs of the two brothers, and found the situation even worse than had been indicated by Stitt's first report. The firm's securities had been systematically appropriated for private speculations; but whereas Alvin Benson had succeeded in covering himself and making a large profit, the Major had been almost completely wiped out by his investments. Markham was able to show that the Major's only hope of replacing the diverted securities and saving himself from criminal prosecution lay in Alvin Benson's immediate death. It was also brought out at the trial that the Major, on the very day of the murder, had made emphatic promises which could have been kept only in the event of his gaining access to his brother's safe. Furthermore, these promises had involved specific amounts in the other's possession; and, in one instance, he had put up, on a forty-eight hour note, a security already pledged—a fact which, in itself, would have exposed his hand, had his brother lived.

Miss Hoffman was a helpful and intelligent witness for the prosecution. Her knowledge of conditions at the Benson and Benson offices went far towards strengthening the case against the Major.

Mrs. Platz also testified to overhearing acrimonious arguments between the brothers. She stated that less than a fortnight before the murder, the Major, after an unsuccessful attempt to borrow $50,000 from Alvin, had threatened him, saying: "If I ever have to choose between your skin and mine, it won't be mine that'll suffer."

Theodore Montagu, the man who, according to the story of the elevator boy at the Chatham Arms, had returned at half-past two on the night of the murder, testified that, as his taxicab turned in front of the apartment house, the headlights flashed on a man standing in a tradesman's entrance across the street, and that the man looked like Major Benson. This evidence would have had little effect had not Pfyfe come forward after the arrest and admitted seeing the Major crossing Sixth Avenue at Forty-sixth Street when he had walked to Pietro's for his drink of Haig and Haig. He explained that he had attached no importance to it at the time, thinking the Major was merely returning home from some Broadway restaurant. He himself had not been seen by the Major.

This testimony, in connection with Mr. Montagu's, annihilated the Major's carefully planned alibi; and though the defence contended stubbornly that both witnessess had been mistaken in their identification, the jury was deeply impressed by the evidence, especially when Assistant District Attorney Sullivan, under Vance's tutoring, painstakingly explained, with diagrams, how the Major could have gone out and returned that night without being seen by the boy.

It was also shown that the jewels could not have been taken from the scene of the crime except by the murderer; and Vance and I were called as witnesses to the finding of them in the Major's apartment. Vance's demonstration of the height of the murderer was shown in court, but, curiously, it carried little weight, as the issue was confused by a mass of elaborate scientific objections. Captain Hagedorn's indentification of the pistol was the most difficult obstacle with which the defence had to contend.

The trial lasted three weeks, and much evidence of a scandalous nature was taken, although, at Markham's suggestion, Sullivan did his best minimise the private affairs of those innocent persons whose lives unfortunately touched upon the episode. Colonel Ostrander, however, has never forgiven Markham for not having had him called as a witness.

During the last week of the trial Miss Muriel St. Clair appeared as *prima donna* in a large Broadway light-opera production which ran successfully for nearly two years. She has since married her chivalrous Captain Leacock, and they appear perfectly happy.

Pfyfe is still married and as elegant as ever. He visits New York regularly, despite the absence of his "dear old Alvin"; and I have occasionally seen him and Mrs. Banning together. Somehow, I shall always like that woman. Pfyfe raised the $10,000—how, I have no idea—and reclaimed her jewels. Their ownership, by the way, was not divulged at the trial, for which I was very glad.

On the evening of the day the verdict was brought in against the Major, Vance and Markham and I were sitting in the Stuyvesant Club. We had dined together, but no word of the events of the past few weeks had passed between us. Presently, however, I saw an ironic smile creep slowly to Vance's lips.

"I say, Markham," he drawled; "what a grotesque spectacle the trial was! The real evidence, y'know, wasn't even introduced. Benson was convicted entirely on suppositions, presumptions, implications and inf'rences. . . . God help the innocent Daniel who inadvertently falls into a den of legal lions!"

Markham, to my surprise, nodded gravely.

"Yes," he concurred; "but if Sullivan had tried to get a conviction on your so-called psychological theories, he'd have been adjudged insane."

"Doubtless," sighed Vance. "You *illuminati* of the law

would have little to do if you went about your business intelligently."

"Theoretically," replied Markham at length, "your theories are clear enough; but I'm afraid I've dealt too long with material facts to forsake them for psychology and art. . . . However," he added lightly, "if my legal evidence should fail me in the future, may I call on you for assistance?"

"I'm always at your service, old chap, don't y'know," Vance rejoined. "I rather fancy, though, that it's when your legal evidence is leading you irresistibly to your victim that you'll need me most, what?"

And the remark, though intended merely as a good natured sally, proved strangely prophetic.

HOGARTH CRIME

Surreptitious slaughter, and the reasons behind it, have never lost their power to enthrall. Old ladies' wills and wilful old ladies, the sleuth in evening dress, the eccentric village squire and the portly butler (who either saw, or did it) continue to exert their fascination.

Some detective stories have worn rather better than others – as a rule, those in which playfulness, assurance and ingenuity are well to the fore.

The Hogarth Crime series, in reviving novels unjustly neglected as well as those by the justly famous, offers a new generation the cream of classic detective fiction from the Golden Age.

R. Austin Freeman
Mr Pottermack's Oversight

Poor Mr Pottermack, living in quiet retirement in a peaceful English village, suddenly finds the misfortunes of his youth catching up with him. Plunged into a nightmare of blackmail, murder, an unexpectedly difficult romance and even the purchase of an Egyptian mummy, he seems to have solved all his problems with an apparently perfect crime. But Mr Pottermack has reckoned without the painstaking investigations of Dr John Evelyn Thorndyke, and his determination to unravel the threads of this most intriguing of criminal capers.

Freeman Wills Crofts

Inspector French and the Starvel Tragedy

Tragedy strikes on the Yorkshire moors when the old house at Starvel Hollow is razed to the ground and its three inhabitants burned to death. But while the ashes are cooling, the mystery hots up, and Inspector French sallies forth from the Yard, and must travel on to Scotland and the Alps before he can unlock the bizarre secrets of the Starvel tragedy.

Cyril Hare

An English Murder

The scene is set for Christmas celebrations at Warbeck
Hall – elegant decorations grace the drawing room, the
faithful butler has laid in a supply of fine wines, and the
five house-guests look forward to tea and plum cake.
Outside, the snow is falling on a hushed world.
But inside, furtive whispers and voices raised in anger
turn all to murderous mayhem in a classic of gentlemanly
detection.

Gladys Mitchell
Speedy Death

At Chayning Court the weekend guests are puzzled. Why is Everard Mountjoy, the intrepid explorer, so very late for dinner? Can he really be lingering so long in his bath? Has he got lost on his way downstairs? They are in for a shock – several in fact – as Gladys Mitchell takes the country-house murder to hilarious heights, unleashing the alarming Beatrice Adela Lestrange Bradley, resplendent in her evening frocks, to deal with the ensuing scandals. A dazzling first novel, *Speedy Death* was to launch both author and sleuth on their brilliant careers.